ETERNAL CHRONICLES BOOK 3

ETERNITY'S REFUGE

BY ZACHARY HAGEN

To Dad
Here's hoping you get caught up and read these.
Just kidding... mostly.
You are the kind of man I aspire to be. May I be the
kind of husband and father you've taught me to be.

AETOM
SUMARA
NANON
REGISTAAN
VIDANIA PR
GABRIELLE'S
BEACH HOUSE
ATLANTIDA
AQUARÉ

FAENACHT
ARBORRIA
NY
FAELAND
AELVBY
RIME
VIDANIA
Lux Terra

Sky Wheel Engine
Misthaven
Isengurd
Ston
Nox T

Mountain Temple
The Lost Fortress
NEBRIDGE
Verdor's Clearing
in the Living Forest
Centaur's Camp
Eternity's Mirror
Terra

ETERNAL CHRONICLES BOOK 3

ETERNITY'S REFUGE

BY ZACHARY HAGEN

Chapter 1
I Was Blind

THE CRASH OF THE WAVES outside Gabrielle's beach house soothed and comforted everyone as they sat together. Elior brought his glass to his lips again. He, Nyx, Opal, Eliam, and Nereza had been talking and laughing for hours about the events of the past couple of weeks and all they had done in Nox Terra while Gabrielle quietly crocheted a blanket in her rocker. Nereza cuddled comfortably with Elior on a loveseat, holding his hand while Nyx recounted a funny joke a dryad had told him while they were dancing in Virdor's Clearing. Then a knock sounded at the door.

The sound of his heartbeat became the loudest pounding Elior could have imagined. He turned to Eliam, Nyx, and Opal. Their faces were as pale as a fresh sheet of paper, crisp yet lifeless. Had they made a mistake in coming back to Lux Terra? Should they have left the other side of the world while they were still wanted for crimes?

Gabrielle stood. "You all hide in the hallway. I'll answer the door."

It wasn't a tough order to follow. As quietly as they could, Elior, Eliam, Nyx, Opal, and Nereza got up and hid in the hallway. Positioning himself so he couldn't be seen from the door, Elior watched from the shadows so he could protect Gabrielle should his gift be needed.

Gabrielle wrapped her cardigan around her waist. Even the beach was cold and windy in the winter. She gripped the doorknob, twisted, and pulled it open, keeping whoever was at the door almost completely out of sight and out of the beach house.

"May I help you, sir?" Gabrielle asked, the air of suspicion in her voice a little too obvious. Elior shifted forward, craning to see if the stranger noticed.

"I hope so, ma'am. I'm looking for the home of Gabrielle Kahn. Mich—" the man caught himself, afraid of using the full name. "A gentleman told me to come here. I was told that my sight could be restored."

The man's voice was familiar.Elior crept forward out of the shadows. There was nothing to fear if the man was blind. In a moment, Elior stood behind Gabrielle, looking over her shoulder.

"Dad?" he asked.

"Elior! Is that you? You made it back from beyond the mirror. I'm so glad! I thought Umbra was going to kill you. Is Eliam with you?"

Inside his veins, Elior's blood ran cold. His face contorted into revulsion, then fear. The man was responsible for so much suffering. Gabrielle had told them what he'd been up to since their trip beyond the mirror. What reason did he have to come here and speak with such familiarity to him? He was Taariq's accomplice, and that djinn was evil incarnate.

Elior was tempted to ball his fists and refuse to answer the man, but something about what he said made him rethink that. "We're both here. Dad, who told you to come?"

Yrahkaz shifted on the balls of his feet uncomfortable. He looked so pathetic, like a scolded child. Elior's anger melted away for the moment.

"Michael told me to come here, Elior. Maybe he wants me to atone for everything I've done to you and your brother and so many others. I don't know. I know I don't deserve mercy from you, but Michael told me that if I came here, I could have my sight restored."

Opal appeared as if from nowhere beside Elior and pulled him down to her to whisper, "Let him in, Elior."

He whispered back to her, "Is that what you think or what Michael and Aelon are telling you?"

"He won't hurt us. There's something different about him. We can get your dad on our side if we do this right. We can weaken Taariq, too! But yeah, I have a strong sense from Aelon that we need to let him in."

Elior stood back to his full height. "Ok, dad. If Michael sent you, come in."

The others emerged from their hiding place as Gabrielle helped Yrahkaz over to a plush chair by the fireplace.

Eliam grabbed Elior's arm. "Are you sure about this? He's never shown much interest in us before. Can we trust him if he was working for Taariq?"

Elior met his brother's eyes. He could see the fear there. It was new since being held captive by a dragon for over a month. He'd seen Umbra interact with Taariq multiple times. He knew how twisted that djinn was.

"Eliam," Elior said, "trust me. Trust Opal and what she said. I will not let anyone hurt you again."

Eliam squeezed Elior's arm. "We'll take care of each other," he pulled out his locket, the one identical to Elior's, "because we belong to each other."

"That's right," Elior said. He turned from his brother and faced his father. He sat there waiting for something to happen. Yrahkaz was blind, defenseless against an attack he couldn't see coming, after all. If there was any doubt about his intentions, he could be killed.

Guilt washed over Elior for thinking that. That wasn't an option. He knew that neither his mother nor Michael would approve of killing Yrahkaz in cold blood. He was a family regardless of what he had done.

"Dad," Elior said, "tell us what happened."

Yrahkaz recounted how Michael appeared to him in lightning and then in his car while he was driving home. He confronted him about the horrible things he did and told him he'd already been blind for a long time. Then, his vision faded and Michael told him to come here to be healed.

Nyx knelt in front of Yrahkaz and raised his hands to heal his eyes, but Opal stopped him.

"Before Nyx heals you," she said, "I have a message from the Great Spirit for you." Opal took Yrahkaz's hand and made him angle his face toward her. "Hear me and do not keep yourself from understanding. The thousands of deaths you caused can be forgiven, but you must give up everything you were before this moment. Your power, your magic, even your name. It's easy to leave your position and name behind. Your magic will be a harder mantle to cast off, but you must be willing. Your sight can only be renewed if you use your influence to do the exact opposite of what you've been doing for the past month."

"What does that all mean?" asked Yrahkaz. "I don't understand."

"Some of it you won't understand until the time is right, but what you must know is that you will not be the *you* you were when you entered this house. That has to be something you're ok with or the healing won't work."

Yrahkaz was silent for a moment. "I don't want to be the person I've been. I listened to someone sing about the Great Spirit and their faith in his power while I executed them for talking about Michael. I don't know why he would give me the opportunity for healing instead of just killing me to protect his followers, but I know I can give up Yrahkaz Almasi for something new."

"Then the moment you open your eyes," said Opal, "you will no longer be Yrahkaz Almasi. You will be called Neander Novak. You will consider Yrahkaz dead and left behind."

"I like that name," he said, tears trailing down his cheeks. "I understand."

Opal stepped back. "Nyx, you can heal him now."

Nyx stretched his hands up to Yrahkaz's eyes. A soft watery glow emanated from his fingers and drenched Yrahkaz's eyes in light. For several minutes, the white, calloused appearance of his eyes didn't change, but then newness washed over them and crystal blue irises appeared.

Nereza clasped her hands and sighed. "Welcome to the world, Neander."

Taariq sat on his throne and relished the feeling of being bowed to again. Before him, Cal, Viola, and Iblis knelt. Black fire burned around the edges of the throne room beneath his palace. A spark ran up his spine and he laughed.

"When you three are joined by the world's population, it will be beautiful."

"Nothing would please us more, master," said Iblis.

"Things are different now that you're a djinn, Iblis," said Viola. "You don't have to be so formal in how you address him."

"Oh, let him have his fun, Viola. I know I enjoy the attention." Taariq crossed his legs and let his vermillion lips spread, exposing his pointed teeth. Flames rippled through his hair and blinked in his eyes.

"Sir," said Cal, "I know we all had business to attend to. Should we get on with it?"

Taariq groaned. His assistant was right, but it just wasn't as much fun as being adored. "Very well. Rise, all of you." He pointed at Iblis. "Let's start with you. What have you accomplished?"

"Since you put me in charge of organizing an infiltration into Michael's following, I have scouted places frequented by those less than loyal, both here in Registaan and in neighboring Vidania."

"Excellent, but do you have other regions covered?"

"The team of djinn you have put under me are spread over the entire Lux Terran world. We will pin-point where they are meeting and how to infiltrate them in every region before the month is out."

"Very good," said Taariq. "It's wonderful to have you back with us from the other side. You're dismissed to continue your outstanding work. Cal, you report next."

Iblis burst into flame, turned to smoke, and swept out of the room.

Cal shifted, nervous to report. "Yrahkaz is missing. We could not find him in the last twenty-four hours."

Taariq chuckled and leaned forward, propping his chin in his hand. "Have you checked his office? The Vidanian palace is quite large as well."

"Sir," Cal said, steeling his gaze against the elder djinn, "when I went looking for him after not being able to reach him, I found his car abandoned on the private road leading to the palace. The unseasonable rain we had washed away any footprints and I couldn't track him. We don't know where he could have gone."

"I can feel that he's alive through the binding I did with the Circle during the Fire Oath Ceremony. He's out there, I don't know where, but you better find him. At least for now, while we establish this nation, I need all the circle members intact. Only when they serve their purpose, can I claim their power as mine. Find him now. Who knows? Maybe some of Michael's followers are bolder than we thought and have captured him and incapacitated him somehow. You're dismissed, Cal."

Cal exhaled and vaporized into smokethe smoke, leaving Viola alone with Taariq.

"Mark my words, Taariq," said Viola, "that human has abandoned the cause and won't be found. At least, he won't be found the way you left him."

"When I left him last, he was studying ways to better kill and torture, using the magic I helped him gain."

Viola exhaled a little purple smoke, which turned to a cigarette in her mouth. She puffed on it. "Maybe, but I saw the way he fidgeted with his hands and stared at that elf girl who sang while we hung her. Something shifted for him, Taariq. You've lost him, and probably to the other side."

Taariq seethed, but he thought back on all the services Viola had rendered to him as a djinn and as a dragon before Aelon ruined them. "If your theory is true, what are you suggesting?"

Viola took a step closer to Taariq, biting her lip. "I think you have the right idea to infiltrate Michael's little underground."

Her tone held the promise of something more. Taariq put his fingertips together, tapping them against his temple. He prompted her, "But?"

"But I think it has to be a little closer to home for Yrahkaz."

Taariq narrowed his eyes at her. "Then, what do you want to do?"

Flouncing her hair and moving closer, she said, "I'm not sure yet, but I'll find the place where he is, and I'll get at him in a way no one else would think of."

"And what do you get out of this, assuming you're correct and you succeed?" asked Taariq, tapping the arrest of his throne.

"When you kill the rest of the Circle and take their power," she said, leaning in and whispering in his ear, "I will be your empress."

Taariq chortled, "Cunning as always, Viola. Very well. If you are correct and you somehow get at Yrahkaz in a way that no one else can, I'll make you my empress when I seize the rest of the power."

She turned to go. "Better schedule the royal jewelers to fit me for a crown, then."

She burst into purple smoke and floated away, leaving Taariq alone to continue relishing his throne and all the plans that would cement him as lord of all creation.

"You ok, Eliam?" Elior clapped his brother on the back as he sat down next to him in the sand.

Eliam chuckled. "Everything is different. You made amazing friends, you have a girlfriend, and our absent father has a new lease on life. It feels almost surreal to be back after being held captive. You're not the same guy that tried to hold me back from running into that building."

Elior held his hands up and turned them over as if examining them for any sign of transfiguration. "I don't feel like a different person. We're still twins, right?" A smirk spread across his face as Eliam laughed.

"You know what I mean! You've grown up."

Elior sat with that for a moment. His brother now saw a new man in him, someone who had grown. Of course, newness brought on new questions.

Turning in the sand so that he could whisper in his brother's ear lest anyone from the house overhear, he said, "Do you think dad will really be any different as Neander than how he was as Yrahkaz?"

"Hmm," sighed Eliam, his mouth twisting into a tight pucker around the answer forming on his lips. "I don't think Michael would have sent him here if he wasn't capable of being different, at least not after what you've told me about him."

Elior grasped at the sand, the small particles of white powder shifting around his fingers and leaving haphazard patterns in their wake. The sound of the waves crashing punctuated his silence.

"Elior," said his brother, "we at least have to give him a chance. Mom is gone, and for a long time, we were all we had. Now, our father has joined us, abandoned his position, and Aelon gave him a new name through Opal. Mom loved him, and I think we owe it to her to do the same."

"I can't withhold forgiveness, can I? My actions caused Michael's death, and the man still forgave me."

Eliam reached out, putting an arm on Elior's shoulder. "Michael forgave you and gave you a gift. You can use that gift to protect our family and everyone else Aelon leads you to. I'll admit, it's hard for me to let dad in, too, but we'll be fine as long as we have each other."

The brothers sat silently in the sand, washed in the ruddy glow of the dying sun, together again at last.

Chapter 2
Leaving the Beach

THE MORNING RAYS OF SUN trickled in through the windows of Gabrielle's kitchen as Elior, Eliam, and Neander cleaned up while the others finished eating.

"You boys didn't have to clean," said Gabrielle, "I'm happy to do it."

"Nonsense," said Neander, "We're happy to help. My sons and I want to be polite guests."

Elior's stomach squeezed. It was fine that Neander had put away Yrahkaz Almasi in exchange for a new persona, but this man still hadn't earned the right, whatever he called himself, to call him a son in such a familiar way. According to genetics, Neander's son is what he was, but forgiveness and ease around him would take time. He said nothing, though. He just kept scrubbing the dishes and exchanged knowing eyes with his brother.

"You all may want to be polite guests, but I want to be an excellent host. Now sit down. You came into my house blind last night!"

"That may be," said Neander, "but I'm seeing better than I ever have now."

Then another sharp knock sounded on the door.

"Not again," said Opal. "I just started enjoying my meal!"

"Not another word," said Gabrielle. "Grab your plates and go hide. All of you! Now!"

They wasted no time scooping up their plates. Elior, Eliam, and Neander shook as much water off their hands as they could and wiped their still damp limbs on their clothes as they hid in the hallway to listen.

Gabrielle crossed to the door, calling, "Coming!"

She unlocked and unlatched the door. On the other side of the entrance stood another woman of similar age to Gabrielle herself, though she was much pinker. Her face was flushed and her hair was powdered in place. Her white hair was pinned in a great big bun on top of her head.

"Ginny! I rarely see you outside of our farmer's market shopping group. What are you doing here?"

Ginny was ringing her hands in the cold, blustery wind. "Oh, Gabby, you won't believe what happened. May I come inside?"

Behind her back, Gabrielle's hand clenched and unclenched. Elior thought she must be struggling to answer. Then words broke through. "Of course you can. I already have the kettle on. I'll pour you some tea."

Ginny came inside acting like a scolded dog. "I have to tell you something, but I'm not even sure what it means or if I should help you at all."

"Well, now you have to say something. You can't just drop a bomb on me and expect me to not have questions. Tell me everything, Ginny, and leave nothing out."

Ginny sat down at the table and took the cup of tea that Gabrielle had handed her. "Ok. I suppose you're right. Before I say anything, I have to tell you not to. Whatever you're mixed up with, if you are mixed up with anything, I don't want to know anything. I don't want to lie to anyone if I don't need to."

Gabrielle sat down and placed a quiet hand on Ginny's wrist. "You have my word. Now, out with it! What has you so tossed up?"

Ginny took a deep breath, inhaling the vapors from the tea. "A group of men came to the market this morning asking questions about you and your family. They asked where your beach house was and everything."

"What did they look like, Ginny?"

"I didn't get too good a look at them because I didn't want to be recognized by them myself, but they had lots of little bits of fire on them. I think they were djinn."

After a few minutes, Gabrielle asked, "Did you hear anything else?"

"I'm afraid not. I left as quickly as possible. Was I wrong to?"

Gabrielle wasn't sure how to answer, so she just said, "Oh would you look at the time! I have an appointment to keep and I need to get ready. I appreciate you stopping by."

Ginny stood. "Of course. We look after each other."

"We sure do," said Gabrielle. "I'll see you later, Ginny."

Ginny walked over to the door and let herself out.

Until that moment, Elior had not realized that he'd been biting his lip, but as the door swung shut behind Ginny, his mouth filled with the coppery taste of fresh blood. His heart slowed down, and he took a deep breath to relax from the fear he'd just bathed in. Relief, however brief, was his for that moment.

When they were all sure that Ginny was well away from the house, they all came back out and sat around the kitchen table, but the happy normalcy that had seemed so present with the sun rays streaming in, was gone. The golden tendrils had lost their color and a pallor of grayness had settled over them.

Elior was the first to speak. "We can't stay here. If djinn are asking questions about us, then we have to go."

"I agree, but where would we even go from here?" asked Opal. "Now that all six of our nations are united, there isn't a safe place for us anywhere on the planet."

Nereza leaned forward in her seat. "That's not completely accurate. Nox Terra is part of the planet."

"While true," said Nyx, "we don't have a reliable way to get there without having to go into Registaan, and that would be suicide right now."

"Not to mention," said Opal, "that Michael said we have work to do here."

Eliam snorted. "I doubt Michael intended for you all to get arrested."

"Don't exclude yourself from the equation," said Neander. "You and your brother share a face. You're in just as much danger as Elior is."

"That's a cheery thought," he mumbled.

Elior leaned with his elbows on the table. "Opal is right. Michael told us we have work to do here, so we can't go back to Nox Terra right now, even if we could.I'm sure we will, but not just yet. Does anyone have any ideas?"

Elior met the eyes of everyone everyone gathered around the table, but they each turned down to their hands when his gaze met theirs.

Gabrielle stood away from them in the kitchen. "Neander, do they know about the underground?"

Everyone looked at Neander.

"What is she talking about?" asked Eliam.

Neander's face was contorted in guilt. "Before Michael stopped me on the road, I was to ferret out Michael's followers. I put a lot of them to death. I don't think I would be well received by them if we went underground."

Opal stood and walked over to Neander, sliding an arm around his shoulders. "Michael could forgive Elior for betraying him and causing his death. If Michael thought you were worth redeeming, then the underground will understand."

"It might also be our only option," said Elior. "We're going to go there whether or not they accept you."

Nereza pinched Elior's leg under the table and hissed in his ear. *"Don't be so harsh with your dad. He's a new person, and we were just reminded of the part you played in Michael's death!"*

She turned in her chair and said, "Grandma, I think you should come too. If they're already asking questions about you, you aren't safe here either."

"I don't mind going," said Gabrielle. "I was thinking about going, anyway. I've been on the outskirts of the underground for several weeks. I'm not in deep enough with the local group members to know how to get to the Vidanian chapter headquarters."

Without an answer apparent to any of them, Elior was about to suggest another course of action until they could get in with them, but then something familiar but still shocking happened.

A cold burst of air rushed out from Opal and the light in the house dimmed to nothing. Opal glowed with a holy brilliance. Her eyes closed and then opened, pouring out liquid silver light.

"What's going on?!" cried Neander, backing away from her.

"Dad," Elior said, "it's ok. She's having a vision."

Opal's voice was joined by two others, as before, when she said, "Go. Do not delay. Pack your things and go to the Delta Pier. There will be a man with a red steel ship. Tell him that the way opens to strangers who are friends. He will know what to do. You will make it to the underground followers. Be warned. The way is treacherous, but I, the Great Spirit, Aelon, have made a way for you. Go!"

It was a brief message. Opal swayed as her mouth closed over the last word, but Nyx was once again able to catch her.

"I guess that settles it," he said. "Let's get our things and get out of here. The underground awaits."

The Great Spirit blessed them all with a new moon and a cloudy night. The six of them, dressed all in black, snuck out of the beach house just past midnight. Cahzpeh, the nearest town, would be asleep. No one would watch as they traveled up the beach to the delta.

Wind whipped down the beach from the east. It was hard walking into it, but the wind disguised their footprints in the sand well. Around one in the morning, it began drizzling.

"How much further is it to the delta?" asked Nereza. "The rain is freezing."

Elior slipped his arm around her. "By the time the sun slips over the edge of the horizon, we'll be at the pier."

They kept walking in silence. Elior wished they could have brought Gabrielle's car, but it was better that they had nothing that could be tracked. They'd even left their cell phones back at her house. Nothing would be the same anymore. There were no safe places left, except for the places hidden from Taariq.

Without warning, a red-hot, blinding flash illuminated the night sky behind them. Gabrielle turned to look at the source of the light.

"By Aelon! My house! They've blown up my house!"

In the sky over the only place they'd been safe in months, a roiling mushroom cloud lit up with flame rose into the sky as djinn circled around it as smoke, fanning the flames.

Nereza grabbed her dumbstruck grandmother's arm and pulled her. "Grandma, we have to go. We can't stop to mourn, we have to go. If we can see the djinn, they can see us."

She was right. Even though the sky had been dark, the flames illuminated the night sky in a blood-red twilight and their shadows were long and reaching on the white sand. Every shadow was a beacon, a harbinger of doom.

Then, the djinn saw them.

Elior turned away from the cloud. "Run!"

Pounding steps ripped into the sand. It was near impossible to move fast enough to avoid the approaching forms. Opal fell behind and face-planted onto the ground.

"Opal!" screamed Nyx. "I'm coming back for you!"

"No," said Elior, "I'll get her, I can protect her, you run!"

A dark ghoulish looking djinn was sweeping down over Opal. Elior ran in leaps and bounds to get back to her. The djinn came close, and their laughter broke through the wind's whistle.

Opal shielded her face as the djinn breathed fire down at her. "Elior! Help!"

A moment before the flames reached Opal, Elior dove in front of her and a force-field of blue energy materialized around them. The djinn descended and beat against it, but not even the sound of his blows made it inside the bubble.

"Elior," said Opal, "draw your sword."

He obeyed and pulled the sword Michael had given him out of its sheath. "What now?"

"Run him through."

With both hands on the hilt of the blade, Elior positioned the sword and aimed at the raging djinn's heart and struck. The blade broke through the force-field and impaled the djinn, who crumbled to ash.

Opal stood. "We have to catch up to the others!"

Elior scanned their surrounding for any help in getting over the sand before an idea struck him. "Hold on to my waist. I think I can catch the wind to get us to the others.

Opal wrapped her arms around Elior's waist as he raised his arms and prayed for his idea to work. After a moment, a hang glider of blue energy materialized over his head and caught the wind, carrying him and Opal towards their friends with the speed of purpose.

Djinn surrounded Eliam, Nyx, Nereza, and Gabrielle. They formed fireballs and were about to launch them at their friends before Elior and Opal dropped in the middle of them.

"Elior!" cried Nereza. "Do something!"

Elior once again raised his arms and a blast of watery blue energy rushed outward, pushing the djinn so far back they were lost and extinguishing the flames painting the sky. In an instant, all was peaceful again.

"I'm shaking," said Gabrielle. "We could have been roasted."

"Then let's not waste a minute more," said Opal. "I want to reach that boat before another team of djinn shows up."

Eventually, the sound of running water punctuated the sound of the surf.

Nyx sniffed the air. "The river is close. It shouldn't be too long now."

Twenty minutes later, they had crossed the High Plains River and were walking up river towards the Delta Pier. As the sun peaked above the horizon, Elior saw the red steel boat that Opal had described.

"That's it!" cried Opal. "That's the boat. Let's go!"

Opal jogged halfheartedly from lack of sleep. The others hobbled after her.

Leaning against the boat with one foot planted on the pier and one dangling between the boat and the dock, was a man of about forty with a short salt and pepper beard and a black hat he wore so low that it hooded his eyes.

"Mornin'," he said. "Awfully early for so many to be up and about. What brings you folk here?"

"We were hoping to travel north a ways," said Gabrielle. "Any chance you know someone or someway we could do that?"

The man pushed himself up onto the pier and tipped his hat up, revealing electric green eyes. "Near as I can tell, all waterways are closed. At least to strangers and people without the proper paperwork. Ya know, new rules from UFSS regulations."

Opal stepped forward. "That may be sir, but the way opens to strangers who are friends."

The man's scowl turned upside down and his eyes lit up with joy. "So you guys are followers of Michael. Part of our little community that believes he started something real?"

"I'd say so," said Opal. She pushed her hair back. "We traveled with him. He helped me and my two friends there," she gestured to Nyx and Elior, "drink from Eternity's Well."

The man's eyes widened, and his voice was much louder. "You mean you're Opal and Elior and Nyx!"

Elior swooped forward and clapped a hand over his mouth. "Quiet! We don't want to attract attention."

The man pulled Elior's hand off his mouth. "My apologies. I understand your concern, but no one will have heard. We chose this pier because it's abandoned."

Elior looked around. The man was right. The docks, except the red steel boat's dock, were in disrepair. The windows of the buildings around the pier were boarded up. This was not a place people were crowding to.

"Sorry. Just being cautious."

The man raised his hand and shook his head. "There's no need to apologize. I'm Marvin, by the way. I can take you to the underground headquarters on the boat. Will the others be coming with you as well?" He gestured to Nereza, Neander, and Gabrielle.

Opal said, "Yes. They've joined us and our mission."

"And now your mission is going to help the underground! Leonis will be so excited to meet you."

"Leonis?" asked Nyx.

"He's the leader of the underground."

"In Vidania?" asked Neander.

"No, of the whole thing, but he is based in Vidania right now. Come on. There's not time to waste. Let's get your things loaded onto the boat."

"I have just one more question," said Eliam. "Won't we be spotted in a red boat?"

Marvin tipped his hat. "Don't you worry, sir. We have a couple defected magitechnicians who joined our number. They created this paint that cloaks the boat at the flip of a switch. It's its own built in glamour spell. I can make the boat look however I like to protect us from prying eyes."

Nereza's eyes grew wide, and she clapped her hands together. "I'd very much like to look at how the system works!"

Marvin chuckled. "You go right ahead, but let's be on our way. When the sun hits the fog at a certain angle, the pier can be seen for miles. It'll be best to be sailing up river before that happens."

The boat driver made good sense. They each brought their things on board and stowed them below deck. Once they were all aboard,

Marvin turned the ignition and the engine hummed to life. It was quiet enough that if you were more than a couple feet from the boat, the engine would be inaudible. Nereza was sure it was more work from the magitechnicians who worked for the underground.

As the boat moved, the red sides glimmered and shifted. Once they had pulled away from the pier, the boat was invisible from the outside. As long as everyone stayed below deck or inside the navigation cabin, they were hidden from view.

Except for Nereza, who was fascinated with the ship, everyone was tired from their walk and settled into cots below deck to get some much needed rest.

Elior woke up to Nereza shaking his shoulder and whispering *"Wake up"* in his ear. His eyes fluttered open.

Sitting up and stretching his back straight, he asked, "Did something happen? Is everyone ok?"

She grabbed his hand and pulled him to his feet. "Calm down, it's not anything bad."

"Then what is it?"

"We're here."

Elior grabbed his things and followed Nereza above deck. The others had already ascended.

The boat slowed as it entered a cave on the southern point of an island between Prime River and High Plains river.

"Black Sap Island," Elior breathed.

"You know it?" asked Nereza.

"A friend and I rescued some people on it before we went to Nox

Terra. No one goes here, so it's kind of the perfect place to have the headquarters. Even better when it's in a cave that's only accessible by water."

The glamour fell away from the boat as the bow of red steel passed into the cave.

Marvin came out and called into the darkness. "Followers of Michael! I have returned with strangers who are friends! Come out!"

The darkness of the cave was an illusion. When Marvin spoke, lights sparked to life, illuminating the darkness.

Hundreds of eyes stared back at them from what had been blackness before. Men, women, and children, the rich and the poor. People from all walks of life were there.

"There's so many more people than I expected," said Neander. "I didn't know, though I suppose that's a good thing."

The boat slid up to a dock in front of an underground village. Huts made of many things stretched far back into the cave. As the boat's passengers disembarked, a gasp of shock ran through the crowd gathered there.

"It's Yrahkaz! He's going to round us up and kill us all!" yelled a woman a few paces back.

A burly man pounded his fist into his palm and snarled, walking forward. "Not if I can help it."

Neander shuffled backward towards the boat.

"Stop!" cried Opal. "This man has left behind who he was before. Michael himself came to him, blinded him and sent him to us," she gestured to Elior and Nyx, "for healing."

Skeptical looks rose from the crowd and murmuring curdled through them.

"It's true!" said Elior. "I am Elior BarVidania. This man who once was Yrahkaz Almasi has been given a new name. He is now Neander Novak."

"We," said Nyx, "are Nyx, Elior, and Opal. We traveled with Michael ourselves and we are wanted across all Lux Terra because of our association with him, just as all of you are."

Opal stepped forward. "If we trust him, then you can, too."

The unease in the crowd wasn't gone, but they no longer looked as if they would kill him.

"You can say what you will," said the gruff man, "but what does he say for himself after all the deaths he's caused?"

Every eye looked at Neander, but his were cast to the dock creaking under his foot. "I can't erase what has been done," he said, "but I can do things differently. I will not take another life. I will report none of you. I don't know why Michael saw fit to spare me after all the evil I've inflicted on his followers, but I'm going to try to be worthy of what he did every day. I regret every life I took and all the pain I caused. I hope you can find it in your hearts to forgive me."

A little girl in a pink dress stepped forward and put her hand on Neander's hand, tracing one of the burn scars with her finger as she held it. "I think that if Michael could forgive him, then I can, too."

The innocence of the comment disarmed the crowd.

"Lily is right." A man at least a head taller than most came forward. He had a powerful jaw and deep set black eyes. He carried himself like a king. Elior was sure that this was Leonis, the leader of the underground.

He continued. "Michael was a healer and a man of kindness. He would forgive, and I can forgive you too, Yrahkaz." He extended his hands as if to embrace all those who had come off the boat.

"Welcome, all of you, to the underground, or as we call ourselves,

Eternity's Refuge."

Chapter 3

Leonis and the Commander

LEONIS LOWERED HIS ARMS AND beamed at them. "I apologize for how some of our number greeted you, Yrahkaz. Fear can make people not trust anything."

Neander extended his hand to Leonis. "It's not a problem at all. If I was in their shoes, I'd understand. But, please, call me Neander. I want to leave Yrahkaz in the past and focus on moving forward past his mistakes."

Leonis shook Neander's hand. "You speak as if your former self is foreign to you. If Michael had anything to do with your change, I suspect that Yrahkaz Almasi is as good as dead!"

The crowd dissipated as they talked there. Opal stepped forward.

"Leonis," she said, "how did all this get here? How did you find this cave?"

Leonis sighed. "I suppose you would be curious about that. Your journey with Michael was the catalyst for this. I'll tell you what, why don't you all come eat dinner with me? I'm sure it was a long journey up the river."

Leonis led them up the path through the refuge. "This cave was an outpost for the navy during the Great War of the fourteenth century. Registaan had pushed her borders all the way to the High Plains river. After the djinn were driven back, this base was abandoned. The infrastructure and buildings remained here, protected and untouched, ever since."

Nyx pivoted around, gesturing back to the dock. "Are the Aquarian barracks still intact below the surface, Leonis?"

The leader raised an eyebrow. "How did you know about those?"

"I was a commander in the Aquarian army. My family has been in military leadership down there a long time." Nyx took a few long strides to catch up to Leonis. "The first General Cascata, my many great grandfather, was the one who allied Aquaré with Vidania in the Great War and built the barracks here."

Leonis raised an eyebrow. "And here I thought the most interesting thing about you was that you traveled with Michael Rex. We should talk more during dinner."

The headquarters of Eternity's refuge was much larger than they had thought. As Leonis led them through the meandering pathways leading to his personal quarters, they passed by shops, businesses, homes, and everything else you'd expect to find in any town.

In fact, it was a town. Children played in the streets. The smell of salted yeast rolls pulled fresh from the oven wafted out of a bakery they passed. It was not part of the world controlled by Taariq outside.

Nyx leaned over and asked Opal, "What kind of vibe do you get from this place?"

Opal thought for a moment. "Peace. It feels peaceful."

"I agree," said Nereza.

Nyx chuckled. "I didn't realize you were listening."

"Not on purpose," Nereza said, "but these streets are kinda narrow. I feel calm here. Elior? You?"

"I'd say almost nostalgic. When Eliam and I were kids, we used to play around the grounds of our cottage a lot."

Eliam continued the thought. "We were so carefree. Eternity's Refuge has a similar air about it. It's almost like… Oh, how to put it?"

"Like we're kids again. No worries." Elior grinned and clapped his brother on the back.

"Exactly! It's relaxing. After being held captive by a carnivorous reptile for weeks on end, this feels like total bliss."

Laughing through his words, Nyx said, "Of course, anything would relax me after that."

Leonis interrupted their conversation as he came to a stop in front of a stone door in the wall on the edge of the cave. "These used to be the main offices when this base was still operational. Now I work and live here."

He pushed on the stone door, and a warm aroma of steaming bread and stewed meat wafted out. "Please," he said, "come in."

With a scent like that, Nyx couldn't resist. He was the first one to step over the threshold. Leonis's apartments were sparse, but comfortable. There were plenty of places to sit. The table didn't have a cloth over it, but it was well lit for being in a home built into the wall of a cave.

Leonis led them to the table, which was just outside the kitchen. The smell of the soup simmering made Nyx's stomach gurgle with anticipation.

"Please, everyone, have a seat," said Leonis. "My cook will serve shortly."

As soon as they were all seated in a chair around the long dining table, Leonis's cook was out, circling the table with a tray.

Nyx inhaled. The stew was richly colored. Chunks of chicken, fish, and lamb swam in a tomato gravy with chopped veggies over a bed of rice and a sweet, lemony scented herb sprinkled over top. When Aelon's blessing had been invoked, he couldn't wait to taste the stew. He took a bite, allowing the sauce to coat his throat as he savored the fish.

"Nyx?"

He looked up. Every eye was on him, and Leonis looked like he was waiting for something.

"I'm sorry. Could you repeat the question?"

Leonis smiled and repeated himself. "You mentioned you were a commander. What was serving in the military in Aquaré like?"

Nyx took another bite, thinking about how to answer. "I loved it. I had great people to work both over and under. The most challenging part was after Minerva staged her coup and seized power. I and the other officers that escaped had a difficult time strategizing, but if the intel we had then had been accurate, we could have turned the tide and reclaimed our country."

"What was the intel that you received?" asked Leonis.

Nyx leaned back in his chair. "We were told there was a book of battle plans and strategies in her stronghold. Unfortunately for

Aquaré, it was an old journal of Minerva's telling about her time as the High Priestess of Aquaré. The information in that book led me to meet Elior and Michael, though, so it wasn't all bad."

"It sounds to me," Leonis said, "that the Great Spirit blessed your plan even though the intended results differed from the planned consequences."

"That much is true," said Nyx, taking another bite of the stew.

Leonis dabbed his chin with a napkin. "So, how did you meet your friends and Michael?"

"Elior, do you want to tell it?" Nyx eyed Elior.

Rousing himself from his bowl, Elior said, "Sure. They were going to stop searching for Eliam, my brother."

"That's me," said Eliam, waving his hand. "I was transported to the other side of the world by a failed magitech experiment."

"Yeah," said Elior. "So Nyx and I tried to find Eternity's Well after we met, but it moved. That's when we went to find Michael."

"Of course you know who he is," said Nyx through a mouthful of a roll.

Leonis snickered. "He is the reason we're all here."

"After they met Michael, they came to my court just before Lord Steelwort betrayed me by forging my signature and removing me from my throne."

"From there," said Elior, "we made our way to the Well with Michael. The waters didn't work at first, but after he died and came back to life, the waters were redeemed. We drank the water and that put us on the path for our next adventure."

"That's when I met them," said Nereza. "They'd had a dream together and one thing they saw was a magic mirror that I'd been researching when I worked at Magitech International. I helped them hack into the mirror. Then we were all transported to Nox Terra, the other side of our world."

"But before that, we found out that the waters gave us powers," said Nyx. "I became a healer, Elior can prevent harm, and Opal has visions and talks with Michael even when he's in the Unseen Realm."

"That's interesting, that you developed powers." Leonis poured himself a glass of water. "I may have some people here who are interested in your talents, Opal. There are several priests who joined us. What happened after that?"

Elior swallowed his bite and wiped his hand on his pant-leg. "We had to repair the sky wheel on that side of the world before we could get to the Lost Fortress where they were holding my brother."

Eliam groaned. "Umbra, Solarium's right-hand dragon cursed me and made us fight."

Elior squeezed his brother's arm. "We made it out without either of us getting hurt. We killed Umbra and could come back to Lux Terra through the other end of the Well.

Leonis whistled. "That's an amazing string of events. I have another question about that mission you were on, Nyx, that set everything else in motion. Were you involved in the planning of or just the acquisition of Minerva's book or other missions as well?"

"In a month of rebellion? I must have planned at least fifteen operations."

"Were they successful?"

Nyx sucked his teeth. "Except my last one, they all went as well as expected, so yeah."

Leonis sat for a few minutes. Nyx caught Elior's eye and asked him if he had any idea why Leonis was asking these questions, but Elior just shrugged and took another bite of his stew.

Leonis broke the silence. "Nyx, you know that members of the Refuge are being targeted, right? You know how bad it's gotten?"

"Yeah," he said, "why?"

"We need serious help from someone who understands military strategy and how to plan for the unexpected. We need someone like you, Nyx."

Nyx cocked his head. "Do you have an army to lead?"

Leonis shook his head and folded his hands in front of him. "We don't, in the traditional sense anyway, but we are fighting on multiple fronts to stay alive. With a good, curated defense, we can keep more people from being lost to the state."

"Then," said Nyx, "what are you asking me to do?"

"Nyx, I think you'd be a phenomenal leader, and I'd like you to serve as General of defense and strategy for how we plan to keep our people safe."

"Whoa!" Elior pushed back from his seat. "Nyx, that's an awesome job. Think of all the good you could do, not just here, but all over the world."

Nereza pulled on one of her coils and said, "I agree. You could help Aquaré this way, even if it isn't what you thought you'd be doing. Any resistance against the UFSS is worth pursuing, right?"

"Nyx," said Opal, "you should take it. Take the job. You'd be perfect for it."

Nyx looked back at Leonis. "I'll accept your offer on one condition."

Leonis beamed. "And what is that condition?"

"Everyone here needs to have a role, too. I don't want to leave them with nothing to do. We need to find something for each of them to get involved in."

Leonis stood and shook Nyx's hand. "You've got yourself a deal."

Chapter 4
A Seer's Place

Opal looked at the directions Leonis had written out for her one more time. She knew she was in the right place, but this cave was massive, and everything looked the same. Many of the buildings were hollowed out stalagmites, almost all of which matched the cave in their enormity.

This stalagmite was the largest of all of them. Actually, it was many stalagmites that had fused together into a giant mass. This was the Temple of the Refuge. All the priests and priestesses who had joined the efforts of Eternity's Refuge in Vidania met here every day to tend to and care for the spiritual needs of their community.

A priestess in pressed white pants and a royal blue blouse peeked through the doorway. "May I help you?"

Opal pulled her attention away from the dozens of stone steeples the structure had. "Leonis sent me."

"Oh? Are you a new member in need of perspective?"

Opal approached her, craning to make eye contact with the woman. "Not exactly. My name is Opal Stronghand. I am the dwarfess that travelled with Michael to Eternity's Well and drank from its waters."

The priestess clapped her hands over her mouth in shock. When she lowered them, she wore a grin from ear to ear. "No one among the priests here has drunk from the Well! You must tell the assembled clergy about your experience!"

Opal smiled while the young woman buzzed with excitement. "I didn't catch your name."

"I didn't realize! I'm Irisa. Please, come in. Everyone is gathered for our morning prayer meeting."

Irisa put out her arm to lead. Opal took it and walked with Irisa into the giant stalagmite. Blue lanterns hung in swirling patterns along the inside. They walked together up a flight of stairs carved into the outer wall of the structure. At the top of the stairs was a room hollowed out from the top of the tallest stalagmite in the fused building.

In the center of the cone-shaped room was a round table where half a dozen other priests sat.

The eldest of them, a somber man with mournful eyes with white robes draped over his lithe frame, stood up from his place across from the doorway. "Irisa, we rarely permit guests into these meetings, my dear, and we certainly don't permit them without advanced notice." He wagged his finger and scowled from behind the table.

Irisa let go of Opal and approached the Table. "Gerald, this isn't a guest. This is Opal Stronghand. She is the dwarfess who traveled with

Michael and drank from the waters of Eternity's Well."

Gerald turned his attention back to Opal. "Is this true, young lady? Did you go through the trials and drink from the Well?"

Opal smoothed out her skirt with her palms and approached the table. "It is. I think that has something to do with why Leonis sent me here. Nyx, Elior, and I all drank the water."

Gerald motioned for you to sit. "Then you must each have been granted a gift. Tell us about them."

"Well," started Opal. "Elior discovered his powers first—"

"Let me clarify something," said an austere woman with knee-length black hair, "the powers you each discovered after drinking belong to Aelon. He allows you to use them at his good pleasure."

"Peace, Alurra," said Irisa. "Opal wasn't brought up to be a priestess. She was brought up to be a queen. It's ok of she gets some of it wrong."

"Allura," said Gerald, "you're right, but let's let Opal continue her story without interrupting her again." Gerald extended a hand as if to cue Opal to speak again.

"Like I was saying," Opal said, "Elior discovered his *gift* first. We were almost killed by a djinn's fireball, but he could form a sort of protective bubble around us which kept us from being incinerated."

Opal peered at each of the priests sitting around the table. Several jaws were set and eyes bulged.

Gerald furrowed his brow and said, "Then?"

"Then," said Opal, "Nyx healed some pretty severe sunburns I had with a touch. My gift was more subtle at first. In fact, I didn't realize what my gift was until we crossed over into Nox Terra. I'd heard Michael's voice when we were in the dessert and again when we had to convince some centaurs to take us to their camp, but it wasn't until I went into a vision that I truly understood what it meant to be a seer."

"Gerald," said Allura, "when was the last recorded instance of a seer, a protector, and a healer all being seen together?"

The old priest leaned back in his seat. "There have not been all three of the gift archetypes present together since the Dragon War began."

"I don't understand," said Opal. She wiped her hands on her skirt again. Her palms sweat, not sure what they meant.

Gerald sighed. "The gift archetypes aren't well known outside of the priesthood. The gifts are magic bestowed on spiritual leaders by the Great Spirit. Protectors, at their most powerful, use their magic as pure energy to form barriers or other devices to protect themselves and others from harm. Of course, the Pure Protector is a rarity. Most protectors know when to plant certain crops or will give advice to people seeking safety during travel."

"Healers," said Irisa, "are more common, but healing with a touch is rare. Most priests granted healing magic still use many herbs and other remedies. The type of healer you describe Nyx being is a Holy Healer, the most powerful of all the healers. If Aelon wills it, Nyx might grow his gift enough to bring back the dead under special circumstances."

Opal put a hand up to her heart. "I didn't know our gifts were so unique."

"You haven't even heard about your own gift, yet," said Allura. "When you went into vision, did silver light pour from your skin and eyes?"

Opal shifted a bit. "Yes, it did. Why?"

Allura continued, holding back emotion. "That means that you're a Seer of Sanctity. That is the rarest of all the gifts. Most seers can hear impressions and the occasional clear voice from the Great Spirit. To hear his voice and then to go into vision in that way? You are truly blessed."

Opal's mouth had cracked, but she shut it, swallowed, and said, "What does that all mean?"

Gerald answered, "It means that many things."

Opal shivered, her mind buzzing with the ramifications of what they were telling her.

"Obviously," said Allura, "we'd be honored if you let us train you to better use your gifts."

Gerald said, "It also means that we'd also be ecstatic if you would join the priesthood."

Opal laughed and shook her head. Getting up from her chair, she said, "You have to be joking! All of Lux Terra would recognize me, and you can bet that if I joined, Taariq would have me killed."

"We aren't talking about joining the main body of the priesthood," said Allura. "We want you to join us here. Not only could we help you and your friends better understand your powers and the gifts that Aelon has blessed you with, but you'd be a great blessing to us as well."

Opal sat back down, her heart pounding. "Ok. I'm listening."

Irisa said, "You were a queen, so you're already a leader. We've been praying for guidance, and then a seer, a *real* seer, comes to us. Do you think that's a coincidence?"

Opal crossed her arms and sighed as the familiar feeling of

Aelon's smiling sigh filled her senses. "I suppose it isn't."

"Then you'll consider it?" asked Gerald.

Opal's mind washed over in a wave of silver light.

Opal, my dear, this is why I called you here. Join them. This is how you can help the world now.

Smiling, Opal answered, "I don't have to consider it. Aelon has revealed his will to me. I resisted my father's insistence on my role as a queen, and my resistance was part of why I was defeated by Steelwort, so I won't resist a call from the Great Spirit and his son to lead here either."

Gerald beamed. "Then welcome! Normally we would anoint you, but you've already had water from the Well, so we can skip that." He turned to the rest of the group. "Let's put it to a vote, then. Considering Opal can speak directly to Michael and Aelon, I motion to replace me as the interim High Priest of Eternity's Refuge with Opal Stronghand."

"I'll second that motion," said Allura.

Irisa stood with her hand high in the air. "All in favor, raise their hand!"

Every priest around the table raised their hands.

"That settles it," said Gerald. "Welcome, Opal Stronghand, High Priestess of Eternity's Refuge."

Opal's face went pale. Allura leaned in to whisper in her ear.

"Don't worry. I'll help you figure out your new job."

"Thank you!" she whispered back. She knew she was going to learn a lot when she came here today, but she never expected to become a leader again. The thought that her father would be proud of her swelled and grew in her heart until a tear of happiness rolled down her cheek.

Chapter 5
The Magitech's Ranks

Nereza slid onto a bench overlooking the dock and the inky water below and pulled out her laptop and keyed in a few strokes. A few moments passed before she was interrupted.

"Naynay?"

The nickname was old and nearly forgotten. "No one's called me that since my days at Vidania U!" Nereza turned in the voice's direction. "Melanie? Is that you?"

"It is!" Melanie sat next to her on the bench. "What are you doing here?"

"Well, my boyfriend traveled with Michael, so we had to join Eternity's Refuge, though I keep hearing people shorten it to ER. What about you? Last I heard, you were a big shot at Magitech. What happened?"

"You happened. After they treated you that way, it was only a matter of time before I had to bail. Then I heard about Michael and all the healing he did, so I had to learn more."

Nereza's eyes bulged. "Wait, were you the one who engineered that amazing built-in glamour on the ship?"

Melanie clapped. "Yeah! My team and I are super proud of that magitechnology."

Nereza closed her laptop and turned to face Melanie. "I loved it. I couldn't stop geeking out over it when we were on our way here from the coast."

Putting her hand over her heart, Melanie asked, "Do you remember that program that would magically find lost things?"

"That was an amazing project! I miss our VU days."

"Well," said Melanie, "since you're here, why not take a trip down memory lane with me?"

"What do you mean?" asked Nereza, pushing a coil of hair behind her ear.

"I mean that there's a team of magitechicians, several you'll remember from school here, and we could use someone of your talent. What do you say?"

Nereza slid her laptop into her tote bag and stood up. "Lead the way."

Melanie hooked her arm into Nereza's and walked her through the base. Eventually, they descended a long flight of stairs leading into a wide open workspace full of computers, glowing projects, and at least a dozen other magitechnicians tinkering or typing away.

Nereza's heart fluttered as she took everything in. "What is this place?"

"Bet it brings back memories of working in the pit under Moss

Hall," said Melanie. "This is a brand new start-up company that Leonis let us start here. We call it Fruit of the Living Tree."

"I remember that legend. It's the one where the fruit that fell away from the tree and rolled down the hill rotted and the seeds grew into a new grove that escaped from harm when the fires descended on the parent trees. Why did you pick that name?"

"I think it would be obvious, considering what Magitech International did to you, Naynay."

"I just go by Nereza now, but please explain. I want to hear more about Fruit of the Living Tree."

Melanie picked up a spinning mechanism from a nearby workbench. Under her touch, it started glowing. "Well, just like you, everyone here got screwed over by the bigwigs. Work was stolen, there were layoffs, and a bunch of people couldn't find any work anymore."

"That's the worst, isn't it?"

Melanie huffed. "Tell me about it. When only one company in the world looks for people with your skill level and they fire you, it kinda thrusts you into uneasy territory, unless… "

"Unless," Nereza said, smiling as realization dawned on her, "you start your own company to compete with them."

"Exactly! You get it." Melanie put the mechanism down and led Nereza further into the workspace. "Besides, we couldn't call ourselves 'Michael's Magitechs,' right? That would have been dangerous for the Refuge. Our company also gives them a cover to have things shipped on and off the island."

Nereza reached up and dragged her hand across some schematics for a turbine that functioned on magical energy rather than electricity.

Clean energy wasn't something that her old company had pursued, but this new one was making huge strides. "This is amazing. I'm super proud of you, Mel."

"Want me to show you around?"

"Do you even have to ask? Of course I do!"

Melanie gestured out. "The area you're in now is home to our research and product development people. We have about a dozen people working here. It's our largest department."

"Are they responsible for that glamour paint on the boat?"

"Yeah. I think Marcus and Jenny—you'll remember them from our micro-circuitry class—had a gigantic hand in that. They did a fantastic job. But there's more. Follow me!"

Melanie led Nereza through a corridor at the end of the room. A few paces down the hallway, the walls opened up to another large room. About eight individual workstations were spread over the room with maps, computers, and all kinds of strange pieces spread across the tables.

"This," said Melanie, "is our magical artifact research wing. We've got someone in here working on how we can harvest, multiply, and harness magical energy from the remnants of magical items that can't be used anymore. We have someone else looking into restoration projects for ancient sites that can be salvaged."

"Wow. That's just… I'm speechless." Nereza walked over to a table and picked up a piece of stone with old dwarfish runes carved into the surface.

Melanie put a hand on Nereza's back. "I know you were working on stuff like this when Magitech International let you go."

Nereza put the stone back and turned around. "You know, after they fired me, I became a bandit for a while.”

Melanie's eyes went wide. “No! You were the Bandit of Obsidian?”

“Yep! The last thing I stole was all the data I created while I was working for them. If you let me come on, I'd love to share what I have. I think I might have a good inter-departmental project we could start.”

“Nereza, stop! That sounds amazing. Of course I'm gonna hire you. Do you want to show me what you have now?” Melanie motioned to an empty table. They sat down and Nereza pulled her laptop out of her bag. She navigated through her files until she found what she wanted.

“Now, I have more stuff besides this, but after the experience I just had going to the literal other side of the world, I'm most passionate about this.” Nereza double-clicked on her files about Eternity's Mirror. “My boyfriend, our friends, and I saw this artifact. Well, more than saw it. I found that Eternity's Mirror was a portal between our side of the world and the other side. They call it Nox Terra.”

“That's amazing! That must have been incredible to be there when you figured it out.”

“It gets better. I was able to use the technology I created to interface with the mirror and got it to work again. It only worked briefly, but that's how we got to Nox Terra! What's better is that I kept a copy of the magical code that made it work.”

Melanie playfully slapped Nereza's arm. “Shut up! No you did not! If the project you want to take on is what I think it is, you're gonna have everyone's support on it. Tell me. I need to know if our college mind-meld is back." Melanie gripped Nereza's arm, staring into her eyes.

"I want to replicate the Mirror's magic and create a new portal between the sides of the world."

Melanie shrieked and threw her hands up. "Yes! Girl, yes! I am so for it. With that in mind, let's find *another* mirror because I need to introduce you to the new head of Inter-departmental Research and Development!"

Nereza leaped up, her coils bouncing as she leaped toward Melanie. "An executive position? Are you sure?"

"Nereza, of course I'm sure." Melanie pulled Nereza into a hug. "You're one of my oldest friends and you were the best in our class. As CEO of FTL, I'd be stupid not to bring you on to be head of your own department. It's perfect for you."

Nereza's heart swelled and she hugged Melanie tighter. "You'll never know how much this means to me. I thought I lost myself, my entire identity when I lost that job."

Melanie pulled out of the hug to look Nereza in the eye. "Your identity has always been more than what you do, but I'm glad that this can help you feel more like yourself because you deserve that." Melanie pulled away and winked at Nereza. "Now onto the juicy stuff, girl. You gotta tell me about this boyfriend you mentioned."

Chapter 6
Advisor and Rescuer

Neander took a sip of his coffee. "I have to thank you for your hospitality, Leonis. It seems like we're all falling into place here."

"I'll echo his praise," said Gabrielle, folding and refolding her napkin. "I see how happy my granddaughter is after joining the other magitechnicians in Fruit of the Living Tree. She hasn't been that happy with her work since Magitech International let her go."

"It's my pleasure," said Leonis. "I told Nyx that we'd find a job for each of you, after all. Of course, that brings me to why I asked you two to join me for breakfast this morning while the younger guests visit with some of our younger inhabitants topside."

"I'm sure they'll enjoy getting some sun," said Neander.

"I imagine they will," said Leonis. "Though I want to focus on why we're here this morning."

Gabrielle took a sip of tea from her mug. "Leonis, did you find a way for this old lady to help?"

"I did. I looked you up, Gabrielle. Now, I'm sure there may have been another Gabrielle Kahn, so tell me if I made a mistake, but were you a nurse and midwife before you moved out to Cahzpeh?"

"You do your homework, don't you? Yes. I worked for forty wonderful years caring for people and helping mothers deliver their babies. My daughter-in-law, Nereza's mother, even allowed me the pleasure of helping her deliver my grand-baby."

"That's beautiful, Gabrielle," said Leonis. "I'm glad that was correct because our health clinic is understaffed, and I would love for you to work there. A few of the women have become pregnant since we arrived here, and they could use experienced care."

Gabrielle chuckled and leaned forward on her elbows. "Well, it's been a long time, but I'm sure most of the parts haven't changed too much. I'd love to help in the clinic."

"Perfect," said Leonis, his eyes crinkling as he smiled. He turned to Neander. "Now, for the moment, that just leaves you. You've spent a long time working with Taariq and the other members of the Dark Circle, that nasty coven of sorcerers. Would you say you know them pretty well?"

Neander's face contorted in a pained expression. "Unfortunately, I do. But I have left that life behind, Leonis. I don't even go by the same name anymore."

"I know that, but I had a thought." Leonis pushed back his plate and turned his chair so he could face Neander head on. "With all the knowledge you have, your opinions and insights would be useful to us. In fact, because you led the campaign against us, you might help us protect ourselves."

Neander thought for a moment, his eyes fixed on his shoes. "What are you asking me to do? I don't want to be involved in anything violent again. My hands have already caused enough death."

Leonis reached out to put a hand on Neander's shoulders. "It's nothing like that, I assure you. One of my advisors stepped down because he wasn't sure he could fulfill his duties anymore. I want you to take his spot."

Neander frowned. "I don't know. I'm still trying to be worthy of my sons' trust. How could I be worthy of such a high honor as to be an advisor?"

"What reason do you have to believe that your sons don't trust you?" Leons sipped lemon water from a glass. "They brought you here, to a place where everyone is someone you hunted less than a week ago."

A tremor ran up Neander's legs and back to the base of his skull as he remembered the few interactions he'd had with his sons. The brief meeting in the hospital as Emily lay helpless and dying, their official introduction at the boys' graduation a few months later, and all the little tension filled pockets of time since.

"I'm less worried about whether they think I can do the job," said Neander, "than I am about whether they know I care about them. I haven't been the best father."

Leonis stood and moved closer to Neander, placing a hand on his shoulder. "A good father protects his children, Neander. By doing this, you can help me protect your children and everyone else who lives here. We need actual information so we can guard ourselves against the enemy."

Neander wondered what Elior would say. A few months ago, Elior might have wanted Neander to refuse, to focus on being more like Emily, the only parent Elior and Eliam had known. Now, he thought, the twins might be more mature, might want to see Neander be self-sacrificing as they had learned to be.

"If I agree," said Neander, "you won't use any information I have or advice I give you to hurt anyone, will you?"

"Absolutely not. I want to use it to protect people."

Neander met Leonis's eyes for the first time in a minute and considered him. "Then I accept. I'd love to preserve life for a change."

A gentle spring breeze swept across the island as Elior sat with his friends and several others who had also come up to the surface. The sound of the wind in the trees was like music setting the tone of an evening in the setting sun. Birds swam and chirped in the still waters in the lake as they all watched and enjoyed nature.

"It's pretty here, isn't it, Reza?" asked Elior as he entwined his hand in Nereza's.

"It's a beautiful area of the lake, for sure. Does it make you nervous that we're so close to the capital?"

Elior looked out over the water. The air was still cold, and the warm water was causing steam to rise all around them. He breathed deep into his chest.

"Elior?"

He shook his head, rousing himself from his distraction. "Sorry. I was just thinking about how you guys all have a job now. I don't know what I'm doing here."

"I don't have a job either," said Eliam.

Elior threw his head back in laughter, toppling onto his back on their blanket. "That's true. I suppose we can be useless together!"

"Hey!" Nereza punched Elior's shoulder. "You'll never be useless, Eli. You know that."

Eliam coughed and leaned in to fake whisper to Nereza. "Kissing doesn't count as a use."

"Shut up, man." Elior shook his head and winked at his brother.

Opal leaned forward. "I'm sure Leonis is looking for a way for you two to help."

"After all," said Nyx, "it was my one condition. You guys have to have something to do before I'll act as general."

"You're right," said Elior. "I'm sorry, Reza. You'd asked something when I zoned out. What was it?"

"If being close to the capital made you nervous?"

"Oh! That's right." He thought for a moment, his head craned to some point in the sky. "No, not really."

Eliam huffed. "I mean, if my dad was still in charge, I think that might make me nervous, but the larger powers are a long way from here."

"It makes me a little nervous." Nereza turned to Opal. "Didn't you leave this area for the beach before we went to Nox Terra?"

Opal stretched her arms overhead. "We did. I understand why you're nervous, but it is a remote part of the lake, and no one comes to Black Sap Island. I heard it was some kind of war memorial."

"Something like that," said Nyx. "They may have commemorated it and made it a sanctuary as a cover, but parts of the island were covered in landmines when the navy base was active."

Nereza gasped. "And you didn't think to mention that before we all came up here?"

"I assumed," Nyx said, "that they had disabled the mines, so it was safe to be up here."

"That makes sense, Nereza," said Opal.

"I'd assume that if Leonis knew about the underwater barracks, he knew about the landmines."

"See?" asked Elior. "There's nothing to worry about, Reza."

They resumed contemplating the beauty of spring's arrival to the world until Melanie came up to them on the shore.

"Hey Nereza! Some of the other magitechnicians from FTL and I are going on a nature walk around the island before we have to go back to work. Do you, your friends, and your boyfriend wanna come?"

"Oh, that sounds like fun! Do you guys wanna come?"

Opal stood and brushed off her pants. "I don't see why not. Let's go."

The rest of them stood and brushed themselves off, sending a shower of pine needles back to the shore of the island. They followed Melanie to her group of friends and they began exploring the beach. Then one of the magitechnicians suggested that they explore some of the wooded areas.

"I don't see why not," said Melanie. "You guys down?"

"I'm a fan of exploring anywhere after being shackled by a dragon," said Eliam. "Let's do it."

The woods were beautiful, but the meaning behind the name of the island couldn't have been more apparent. Black sap oozed from the pine trees. It coated the forest floor. By the time they had walked a quarter mile into the woods, their shoes were caked in sap and pine needles.

Then, Nereza got her foot caught on a knobby root.

"Elior," she said, "I need help to get unstuck."

Chuckling, Elior said, "I'm coming."

He gripped her hand and pulled.

"Eliam, I'm gonna need some help. She's really stuck. Can you grab my waist to give me some extra leverage?"

"Sure thing, brother." Eliam hooked his arms around his brother's waist and they pulled. They pulled and pulled until there was a loud snap of bark breaking off the root and they all fell down.

Eliam landed hard, and a click echoed in the surrounding woods.

"What was that?" asked Nyx. "What clicked underneath you?"

Eliam shrugged. "I don't know. Could someone help me up?"

"I've got you," said Melanie. "Take my hand."

"Wait! Don't!" screamed Nyx, but it was too late.

Everything slowed down. As Eliam stood up, a spark flew from where he had been sitting and the hiss of gas rang in the air. As soon as the fire ball formed, Elior's hands shot up. A blue force-field enveloped the exploration party.

When the smoke cleared and the adrenaline subsided, Elior lowered his hands and the force-field that had kept them alive dissipated into the air.

"Every needle off the trees within twenty feet is burned to a crisp!" said Opal.

"I think my life just flashed before my eyes like some sort of stupid cliché," said Melanie. "What would we have done without you, Elior?"

"Auto-barbeque?" suggested Eliam.

Elior slapped his brother up the backside of his head. "Not funny, man!"

Eliam snickered. "Then why am I laughing?"

"Well," said Nereza, "I guess we all handle shock differently."

"Seriously," said one of the magitechs, "that was incredible. I'm very glad not to be burned alive like these trees."

Elior turned around. Not only were the needles falling to the ground as ash, but parts of the trunks were smoldering and catching fire still.

"I don't think it would be good to leave the forest looking like this. On the off chance a scouting boat from the city comes out here, they should see only green. Nyx, do you think you could do something?"

"I can try, man. Let's see."

Nyx took a deep breath, cracked his knuckles and touched the root where Nereza had been stuck. A watery wave of healing magic rushed from his finger tips. Needles went back into place, fires extinguished, and life was restored to the barren landscape around them.

"You know what?" asked Melanie.

"What?" asked Elior.

A huge grin spread across Melanie's face as she said, "I think I know what you should do to help Eternity's Refuge. Let's go back to see Leonis."

When they had returned to Leonis and Melanie had told him about what had happened above the surface, the leader said, "I had wondered what that explosion we felt was. I'm glad no one was hurt."

"Yes," said Melanie. "We are lucky to be alive. After all, most of us can't survive fire the way djinn can."

Picking up a pen and jotting a note down, Leonis said, "Very true. So, are you just reporting, or did you have something more to say about what happened, Melanie? Do you want permission to study Elior or what?"

She sat in a chair across from him and motioned for Elior to do the same while the others stood behind them. "No, I don't want to study Elior. That isn't the kind of magic I'm interested in anyway. I am interested in what he could do for us all."

"Ok," Leonis said, leaning back in his chair. "You have my attention. What do you think Elior should do?"

"I'm curious myself," said Elior. "She didn't tell me anything about the idea she has."

"That's because I like surprises," Melanie said, pulling her blonde locks back revealing purple streaks. "You know how many members of the underground are prisoners, don't you?"

"Unfortunately, we lost count weeks ago." Leonis sighed and stood up. He sat on the edge of the desk nearest to Elior and Melanie. "Taariq's initiative to round us up is relentless."

"Exactly. And, there are no plans to rescue any of them, correct?"

Leonis rubbed his eyes. "We don't have the resources to even attempt that, Melanie."

"That's where you're wrong. Our biggest concern is being able to keep the people who rescue the prisoners safe. Before now, we didn't know how to do that."

She stood up, gesturing at Elior, and continued. "Nereza told me he was a search and rescue operative before all of this started, and he has magical powers of protection that just saved all of our lives. He can be the solution we need to bring our people home."

Elior felt like he'd had a bucket of ice water dumped on him. Shocked, invigorated, scared, and enlivened at the idea all at once, he said, "I can do that. I'd love to help that way. Taariq shouldn't be able to hold anyone who follows Michael captive."

"Then not only is he the answer to our problem," said Melanie, "but he's willing, too. C'mon, Leonis. What do you think?"

Leonis held his chin and mouth in one hand while he cradled his side with the other. Several moments passed while he stared at Elior and Melanie before he spoke again. "Elior, since you're willing, I'm putting you in charge of a brand new department. You'll pick and train your staff and lead your own operations. I'm appointing you the High Commander of Rescue."

Elior turned back to Eliam. "I already know who my second in command is." He swiveled back to face Leonis in his chair. "My brother is the kind of man to charge ahead and risk his own life to save someone. I can't imagine anyone better to have by my side."

"Then it's all settled," said Leonis. "Welcome to the team, Elior. I look forward to working with you."

"I guess that means I'm officially accepting your offer, too," said Nyx. "Everyone has a place. Everyone is helping, and that's what I wanted. So, where do we start?"

"We start with you getting to know my head of household and business, Demetri. He's new here like yourself, but he's been an excellent help in getting us more organized. I asked him to meet us here so you could get to know him, knowing you'd accept."

Neander laughed. "Confident, are we, Leonis?"

"Only when I know I'm right, Neander. Only when I know I'm right."

Chapter 7
Rescue

IBLIS'S BOOTS CLOMPED AGAINST THE stone floor as he walked down the hallway to Taariq's office. The sound was so forceful that if he closed his eyes, he could almost picture himself back in his proper body. He missed the sway of his tail behind him and the leathery wrap of his wings. But his revenge was in motion, so maybe it wasn't so bad after all.

As the djinn came to the end of the hallway, he raised his fist to rap on the door, but it swung open, almost of its own volition.

"I could hear you all the way at the other end of the hallway, Iblis," said Taariq. "Try not to be so loud. You aren't a two ton beast anymore."

Iblis growled in his throat. "I suppose old habits die hard, master."

"Hmm. I suppose they do. What do you have to report?"

Iblis walked over to Taariq's desk, careful to step lightly so as not to further annoy his liege. Sitting down, he said, "The plan is in motion, Taariq. Every one is ready to work."

"Good," said Taariq. "Tell me more."

"I've installed a plant in each of the six strongholds of Michael's power in the six corresponding regions on our side of the world. As we speak, they are ascending into power in their respective assignments."

"Are they all djinn?"

"A mixture, sir. There are some members of the other races who are more than willing to help my cause."

"Good," said Taariq, standing and circling his desk. "It wouldn't do for the others not to feel involved in this, too. And how are they ascending into power?"

Iblis chuckled. "Each of the selected moles was chosen for their excellent acting skills. Where they lacked, I trained them or cast enchantments to bolster them, but acting was the most important part."

"Why is that?" Taariq folded his hands.

"Because each of them will have to prove that they are faithful to Michael's cause and Aelon's dominion in order to advance to high stations. They will fool those idiots with little effort."

"Acting alone won't endear them to the deepest sympathies of the enemy. What else?"

"Well, any plan this important has multiple layers to it. The plant in Vidania has leaked a fake article about the former dwarf queen's mother and aunt."

"You've got my attention, Iblis," said Taariq. "What was in the article?"

"It details their capture and where they are being kept."

Taariq stood and stomped his foot. Smoke and fire filled the air around them for a moment. "Are you out of your mind? They are some of the best bargaining chips we have."

"When have you not trusted me, master? Would you like to hear why I've released this information in this way?"

"You'd better have a good excuse."

Iblis sniffed and turned to walk to the bookcase. He pulled a title carelessly off the shelf and leafed through it. "Leaking mildly important information through the plants helps foster a sense of trust. If the leaders trust them and see that they are useful, their guards will lower."

"I see," said Taariq, sitting back down and letting his anger roll away.

Iblis replaced the book and spun back to pull Taariq's eye contact to himself. "I was named your second in command for a reason, Solarium."

Taariq bristled at his old name. "I have a new name now. How many times must we go over this?"

"You may have a new name, but your fire burns just as brightly as it did when you drenched the very sky in flames bursting from your red maw. We have to keep remembering the old times if we desire a chance to bring ourselves back to our former glory."

"You have a point," said Taariq, strolling to his window. "But every time I hear my old name roll off your lips, in this form, everything feels a little more hopeless."

"No, master," said Iblis, moving to stand behind him. "You will be the greatest dragon to ever fly once again. I swear I will make it happen."

"If you don't, then I'll have to kill you." In Taariq's reflection in the window, Iblis saw his eyes turn as black as a starless night and a chill ran up his spine. His master meant exactly what he said.

Elior walked swiftly through the maze of alleys and byways on his way to Leonis's conference room with Eliam trailing close behind him.

"Do you know why he called this meeting?" asked Eliam, buttoning his shirt as they walked.

"I'm not sure," said Elior, tucking his shirt into the back of his pants. "All I know is that he said it was urgent. I don't know more than that."

"Has to be serious to call us together this early." Eliam yawned. "I hope we can catch some more sleep when we're done talking."

"Something tells me that is not likely to happen."

"Worth hoping for, anyway."

Soon they arrived at Leonis's quarters and were shown to his conference room. Leonis sat at the head of the table and was flanked by Nyx, Opal, and Neander.

"Good," said Leonis. "Now that you two are here, we can start. We have some intel I want to discuss, and I think you should all be part of the decision about what we're going to do."

"Intel?" asked Opal. "I'm not sure what I would have to add to the conversation. I'm a priestess."

"The high priestess," said Nyx.

"While that may be," she said, "I'm still not sure why I would need to weigh in on intelligence reports."

Leonis cleared his throat. "Ordinarily, I wouldn't include you in this kind of conversation, but considering the subject, I think you would have been angry if I hadn't included you."

Leonis motioned for Eliam and Elior to take a seat and continued. "We received some information about some specific prisoners, which Neander confirmed. Neander, would you like to explain?"

"Of course. Early this morning, another advisor told Leonis that two noble dwarf women were being held captive in the palace dungeon. Since I was there recently, Leonis called me to corroborate the story, and I did. I had forgotten, but the dungeon is currently housing your mother and aunt, Opal."

Opal shot to her feet. "Are they hurt? Are they still alive? How could you not mention this to me before, Neander? I swear, if Michael hadn't—"

"Opal!" Nyx cried. "We wouldn't be here if there wasn't a plan. Sit back down and let's talk about this."

Opal tilted her head and narrowed her eyes at Nyx. For a moment, Elior expected her to argue, but her expression shifted and she uttered only one word.

"Fine."

She sat back down, and Leonis picked up where Neander left off. "With that in mind, and Opal's obviously powerful feelings on the subject, I would like to propose a rescue mission. I don't think it does any good having the high priestess's family behind bars."

"I agree," said Opal.

Leonis turned to Nyx. "Can you think of any reason rescuing Opal's mother and aunt would be a bad thing? Does it make strategic sense for us, given our current state of affairs?"

Nyx didn't look at Leonis. He kept his gaze fixed on Opal as he said, "I don't think that matters. Regarding rescue efforts, I have to think about what Michael would do, and he was the type of person to leave no one in harm's way. I will tell you that my strategy would include reuniting Opal with people she loves. I'm in favor."

"Neander," said Leonis, "can you think of any objections? Would there be any specific reason that we should not send a rescue party?"

Neander thought for a moment. "If Elior is going, I'm sure that the Great Spirit will provide a way for him and whoever accompanies him to avoid danger. That's why you appointed him the High Commander of Rescue anyway, right?"

"Then that leaves only you, Elior," said Leonis. He slid a file folder across the table to him. "Does this sound like something you, your brother, and your men can handle?"

Elior opened the folder. Schematics, details about guards, and various other pieces of pertinent information were compiled. Eliam looked over his shoulder and made little noises as he read.

Eliam whispered in Elior's ear. *"I don't see any reason we shouldn't, assuming we do it quickly and we take weapons, just in case."*

"I agree with you," said Elior.

"Tell Leonis, not me!"

Elior sat up straight and folded the file shut. "I think it's doable. My men and I can leave by dusk."

The sword that Aelon had imbued with power glittered in the light of the setting sun. Elior sheathed it as he turned around to face his small team of men. Two former policemen rounded out a four-person team with him and his brother. Jonas and Marcus had been part of the special missions team that raided hostile crime scenes while still in action, so they were an obvious choice.

"As soon as the sun dips below the horizon," Elior said, "we'll move out."

Jonas picked his teeth. "Whatever you say. I'm just glad we're getting out of the cave."

"I was goin' nuts," said Marcus. "At least now we'll see some kind of action. Hey, boss, do you need some armor? I can go back and get my spare bullet-proof vest real quick before we row to the mainland."

"Nah," said Eliam. "He doesn't need that. If someone tries to shoot at him, he's just gonna put up a nice blue bubble of protection. He won't feel a thing."

Marcus whistled. "I might shoot him just to see that."

"Please don't," Elior said. "I've never tested my powers in a situation that wasn't actually life or death, and I don't want to go using it as a party trick."

"I can respect that," said Marcus.

"Still hope we get to see it," said Jonas.

"And I'd like us all to make it back in once piece with no threats to our lives. Unfortunately, only one of us will get what he wants, and I think it's more likely to be you, Jonas."

Elior kept his eye on the horizon. The moment the sun glittered over the edge of the world and blinked out to make way for the moons and their glories, he pushed his oar into the sandy bank, and they rowed through the water.

Mist and steam still rose from the water. He prayed a silent prayer of thanks. In the darkness of night and the mystery of the fog, even the most skilled watchmen would have difficulty spotting them.

The night only got darker as they rowed. Clouds rolled in from over the northern mountain and a light drizzle of rain washed the banks and the lake as they rowed.

Elior guided them to the corner of the lake that was closest to the royal estate. Nearly an hour and a half after leaving Black Sap Island, they were standing in the mud within eyesight of the palace.

Guards circled the grounds around the palace, but Neander had told them about a small evacuation shaft that led directly to the dungeon. Apparently, Elior's father had found it while traveling by smoke, which he found hard to understand.

"The grate Dad told us about should be that way," said Eliam, pointing to the edge of the wood that separated the palace grounds from the acreage of their childhood home.

"Then what are we waiting for?" asked Jonas.

Not another word was spoken. As noiselessly as possible, Elior led the way across the grassy bank to the edge of the woods.

He kicked at the leaves in the area where Neander had indicated.

"Everyone, help me look. The entrance has to be around here somewhere."

Eliam, Jonas, and Marcus kicked around in the grass. Several minutes later, Elior turned to hush Marcus as he suppressed a curse.

"Quiet! We don't want to attract any guards over here."

"I'm sorry! This thing is just a lot harder than I thought it was going to be."

Jonas snickered, trying not to full on laugh. "No one told you to swing your leg like you were trying to turn a perp into a soprano, Marcus."

"Shut up!" hissed Eliam. "At least he found the entrance. We're all going to work together to move it. Now come on, one man on each corner. Let's go!"

Elior positioned himself with his three helpers and squatted. He mouthed a countdown, and when he got to one, the four men lifted the stone grate into the air and moved it about three feet to the side before they had to drop it.

As they gathered around the shaft below it, Marcus whistled. "That is a deep shaft. Are we supposed to slide down there?"

"No," said Elior, "There's a switch on the corner that pops ladder rungs out."

Elior punched an otherwise unremarkable brick, and stone rungs jutted out of the side of the shaft. He climbed in and led his men down into the dungeon.

After what felt like forever, Elior planted his feet firmly on the damp stone floor of the dungeon. The air was stale with the stench of waste and vomit. He couldn't imagine Opal's mother, the regal woman he'd met those few months ago, in a place like this.

Eliam, Jonas, and Marcus joined him on the damp floor. He ducked and pulled them into a huddle. *"Stay close,"* he whispered. *"There are a ton of guards down here. I don't want to kill anyone if we don't have to, so don't make a move that we didn't plan without my say so."*

Eliam and the others affirmed their understanding, and they stood, ready to pursue their mission.

Elior peeked around the corner. For the moment at least, their way forward was clear. Elior led his men down the corridor towards the place they had been told Ruby and Saphira were being held.

As they eased their way through the dungeon, Elior wondered where the rotation of guards was. There should have been a lot more men there, or really, any men guarding the prisoners at all.

"Elior, wait," said Eliam. "There's something weird happening."

"What is it?"

Eliam pulled Elior's shoulder to make him look at the cell they were about to pass. "This is the tenth empty cell we've passed. If they are keeping so many people form Eternity's Refuge in here, then where are they? We haven't had to incapacitate a single guard. I just think that there's something wrong."

"You know, we were kinda thinking the same thing," said Jonas.

Marcus kicked a loose piece of stone on the floor. "Something doesn't feel right."

"I hear what you're all saying," said Elior, "but we have our orders. We can't stop now." He took a deep breath. "Let's get to their cell as quickly as possible. Draw your weapons, just to be safe."

Eliam, Marcus, and Jonas all drew guns, but Elior preferred the sword that Aelon had blessed. It had helped him and his friends slay Umbra, and Elior was sure that it could help him defend against any foe in their way.

A few moments later, they were in front of Saphira's and Ruby's cell.

Elior sheathed his blade. "Saphira! Ruby! It's me, Elior!"

Saphira turned. "Oh, thank the Great Spirit! I was afraid we were going to be stuck here, alone forever. Aspen! Elior is here to rescue us."

"Wait, Aspen is here too?"

The elf stood up out of the shadows, revealing his form for the first time. "They brought me here, along with Elowynn. They killed her and kept me here to keep from continuing her work. She was spreading the news of Michael's power in our community."

"That's horrible!" said Eliam.

Ruby smiled. "At least you've been able to rescue your brother! You must be so happy."

"I am," said Elior. "Now let's get you out of here." He turned his neck to his brother, Marcus, and Jonas. "Guys, cover me while I pick the lock."

The three men behind Elior raised their guns and cocked them so they were ready to shoot as Elior worked on the lock.

It was slow going. There were more pins than usual in the lock, and some of them were extremely resistant to being used. Then, in one shining moment, the lock popped open, and the door slid open.

Saphira embraced him. "Praise be to Aelon for sending you, Elior! Now, let's get out of here. They've left us alone for days without food or water."

"That's horrible! Don't worry, there's plenty to eat and drink where we're going," he said, releasing her from their embrace.

"That may be," said a gravelly voice, "but you'll never make it back."

Three djinn materialized out of thin air. Elior's men trained their guns on the newly appeared enemies and fired, but no sooner had they pulled the trigger than had each djinn erected a wall of fire in front of their hearts. The bullets fell to the floor in melted heaps.

"RUN!"

No one was sure who had screamed it, but it was the only thing to do. The dwarves and the elf didn't have the strength, though.

"Your guns are useless anyway," said Elior. "Each of you grab one of them and carry them back out. Hurry!" They followed their commander's instructions, leaving him to face the djinn alone in the dungeon's dank corridors.

Elior turned to the djinn, smoking with anger, and drew his blade once more. "Not another step, or I will end you."

The gravelly voiced djinn laughed. "Alone? At least with the other three humans, you had a slight advantage in numbers, but this? This is just pathetic." He turned to his companions. "Attack."

The other two djinn launched themselves at Elior with the force of a rocket. He raised his blade and their momentum pushed him back several yards. The djinn stumbled at the end of their push. When they regained their balance, they swung their fists at Elior from opposing directions.

He ducked, falling out of the line of their assault and their knuckles collided, spraying sparks across the floor and singing Elior's hair.

Springing up, Elior swung his sword at the djinn, catching one on the chin and the other on the shoulder. Hot, steaming blood blistered out of the razor thin cuts he'd inflicted.

Anger spilled out of their pours in liquid fire. They burst into flames, sending waves of heat towards him, but Elior's gift enveloped him in a cooling blue light.

"Elior!" Eliam yelled.

"What are you doing here? I told you to take them out."

"I couldn't leave you alone against three djinn."

"I'm fine, get out of here!"

The gravelly voiced djinn laughed. "Oh, I see. You want to protect him and you're worried that if we fight the two of you, you'll miss something. After all, you just got him back." The djinn dissolved in smoke and reappeared behind Eliam.

He wrapped his arm around Elior's throat. "Resist anymore, and I will pinch his head off and enjoy the gush of blood that will bathe me when his neck bursts."

Elior sank to his knees. He was about to drop his sword when the choking, gurgling cry of Eliam reached him.

"Don't—stop—fighting!"

His brother wouldn't stop, so neither would he. Concentrating all his will power on calling on Aelon and Michael and the gift of the waters, Elior opened his heart and prayed for what he needed.

Bright blue light spread from a reflection on his locket like wind and blew back the other two djinn. They hit the ceiling with such force that they passed out. The moment of victory felt short lived.

Eliam started screaming as the djinn squeezed his neck.

"NO!" cried Elior, throwing his sword at the djinn's face.

A sickening thunk echoed off the stone walls as the sword embedded itself into the djinn's forehead. Eliam gasped for air as the djinn's strength failed and the fire in his eyes died to an ember and then went out.

Elior rushed to help his twin up from the ground where he had fallen with the djinn. "Are you alright?"

"Yeah," he choked, rubbing his throat. "I'm gonna be fine. Grab your sword."

Elior reached for the hilt of his blade and pulled. The sound of the djinn's skull against the steel made his spine shiver. "Let's get out of here before any reinforcements come."

"That sounds like a good plan. I think I should listen to you more."

Elior laughed. "That might be a good policy from now on."

Chapter 8
Plans

WHEN THEY RETURNED, ELIOR LET Marcus and Jonas go enjoy a well-deserved break while they went to meet their friends and Leonis.

Elior beamed as he watched Opal embrace Saphira and Ruby. Leonis strode over to him and shook his hand.

"I had my doubts about Melanie's idea, but you really pulled through. You rescued them, fought off djinn, and made sure that all your men came back safely."

Elior blushed and turned away. "I really can't take all the credit. The gift I have came from Michael. Everything else is just training that any other search and rescue operative would have had. I'm glad I could be of service."

Opal turned to Elior. "I can't thank you enough. I feel like I can actually do my work now that they are safe. From the moment I found out where they were until you brought them into those doors, I was on edge."

"You would have done the same for me, Opal."

She walked over and hugged him. "Of course I would. I sort of already did when we went to Nox Terra."

"And who could forget all those good times?" asked Eliam. "If only I had been as easy to rescue, right, Elior?"

Neander stood from where he'd been sitting. "While we are thrilled that Saphira, Ruby, and Aspen are safe, there was another prisoner that was supposed to be there as well."

"Who?" asked Elior.

Leonis sighed. "One of my other advisors. She was rounded up in one raid on the city. Somehow, Taariq, or whoever, is in charge of their campaign of oppression, found out exactly what their role was."

"What would they have done with her after that?" asked Nereza. "If she wasn't there, do you think they killed her?"

"Not if they wanted information, which would make sense," said Nyx. "What do you think, Neander?"

"More than likely," he said, "they've transferred her to the new top security prison under the surface of the plains."

"We need to get her back," said Leonis. "She knows so much about us, and that's a huge weakness. We don't know what she's told them and what she hasn't, or if she's even cracked at all. It's a giant liability. Even if we have to make some changes, we need to know what to change to protect Michael's followers."

"Then I suppose you'll want us to go rescue her?" asked Elior.

"Yes," said Leonis, "but this time it's going to take more preparation. Neander was telling me about this prison. It has the best security system ever designed. Without proper preparation, it's going to be immensely difficult to infiltrate and impossible to escape once you're inside."

"I think I have an idea that can help with that," said Nereza. "Melanie and I will take care of the details and have something ready for Elior and his team by tomorrow morning."

"Excellent," said Leonis. "Let's rescue our missing advisor."

Elior walked into Leonis's office. His father and girlfriend were already there with their leader, waiting for him.

"Are you and your men ready to go?" asked Leonis.

Elior handed Leonis a report of the equipment and men he was taking. "Yes, sir. Everything is packed for the journey. Eliam, Marcus, and Jonas are ready to row out to meet our driver at the drop zone."

Leonis turned to Nereza. "And you're sure your devices will work? They will hide them as they infiltrate the prison?"

In answer, Nereza lifted her wrist and pressed a button on her smart watch. In an instant, her form glittered out of sight. "As you can see, the glamour watch is in perfect working order. Every bit of me has been hidden by the charm."

"That's amazing!" said Neander. "It took me months to learn how to do a basic glamour, and I could never fully master invisibility."

Nereza reappeared. "We based it off the paint on the boat we sailed in on. After that, it was as simple as using the AI of a smartwatch to create a physical map of the user's body on which to project the charm."

"Well done," said Leonis. "We're glad you joined our magitech team."

"Let's go over the plan one more time," said Neander. "Your driver will drop you off in the forest, three miles from the prison gates. Once you are within eyesight, you turn on your glamours and find an opportunity to get inside. Find the advisor and any other high profile ER prisoners, give them the spare devices, and escape."

Elior laughed. "You make it sound so simple, Dad. Yeah, I understand. It's the basic get in, get out."

Nereza reached out and took Elior's hand. "Be safe out there. I need you to come back safely."

"You have my word."

Elior turned to go, but as his hand landed on the knob, he swiveled. "Other high-profile prisoners? Are there others besides your missing advisor, Leonis?"

The leader winced. "There's a possibility, but we don't know for sure. We don't have anyone on the inside, so most things we hear are rumors. Neander's information has been the first genuine news from the inside we've ever had."

"And," said Neander, "some of what I know may have changed. Taariq doesn't like to have loose ends, and I'm a huge one for him right now. As far as I can tell, he hasn't figured out where I am, and I'm going to keep it that way."

"So what other prisoner would I be looking for?"

Neander rubbed the back of his neck. "Let's just say that one of your friends would be thrilled if you found who I think is there."

"That's cryptic," said Elior.

"Son, I'm not interested in giving false hope."

Elior turned back to the door and chuckled. "In any case, I'm sure I can handle the mission at the basic level we've discussed already.

Come see us off?"

"Ok, I'll be there shortly."

While Marcus and Jonas checked and double checked the equipment they would need for the journey, Elior and Eliam stood aside with their father. Neander stood, fiddling with his pockets, turning them in and out.

"Are you ok, Dad?" asked Eliam, taking a small, awkward step forward.

Neander shoved his hands deep into the linen folds and sighed. "I don't know how to say what I want to say without sounding disingenuous."

Elior's chest tightened as he stood before his father. The man carried the weight of years beyond his own, with hunched shoulders and a pinched expression full of pain. Compassion compelled Elior forward, and he swallowed his pride as he stepped forward to embrace Neander.

For a moment, Neander tensed as Eliam joined his brother in the embrace, Neander sobbed and hugged his sons into him. The out-pour from Neander brought tears to the eyes of Elior and Eliam, and they stained Neander's shoulders with tears. A couple of minutes passed, and they pulled away slightly.

"Dad," said Elior, "we know you're going to be real with us. I trust you." Elior hadn't expected to say it, but he meant it. This was a new man, not the father who had abandoned him.

"I need more moments like this," said Neander. "Come home safely, so we can have more moments like this."

"We will, Dad," said Eliam.

Elior smiled and squeezed Neander's arm. "We'll all have plenty of time. We're a family now, dad, and nothing can change that."

"Just come back safe," said their father.

"Of course we will," said Eliam. "After all, we belong to each other."

The familiar line settled over them like a soft blanket, and for a moment, it was as if their mother, Emily, was with them. She'd be thrilled with where they were now.

After a short row and a long drive, Elior and his men were within sight of the prison's gate.

"Turn on your stealth devices," he said.

As soon as they did, all traces of them, except for their shadows, disappeared. Even those were fuzzy and indistinct in the dying sunlight. Thankfully, there was a failsafe for users in a registered group, where they could still see each other within five feet of one another.

Eliam clapped his brother on the back. "Remember, our leader told us to stay close. We don't want to lose anyone in there."

"Stay close together, don't get caught," said Marcus. "We get it."

Jonas gave a thumbs up. "Nothing to do but to do it!"

They moved forward. The terrain leading up to the gate was rocky and hard to cross. Of course, why would they put a prison in prime real estate? The gate was the only part of the prison that was above ground. Part of the reason it was so hard to break into or out of this place was that there were no air vents larger than a coin, no shafts larger than a hand, nothing leading in. The only way in or out was through that gate.

Elior, his brother, and their assistants knelt by the gate, waiting for the guard on duty to open the door. Then, an enormous truck pulled up to the gate and a severe man with a scar across his face and dark military fatigues stepped out.

"Warden," said the guard, "welcome back."

Elior turned to his men and signaled for them to trail the warden.

The warden strode toward the gate. "It's not exactly a warm welcome, but I'll take it. Anything to report, Morisson?"

"No, sir," said the guard. "Shall I open the door, sir?"

"Well, I don't pay you for the stimulating conversation, do I? Yes. Open the door."

The guard did an about face and flipped a switch. A retinal scanner emerged from a hidden panel. The guard scanned his eye and whispered a passcode. Then the door opened.

I sure hope escaping is easier than getting in, thought Elior.

He stuck close to the warden, trailing his steps as silently as possible as he slipped inside. Then the unthinkable happened. Marcus was locked outside the door.

Elior, Eliam, and Jonas all eyed each other with silent horror as the elevator behind the door descended and they left their fourth group member behind.

Their wrists buzzed with a notification.

Don't worry about me, guys. I'll make sure the door opens when you come back. I'm tracking your location.

It wasn't what they'd planned, but as many steps as were necessary to open the door, it was probably better that Marcus was stuck behind.

When they had descended to the body of the prison, the warden walked off towards his office and Elior, Jonas, and Eliam got their first view of the inside of the prison. The entire structure was one long spiral descending into the depths of the earth in sterile white. Guards in silver roamed and observed the doors.

Elior made sure they were outside of anyone's hearing and said, "This is going to be a lot harder than when we rescued Ruby, Saphira, and Aspen. We are going to need an enormous distraction."

"No kidding," said Eliam. "Why don't you find Leonis's advisor and any prisoners from the Refuge with them and we'll work on the distraction."

"Sounds like a plan to me," said Jonas.

"Fine," said Elior, rubbing his temples. "Just don't get caught. I just got you back."

Eliam put both hands on his brother's shoulders. "We're gonna be fine. Go find our people."

His remaining men turned and were out of Elior's bubble of sight. He turned and walked down the spiral, careful to avoid the paths of any guards he saw. Each of the cells was labeled with the prisoners' names and their offenses.

Four levels down, Elior found his mark. Two prisoners sharing the same crime, supporting Michael Rex and state treason, shared a cell. The current round of guards was switching out, so Elior whispered as loud as he dared into the cell.

"Hey, lady," he said, "are you Leonis's advisor?"

She jumped. "Who's there? I can't see anyone. I must be hallucinating."

"No," said a voice from the other side of the cell, "I heard it too."

"Really?" she asked. "Then where are you?"

Elior toggled his stealth briefly, so they could see him. "I've got some stealth magitechnology from the Refuge. I've got some extras for you, too." Elior held two watches through the bars. "Put them on while I pick the lock."

"What a relief," said the advisor. "I didn't know Leonis was planning a rescue. We rarely do that."

"I'm new," said Elior. "We just started doing this."

The other prisoner stepped forward. This prisoner looks a bit like Nyx. "Are you from Aquaré?" he asked the man.

"I am," said the merman as he put on the watch and toggled it on. "I'm a member of the refuge down there. A leader, actually."

"It's a pleasure to meet you. Now, let's get you guys out of there!"

Elior sent a message for a distraction on his watch and then went to work on the lock. The moment he tripped the lock, there was an explosion below him and alarms started blaring.

"Let's go!" Elior yelled.

He led the two prisoners he'd freed up and up through the spiral. Guards ran down past them, narrowly missing them in their cloaked state. They reached the elevator doors, where Elior slowed and turned to wait.

"Why are we stopping?" asked the merman. "Don't we have to take this elevator up?"

"Yeah," said Elior, "but my men need to return first."

The merman flared his webbed fingers and snorted through his nose. "Well, they better get here fast or you'll have rescued us for nothing."

Aching seconds passed. Elior kept his eyes fixed back toward the explosion. He was about to give up for the safety of the mission when Jonas and Eliam came into view.

"Thank Aelon, I thought you were caught," he said. "Let's ride up."

They got into the elevator. No one said a word as they rode up. Elior sent a message to Marcus telling him to get ready to open the door, but he didn't respond.

Elior chewed on the inside of his lip. His mind was on fire as he waited for a reply, but none came. As they neared the top, he prepared to be sent back down. The mission had failed.

Then, when they slowed to a stop, the doors slid open. Marcus dropped the guard's unconscious body to the ground and laughed with relief.

"I'm so glad that worked, I wasn't sure if it would. You're all safe! And you rescued the marks. Let's get out of here before he wakes up."

"I don't want to stay here another minute," said the advisor.

"Agreed," said the merman. "I'm ready for a change of scenery."

Nyx sat in Leonis's office waiting for his friends' return. It had been nerve-racking waiting for word of success when Elior infiltrated the prison, but as soon as Leonis had an estimated time of return, he made sure that they would be gathered here to greet Elior, his men, and those he had rescued.

Tapping his nails on the armrest, Nyx said, "Leonis, do you have an update on that ETA?"

"I'm afraid not," said Leonis, jotting down a few notes.

"Don't worry, Nyx," said Neander. "I'm sure they'll be here any minute."

Nyx sighed and stood up. "I've been by Elior's side almost constantly for the past six months. I'm glad he's doing something useful, but I don't want to lose another friend."

"I know losing Mason was hard for you," said Opal, "but Elior has his gift and three other men with him. He'll be here."

That's when the door opened. Elior led Eliam and Leonis's advisor inside. Then another figure entered.

Nyx's jaw felt like it dropped all the way to the floor. He gathered his wits and cried, "Mason?!"

The merman Elior had rescued froze and turned to Nyx. "You're here, Nyx! This is amazing!"

Nyx rushed to his friend and embraced him. "How is this even possible? I thought you drowned!"

Leonis cleared his throat. "It looks like this is a reunion that's long overdue. I'll talk to Elior and Eliam with Neander and Opal. Why don't you go catch up with your friend, Nyx?"

"Thank you, sir. I appreciate that," said Nyx as he led Mason out of Leonis's office and to his own quarters.

Once they were settled and they both had a mug of hot tea, Nyx said, "I just can't tell you how happy I am to see you, Mason! Tell me everything. Leave nothing out."

Mason chuckled. "If you say so. It's a long story."

"I'm sure. I'll just drink my tea and listen."

Mason adjusted himself in his seat. "Guess I better get comfortable then." He cleared his throat. "After you swam out the window, Minerva caught me and held me down. Just before I drowned, she removed her curse and I could breathe again. She told me that if I didn't help her, that the rest of my life would be spent on the verge of drowning."

"That's awful!"

"Yeah, so after a couple times experiencing that, I'd had enough. I asked her what she wanted to know."

"Oh, Mason … "

The merman looked down and rubbed his arms. He shuddered as if the memory had pulled a physical response from his body. "I know I shouldn't have, but it was torture."

Nyx gently put a comforting hand on Mason's shoulder. "I don't blame you. I'm sorry you had to go through that."

"Right. So she asked how the resistance worked. You know, location, numbers, strategy, things like that. I lied a couple times, but when she would test the intel, she'd come back and torture me." Mason lifted his shirt. Burn scars spiraled around his torso.

Nyx reached out with a shaky hand. "Do you mind?"

Mason shook his head, and Nyx touched a scar. It was hard and rippled. It felt nearly identical to shark fins. Prickly and cartilaginous.

Mason lowered his shirt. "I don't think I can talk about how these felt when they were inflicted. When high tide came in and pelted me, my skin tore and little scavenger fish would eat the burned stuff while my body tried desperately to heal."

"Mason, if I had known—"

He put his hand up. "Stop, Nyx. I'm ok now, and that's what matters. Anyway, I'd had enough. I gave her actual information when she asked again. She put a curse on me and used me to go execute her plan. She used me to dismantle the rebellion from the inside."

Mason stood and turned away from Nyx. "I'd never felt lower. Thankfully, the priest I knew saw the signs of the curse and helped me break it before Minerva called me back to kill me. I recovered, and then the news was talking about how our leaders were merging our nations. Your name popped up as wanted because of your relationship with Michael. That's when I knew I had to join the underground. I actually helped to start the Aquarian chapter."

"That's truly amazing, Mason." Nyx wiped a tear from his cheek. "I'm so glad Elior rescued you."

"Me too," said Mason. "You have to come back with me. I know so many people who will be thrilled to find out that Commander Cascata is alive!"

"Actually," said Nyx, leaning back and putting his hands behind his head, "I've been named the general for the Refuge, so I fulfilled my dad's dream for me, anyway. I became what he always wanted."

"That's awesome!"

"I would like to go back, though. I might work from the sea, but how would we even do that? I have the gift of healing now, but so far, it hasn't worked on this curse."

Mason pulled a smooth stone out of his pocket. "This charm will work, though. When Minerva sent me in as a spy for the rebellion, she required me to report to her on land if she was ever up there attending to matters for Taariq. This stone is a charm that allows for the spell she used on us to be cast and reversed at the bearers discretion."

Nyx reached out for the stone, lifting it out of Mason's palm. "Do you think I could give this to Nereza? She's a magitechnician and she could duplicate the charm so that we can both have one of these."

"Of course," Mason said, "if you think it will help."

Nyx embraced his friend. "I can't tell you how good it is to see you again, Mason. I thought you were gone."

Mason wrapped his arms around Nyx. "Praise Aelon for giving us our friendship back."

Chapter 9
Assassination

"TWICE!" SCREAMED TAARIQ, LAUNCHING FIRE balls at the objects in his office. "Two separate times has that little brat bested us and gained prisoners back from our clutches!"

Iblis glanced around and gestured at the various fires burning in Taariq's office. "I don't think you're hurting him by doing what you're doing here. You're only going to force yourself to replace these books and maps."

Taariq wheeled on Iblis, catching him by the throat. "Do you think I care about books and maps?"

The darker djinn slipped his hand around Taariq's neck and lifted him up. "Don't forget who your friends are, Taariq. I followed you before anyone."

In a silent agreement, both released the other's throat.

Taariq sighed, his fire calming for the moment. "I'm sorry, friend.

I'm frustrated. You said to trust you and now we've lost bargaining chips."

"Kill any remaining prisoners, so there is no one to rescue. That way, there isn't anyone else they can take. Show your power."

Taariq extinguished the still smoldering fires and cast a spell repairing the damage. "Iblis, I got to where I am now with a lot of diplomacy. The other heads of state still think they have power. They take care of the day-to-day issues of their respective countries, except for Vidania since Yrahkaz's disappearance, and I take care of everything else. Aelon's influence must be destroyed if we are to keep the world under our power."

Iblis scoffed. "What does diplomacy matter now? The entire world is at your feet! You can do anything and no one will stand in your way. Don't you want to take advantage of that?"

"If I wipe out all the followers of Michael, we have in custody at once," said Taariq, "the people will rebel. I may have immense power, but I cannot withstand a planet-wide insurrection. Magic can only do so much."

Iblis stood and paced the perimeter of the room.

"What are you doing?" asked Taariq.

Iblis waved him off. "Let me think a moment." After several minutes of pacing, Iblis stopped. "Don't bother with the prisoners anymore. Instead, wipe out their rescuer. Kill the royal. After all, as long as any of them remain, there is a claim to the human throne. Take away the rallying point."

"You mean Elior? You think he's a rallying point? He betrayed Michael when I asked him. He's hardly dangerous."

Iblis growled. "You forget what I went through. That young man slew my dragon form, Umbra. He has powers of shielding. He has led the rescues. Aelon is setting him up as a symbol of divine power, and if we don't end him, the enemy will use him to end us."

Taariq puzzled at his feet. "How did I survive all these millennia without you, Iblis? Of course, we must destroy Elior. But how? The locations of their strongholds have been hidden from my sight."

Iblis sat and folded his hands in his lap. "Don't trouble yourself with the details," he said. "I have someone on the inside already who can end this problem once and for all."

Taariq stood and stretched. "Good. Since you have that taken care of, I'm going to go enjoy a night out. I need a stiff drink to deal with the stress of this day."

The sensation of slipping into a dream from Aelon was becoming familiar to Opal. Tendrils of velvet wrapped around her as she flew into the sky to watch whatever Aelon wanted her to see that night. He'd shown her assassins, magic rings, and glimpses of the beginning of the world. Mostly history, but tonight had a distinct feeling. This felt like something that was currently happening.

With velvet wings, she hovered over the interior of the cave. The town below her slept with all the security of a warm blanket in winter. At first glance, the whole town was asleep. Then, out of the corner of her eye, she saw a hooded figure slip out of their home and up the street.

Michael's voice whispered in her mind. *"Follow him. No one slips through the shadows like a rat if their intentions are pure."*

Opal leaned forward, moving with the figure and descending to his level. At the slightest noise, he would duck behind a stalagmite or a stray crate until silence settled once more. As her hovering form followed the hooded man, Opal tried to figure out where he was headed, but it was like he was trying to lose someone. She knew he couldn't see her. After all, she was only here in a dream.

His meandering path eventually leveled out as he reached a back alley. He dashed along until he reached the residence that Leonis had assigned to her, Nyx, Elior, Eliam, and Nereza. Chills ran up her back as he began fiddling with the lock on the door. He was so careful and silent that he made no sound.

She tried to rouse herself from sleep, but Aelon must have wanted her to see more because, as the hooded man slipped into their house, she was still deeply entrenched in sleep. With horror, she watched as the man slinked up the stairs and down the hall. As he reached the end of the hall, he opened the door to Elior's room and pulled out a long, curved knife.

Past the hooded figure, she could see Elior, sleeping peacefully and entirely unaware of the danger he was in. That's when she woke.

Opal sat up and ran to her door, screaming at the top of her lungs, "Elior! Wake up!" She ran to his room.

From the hallway, she caught the bright flash of blue light as the hooded figure was blown back against the hallway wall. The noise was enough to rouse everyone else and bring them out into the passage, too.

Elior emerged from his bedroom, rubbing his throat. "Your scream saved my life," he said. "How did you know?"

"I had a dream."

Nereza walked up to Elior. "Are you hurt?" she asked, pulling his hand away. The thinnest line of blood beaded on the surface of his skin just above his Adam's apple.

He took her hand and kissed it. "I'll be fine as soon as the bleeding stops. He just nicked the skin. No damage to major blood vessels, thank Aelon."

Eliam put his hand on his brother's shoulder. "I don't know what I would have done if I woke up and you were dead." Turning to Opal, he said, "Must have been some dream."

"My question," said Nyx, stepping over to the hooded figure who had been knocked unconscious, "is who would do this here? I thought everyone here was on the same side!"

Nyx threw back the hood and recognition painted his face as he balled his fists.

"Who is it?" asked Elior.

"Demetri," said Nyx. "He's one of the council of elders. I don't know why he would do this!"

Nereza leaned down, pushing Demetri's hood further from his neck. "Has anyone seen a tattoo like this before?"

The tattoo was djinni script, arranged in a straight line and flanked by dragon wings. Nereza reached out to touch it, but as soon as her hand made contact, she jumped back.

"What happened?" asked Opal.

"The tattoo is hot! It burned me." Nereza held up her hand. Little red blisters were already forming on her fingertips.

"Nyx," said Elior, "can you heal her real quick?"

Nyx ran his webbed hand over Nereza's fingers and the blisters receded, leaving clean, healthy skin behind it. "We need to tie him up and take him to Leonis immediately. Something terrible is going on here if Demetri tried to kill you."

"And Demetri almost slit your throat?" asked Leonis, one eyebrow raised.

Elior pulled the scarf he wore down, revealing the wound that was scabbing over. "There's the proof, right there. I don't know why, but I know he tried to kill me."

Demetri sat restrained in the corner of the room. He was silent, glaring at everyone gathered in Leonis's office.

Nyx cleared his throat. "There's a tattoo of djinni script and dragon wings on his neck as well. I almost think that he may have been a plant put here by Taariq."

Nereza laced her fingers between Elior's. "There has to be something we can do to prevent this from happening again! If Demetri is a plant, there may be others, and we need to find them all."

Opal sighed. "Nereza is right. We can't just sit around and wait for an eventual successful attempt on Elior's or any of our lives. We were lucky Michael gave me the dream he gave me. If it weren't for that, we would have woken up to Elior dead in a pool of his own blood, and we would have no clues about who did it."

"If we aren't able to trust our own people," said Leonis, "our organization will crumble." He went to kneel by Demetri. "Friend, I took you in, clothed you, fed you, but now you've betrayed us. What are we to do with you?"

"I betrayed Michael once," said Elior. "He forgave me and told Opal and Nyx to do the same. Maybe, if he's sorry, we should do the same."

"I'm not sorry, nor will I ever be," said Demetri. "The Great Spirit is not a good god. He let my family die and let me lose everything."

"It isn't like he controls everything like a puppet master," said Opal. "Sometimes bad things happen because there are bad people in the world and horrible accidents that happen purely out of chance."

"Maybe so," said Demetri, "but the people you claim to be so bad are the ones that have helped me the most. Kill me if you must, I'm sure Iblis and Taariq will resurrect me when they finally defeat Michael and his *father*."

"If you believe that," said Neander, "then you're even more deranged than I was when I served Taariq."

"Wait," said Nyx, "he said something I need to know more about. Demetri, who is Iblis?"

Demetri laughed, his chains rattling. "He's only Taariq's right hand, djinn. He cast powerful spells on me so that I would know what to do in my assignment here. He is my boss."

Elior's heart skipped a beat. "You don't think that…"

"That we somehow triggered the creation of another djinn when we defeated Umbra?" finished Eliam.

Nyx groaned. "That's probably exactly what happened."

"Does no one stay dead anymore?" asked Neander, chuckling and shaking his head.

Opal patted Neander's arm gently and said, "Too soon."

Leonis groaned and stood from his crouch. "Are you the only plant from Iblis and Taariq, Demetri?"

Demetri was done talking. He simply stared forward and hummed a strange tune to himself.

"We're probably not going to get any further with him," said

Elior. "Still, we have to decide what to do from here."

Leonis sat back down at his desk and began writing something. "The first step is easy, but let's wait until Demetri is removed from my office."

A few moments later, two guards took Demetri away. Leonis flipped a switch on the wall behind his desk and a quiet whooshing sound played from each corner of the room and above the door.

"That's a neat feature left over from the military. The whooshing disrupts any bugs or people listening from outside."

"So, what do you see as our first step, Leonis?" asked Nyx.

Leonis folded his hands. "The six of you have to move. If Taariq knew you were here, there's no reason he won't be able to send others after you. Even if he doesn't know our exact location, he knows your general whereabouts, and that's bad."

"But where would we go?" asked Opal. "And can we bring those we've been working with along?"

"You're the high priestess for us, Opal. I'll leave that decision to you if you need someone specific. I think Mason should go with you. Nereza, I'll leave the choice of whether Melanie comes with you to her. As for Jonas and Marcus, I'd like them to stay here. I want to suspend the rescue program for now while we find out if there are other plants and where they are."

"There's certainly a lot to consider," said Opal. "I'll take Allura with me, she'll be helpful. I think we should leave by sunrise."

"But where will we go?" asked Elior. "Isn't there a danger anywhere?"

"One of our outposts is significantly safer than we are here for you. The Faeland base is far from their capital city and the seat of power. Even if there is a plant there, it will take a while for any action to be taken since electronic communication is jammed while within the confines of our refuge bases."

"Then I suppose we'd better pack," said Eliam.

"We'll stay in touch," said Leonis. "We have ways of doing that which are specific only to the people I grant access to. Neander, I'll give you the communication device. I'm sure that you can duplicate it, Nereza." He handed Neander a black disk. "Tap on that three times and you'll be able to speak telepathically with me. I'm putting you in charge of the investigation into any more moles."

Neander crossed his arms. "What's going to happen to Demetri?"

"The only thing we can do," said Leonis, "is to execute him for treason against the cause."

Chapter 10

Up the River

ONCE AGAIN, IBLIS STOOD BEFORE the door of Taariq's office. He tucked the tablet he was carrying under his shoulder, but before he could even knock, the door swung open. Taariq was sitting in his chair, facing the window.

"Are you aware that your breathing is exceptionally loud, Iblis? I could hear you coming halfway down the hall."

"Apologies, sir. I think I'm still trying to breathe enough for my previous size, and these lungs don't have the capacity."

Taariq laughed and swiveled toward him. "To have the problems of remembering being a dragon so vividly. I'd feel sorry for you, but this bipedal body with soft flesh feels all too familiar. I'm sure you had something to tell me if you've left your important work of collecting data from the spies to come talk to me."

"That's just it, Taariq," said Iblis. "One spy has ceased

communicating."

Taariq rotated his chair back to the window. "What? Were they magically converted to the enemy's cause, Iblis? If so, we'll have to be choosier in who we send."

Iblis sat, bracing himself for the rage Taariq was about to inflict on him. "No, sir. Demetri, the one we ordered to assassinate Elior BarVidania, has been executed."

Taariq laughed. "If he was executed, how did you find out?"

Iblis held the tablet up. "I put a spell on the non-djinn recruits so that I could track them and transport them by smoke if I needed to. I stepped away for a meal, and when I returned, Demetri's mark on the incantation slab was burned out." Iblis pointed to the stone tablet and pointed to an engraved circle, like others on the tablet, but this one had no djinni script or wings inside it like the others. Instead, a dark, sooty stain smoldered on the rough surface.

Taariq's face grew colder even as the heat from the flames whispering along his skin grew hotter and more ferocious. "Then this is the beginning of your second failure in such a short time. You lost to weaklings on the other side of the mirror, and now they are exterminating the rats *you* put in place!"

Iblis leaped backwards and covered his face as Taariq screamed and blew fire all over his desk, incinerating it and everything on it to faintly glowing charcoal in seconds. "Sir," said the black djinn, "I can fix this! Just give me a chance!"

"You'd better," said Taariq, "because if you cannot deliver on the promise of your presence here, I will burn you like that desk and I will feast on your bones."

Iblis sighed. "If I was the leader of the underground, I'd move

Elior and his friends. Clearly they aren't safe there, so they're going to change things to throw us off."

"Well," said Taariq, "that's true. You aren't completely useless. Guess I'll have to see that they have some trouble on their way out, then."

Taariq brushed roughly past Iblis, leaving him alone in the office to watch the embers of the desk smolder.

Black Sap Island faded from view in the early morning mist as they glided up the river, barely making a splash. Elior was grateful for the extra cover that the mist brought. As much as he trusted the magitechnology that kept the boat hidden, a little extra assurance never hurt anyone.

Nereza came up from behind and leaned on the railing beside him. "Do you think we'll be safe in Faeland?"

"I don't know," he said before leaning over and kissing her shoulder. "To be honest, I haven't felt completely safe since our plane crashed before we met Opal. It's been one thing after another."

Nereza's coils bobbed as she turned to him fully. "Do you think that we'll ever be safe again?"

"Of course! I mean, if Aelon and Michael are working to stop Taariq, it's only a matter of time before we'll never have to face him again."

Then, a dark voice met their ears from the mist. "What a lovely fantasy," it said, "but even if that were true, today will not be that day."

Without being noticed, Taariq had traveled to them in a smoky cloud hidden by the mist. His form condensed on the deck of the ship. Liquid fire dripped off his body, landing on the metal deck and making the condensation sizzle like bacon in a pan.

He sneered at Nereza and Elior. "I might have missed your departure if you two hadn't also been coated in the same paint as the hull of this boat. Thanks for sticking out like two pathetic imbeciles."

Elior reached for his sword, which he'd grown accustomed to carrying since being enlisted as the High Commander of Rescue. "What do you want Taariq? We have no business with you!"

The djinn laughed. Something was different about it, something unhinged.

"Any business you're in since you aligned with my enemy is my business, boy." Taariq spit and a boiling globule landed mere inches from the toe of Elior's boot.

Taariq took a step toward them, but Nereza put on her brass knuckles and shouted at the djinn. "Don't come any closer!"

"Why?" Taariq examined the weapons. "Sure, those weapons have obviously been blessed by Aelon, but you'd have to actually catch me before I killed you for it to be of any use."

Nereza puffed out her chest and bared her teeth. "If you try anything, I'll use the magitechnology I installed in my weapons to disable your powers. Then what would become of all you've done?"

The djinn bared his teeth in a white-hot sneer. "There's no way you're telling the truth," he said. "Nothing like that exists!" Taariq laughed again, causing the flames on his clothing to change colors and grow brighter and dimmer.

"Test her bluff, Taariq," said Elior. "But on the off chance she's telling you the truth, you might just be handing yourself over to end it all today, and you will lose."

The djinn took a step back. "My powers go far beyond magic, as you know. If you keep tampering with the new world order, I will end you, the underground of Michael's followers, and everyone you love will die, Elior. I'll make sure of it, *personally*."

"I've learned from my mistakes," said Elior. "I don't trust one slimy word that drips from your disgusting mouth. Now, get off this ship in the name of Michael and Aelon!"

Taariq's face contorted in anger and he lunged forward, clearly intent on ripping Elior to shreds. Nereza turned in to Elior's body while he raised his hand. A wave of blue-tinged energy surged forward and blasted Taariq off the boat and into the forest on their starboard side.

"Let's get below deck so he can't find us again," said Elior.

Nereza sighed as if she'd been holding her breath. "That sounds like a good idea."

Elior put his arm around Nereza's shoulders. "One thing, though," he said. "Did you actually put something in those brass knuckles that could disable his powers?"

Nereza threw her head back and laughed. "I wouldn't know where to start with that. It was a total bluff."

"*By Aelon*, never do that again!"

Viola snuck through the mist, watching the boat closely, waiting for just the right moment. Then she saw her opening.

After the ordeal of the morning, the peace in the boat's lower deck was welcome. The boat rocked and swayed with the gentle wind. On the lower deck, Elior and Eliam were playing a board game, Neander and Nyx sat discussing important information for the well-being of the Refuge while Mason listened, Nereza and Melanie tinkered with the beginning of the portal project, Ruby and Saphira read magazines, and Opal sat meditating with a woolen blanket wrapped around her while Allura tended to a stick of incense burning in front of her.

Impressions rose and fell in her mind as Aelon pieced things together like a woven tapestry in her consciousness. Then, a full thought came together.

"Guys," she said, "Aelon just revealed something to me, and it changes everything about what we're doing."

"What do you mean?" asked Elior.

Opal stood up to pull everyone's attention toward her, letting the blanket fall. "Aelon has told me we're in more danger than we realized."

Melanie did not look up as she continued to work on her project. "What makes you think that?"

"Because it has been revealed to me that Iblis and Taariq have planted a spy in every refuge. Nowhere is safe."

"What can we possibly do about it?" Nyx stood up and put a hand on Opal's shoulders.

She met his gaze with eyes watery, but not tearing. "We're going to have to split up. We need to find every informant and arrest them."

"Is that the best idea?" asked Elior. "We haven't been apart, at least the three of us that were with Michael, since before winter began, and now the snow is almost entirely melted."

"Besides that," said Eliam, "Elior and I were just reunited. I'm not exactly eager to go our separate ways yet."

"What would happen to the projects I'm working on with Melanie?" asked Nereza. "I don't want to slow down our progress."

Neander slammed the mug he'd been sipping from down on an end table. "Did none of you hear what she said? Taariq has *spies* in every corner of the world just waiting for a chance to bring us down. If we don't follow Opal's advice and separate to take them down, Taariq will make another attempt on Elior's life and will probably kill all of us along with whatever residents are in the refuge we're stationed in."

Everyone fell silent.

"I won't

There wasn't more to be said after that. Neander was right. Nothing would change that, no matter how little anyone wanted to separate.

"The separation won't be forever," said Opal. "I think that a week at most will be enough, and then we'll all come back together in Faeland and move on like nothing happened."

Nyx stood. "Let's drop any complaints. Ultimately, if Aelon reveals something to Opal, we're fools if we don't listen. Let's rest in Faeland for the evening, but then we need to go our separate ways."

"Just temporarily," said Opal. "No one says that you have to stay where you go."

Nyx smiled briefly. "Of course, that goes without saying."

The boat stopped. As they ascended to the top deck to disembark, the stars twinkled delicately as they swirled overhead in their dance. In the trees nestled between the rocky crags of the mountains, a network of bridges and structures swayed in the gentle breeze. A fairy flitted down from a tree-house and alighted on the dock as they disembarked.

"Welcome," she said. "I am Moretta. Leonis sent word to expect you. I'm sure you've had a long journey. I'll show you to where you'll be staying and we will have breakfast for you in the morning."

They all followed her, their impending separation weighing heavily on all their shoulders.

Chapter 11
Departure

Nereza turned the charm she was duplicating for Nyx over in her hand again. Her eyes smarted from being open all night. Without looking up, she heard the ruffle of covers and a yawn come over from Melanie.

"Oh, Nereza," she said, "don't tell me you never went to sleep!"

Nereza yawned deeply. "If I could tell you that, I would, but I wanted to make sure that Nyx had this ready before he had to leave today."

Melanie stood and walked over to Nereza, leaning on the desk. "Would it really have been such a bad thing if he left a little later?"

"Maybe not, but I have to go soon, too, Melanie. Actually, that reminds me, are you coming with me?"

Melanie scrunched up her face. "I feel like I'd just get in the way. I'll stay behind and keep our project going."

"If you're sure," said Nereza, placing the charm in a small simulation chamber by her computer.

Melanie pulled a chair up beside her. "Actually, I was hoping to get some more face time with Eliam. Do you think that could be a possibility?"

Nereza pressed a button to run the simulation to test the charm and pushed back from the desk. "Why do you want that?"

"Well, he's super cute, and I just thought that maybe I'd like to hang out with him," she said, looking down at her thumbs.

Nereza smirked. "While it feels weird knowing you think he's cute when his identical twin brother is *my* boyfriend, I guess I should be glad that there are two of them."

Melanie giggled and brushed one of her auburn waves behind her ear. "So, do you think you could kinda plant that seed?"

"No," said Nereza, "I don't want to be that girl who thinks the answer to life's problems or trauma is a relationship, so I won't push Eliam into anything. I also don't want to be accused of trying to keep his brother to myself after what they just went through, but I will tell you where his room is so you can pop by before breakfast."

"You're such a jerk, girl!" said Melanie as she playfully slapped Nereza's shoulder. "You really had me going there for a second." Melanie sighed and wagged her finger in a mock scolding. "Ok, I'll take what I can get. Where is his room?"

Nereza picked up a pen and scratched a little map on a piece of scratch paper. "He's three doors down on the right on the floor below us. If you wait twenty minutes, you'll probably catch him alone. I'm meeting Elior on the roof for a little alone time before everyone gets there."

"Ooooh! Alone time with Elior!"

"Stop," said Nereza, "it isn't like that. We just need to spend time together since we've been in crisis for our entire relationship. At least mostly."

"No need to explain things to me, Nereza. Believe me," said Melanie, "I've had my share of complicated relationships. I fully support your need to take time alone, away from all the stuff that has happened in your life for the past couple of months. Are you leaving now?"

"I'm going to splash some water on my face first, probably change. After that, I'll be heading out."

Melanie replaced her chair. "I suppose I'll see you up at breakfast, then."

"Yeah," said Nereza. "I'll see you up there."

Elior sipped a mug of tea in the cool morning air at the top of the trees. Nereza stood next to him, rubbing her eyes.

"Did you sleep ok?" he asked.

She snickered. "Sleep? What's that?"

"I'll take that as a no, then?" He set his mug down on the railing around the top deck and stretched, arching his back until it popped. "Oof! Sleeping in a hammock did not agree with me."

"I didn't even get a chance to try," said Nereza. "Melanie and I were up all night working on duplicating that charm Mason had so that Nyx can go back to Aquaré with him and adapting our cell phones to communicate magically rather than just electronically."

Elior's mouth dropped a bit and his eyes widened. "You did all that in one night?"

"Well, with help."

"Still," he said, "that's pretty amazing."

"What is?" asked Nyx, as he came up behind Elior with a plate of food.

Elior turned to face his friend. "Nereza and Melanie could duplicate Mason's charm so you can go back to Aquaré with Mason."

The eggs and sausage and fruit on Nyx's plate slid off onto the floor as his arms went slack. As his tears flowed, Nyx threw his arms around Nereza. "Thank you so much! I never thought I'd get to see my country again, but you made it possible!"

Nereza returned his hug. "If it means helping you and helping our cause, I'm happy to do it. That's why I came back to Lux Terra, anyway."

The others ascended to the deck and Eliam said, "Don't tell me you're already saying goodbye. It's so early!"

Nyx let go of Nereza. "No. Nereza just gave me a gift."

"Good," said Neander, "because we still need to discuss where everyone is going. Obviously, Nyx, you and Mason are going back to Aquaré."

Opal grabbed a plate from the buffet line. "My aunt, mother, Allura, and I are going to Nanony."

Neander poured himself a mug of coffee. "Of course. Nereza, you'll go to Arborria. Elior and Eliam, since the refuge in Registaan will probably be the most dangerous, you'll go there since Elior's gift can protect you."

"What about you, dad?" asked Eliam.

Neander swallowed a gulp of coffee and sat in a plush chair.

"Leonis has told me to stay here and establish Faeland as the new headquarters. He thinks the remote location here in the mountains is betters suited to our needs than the proximity to Vidania Prime that the refuge there has."

"What about me?" asked Melanie. "I want to help, too."

"Actually, dad," said Eliam, "I think Elior might need to go alone. Traveling into djinn territory is bad enough, but I can't defend myself against magic. Maybe I should stay here with you. I can work with Melanie to help beef up security for all the refuges or something."

Neander thought for a moment. "I suppose that would be alright." He sighed and rubbed his coffee mug with his thumb. "And you're probably right that Elior would be safer going in alone. There's only safety in numbers when we're talking about a conquest, and without a gift, you're someone he'd have to protect if anything went wrong."

"This is just so weird," said Opal. "I don't like that we have to split up. I haven't been away from Elior and Nyx since before winter, and now all the snow is melted. And Nereza, you've been with us for months."

"But we're both going home, Opal," said Nyx.

Elior slipped his arm around his brother's shoulders. "And I have my brother back. Not only that, but my dad came around and is in our lives now."

Opal chuckled. "I know it's strange, but I'm actually looking forward to seeing you all again when this is over. When we've gotten rid of the threat within, we can start really working to dismantle Taariq's power once and for all."

"Well," said Nereza, "let's enjoy our breakfast and get on the road. The sooner we get to work in our assigned areas, the sooner we can be together again."

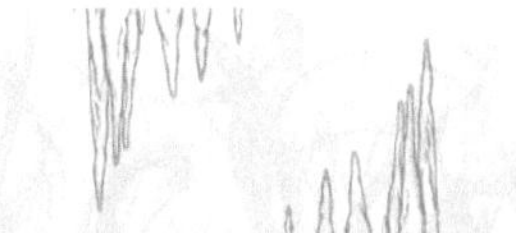

Nyx sat on the bank of the river turning the charm Nereza had duplicated for him over and over in his palm, Opal's words turning in his head like a revolving door.

The soft crunch of leaves behind him pulled him out of his thoughts and he turned just in time to see Opal put her hand on his shoulder. "What are you thinking about?"

"I didn't expect to see you," he said, putting his opposite hand on hers. "I was just thinking about what you said at breakfast."

She sat beside him, smoothing her skirt around her ankles and pushing a few scattered twigs into the water. "What do you mean?"

"I've seen you every day for months. We've talked, shared meals, been in danger, and celebrated every day since the day we left your palace in Nanony."

Opal shuddered. Nyx craned to see her expression, but her hair was loose, cascading around her shoulders and hiding her face from him. "I know. We've been through a lot."

Nyx slid the charm into his pocket and angled toward Opal. "I didn't realize how much until you said something. Do you realize that without this whole elaborate plan of Taariq's, all the planning he did in putting together the Dark Circle, and taking over our countries, that we never would have met?"

There was warmth in her voice when she said, "It almost makes you grateful that it all happened, doesn't it?"

He picked at the grass on the bank. "Does it?"

She turned to him, revealing the smile on her face. "As much as I hate what Steelwort did to my people in order to follow Taariq's plan, I'm glad I got to meet you and become your friend."

"Friend? Opal… Elior is a friend, Nereza is too. You—you're something more."

Opal stood and hugged her arms in as a breeze caught the ends of her ebony hair. "You're going back to Aquaré, Nyx. If we defeat Taariq, I'll be a queen again."

Nyx stood and sighed, putting his hand gently on her shoulder. "Even with those truths, you didn't tell me you don't feel the same."

Without turning or removing his hand, Opal said, "Nyx, I won't lie to you, and I don't want to hurt you, but reality is reality. We both have always had our own countries to think of. What would you do?"

Nyx stood. "I wouldn't trade anything for a world where I don't know you. I may have started this journey desperate to get back home, but now I have something that can let me come and go as I please. I don't want to lose you, even if that means my home is only a place that I visit."

"This is a lot to think about right now, Nyx," said Opal. "Let's think about it while we're apart. You might feel different when you're home than you think you do now. I don't want to color how you feel about home by telling you I feel.

"But—"

Nyx tried to continue, but Opal put a finger on his lips and silenced him. "I told my mother, aunt, and Allura that I'd meet them where the river shallows upstream. When we've found the traitors in our assigned countries and we're back together, then we'll talk."

Then she walked away, the wind rustling and blowing the pale blue of her skirt and her raven black hair in patterns that broke and healed Nyx's heart all at once.

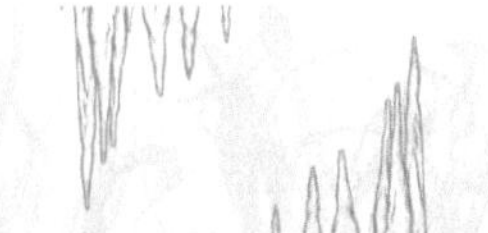

Elior savored the warmth of Nereza nestled into his arms while they swayed in a hammock in a high bough. The weight of her head on his chest was as comforting as a thick woolen blanket on a cold winter's day. After spending the night here in the Faeland refuge, she smelled of pine and herbs.

"Are you scared?" he asked her.

She stroked his fingers with hers, entwining them one at a time. "Depends on whether you mean for myself or for you."

Elior breathed deeply, trying to sort out exactly what he meant. "I guess just all of it. One of these spies almost killed me. If it wasn't for Opal's dream, he would have succeeded."

"And that would be why I'm scared for you," Nereza said, sitting up. "You're going into Registaan. While I'm glad that even that Spirit forsaken country has some citizens loyal to Aelon, I wonder if they are worth saving. Is it worth it to go there, exposed, and be at the mercy of a spy who not only shares Demetri's views but has magical powers?"

Elior took his eyes off Nereza and fixed them on the thinning canopy overhead. They were so high in the trees that the blue of the sky was taking over the green of the trees. "When this whole thing started, Eliam ran into a building to save one woman. We'd already pulled out dozens of victims from that research lab. Nereza, if things were even just a little different, you could have been in that lab."

"But I wasn't, Elior. I'd already been fired, and I was stealing software from Magitch and other companies to sell on the black market just so I could eat and live."

"That's not the point," he said. "I love you, and everyone in that building had someone they loved. The last time I made a choice to protect myself, I hurt Opal and Nyx."

She sat up a bit. "You mean when you betrayed Michael to Taariq?"

Elior bit his lip, hating to relive the memory. His actions had caused the death of Aelon's son. "I never want putting myself first to be my default again. I can't be that person."

"I think I understand, Elior," said Nereza with a sigh. "Just because it might be dangerous, you don't want to put more people in danger. There are families and people who love each other in Registaan, too. Even djinn are worth the risk."

"Eliam said it best," said Elior. "Every life is worth the risk. If I don't go, who knows what that spy will do? I doubt Taariq is thrilled with his own people turning on him."

Nereza swung herself up, so that she was on top of Elior, her hair creating a coiled cocoon around their faces. "Don't you dare die on me. When this mission is over, I want us to be right back here doing this again." She pressed her lips to his. His heart beat faster and heat rose in his cheeks.

When she drew back, he sighed. "I promise I'll come back."

She pushed herself off the hammock to the platform beneath it. "I'm going to hold you to that."

Neander released his sons from a bear hug. "I can't believe all I missed out on. These last several weeks being able to get closer to you both have been the best of my life."

"Dad," said Elior, "don't launch into another speech about wanting me to be safe. I've heard it from everyone. I don't need another one."

"That isn't what I was going to say," said Neander. "I'm truly just grateful for the time we've had so far."

"Seriously, though," said Eliam, "come back in one piece. This family just got put back together."

"Well," said Elior, "it isn't like you two aren't also in danger here. We haven't identified the spy here yet. Are you sure you guys can do it? I mean, Opal, Nyx, and I will all be gone."

Neander chuckled. "Don't worry. While I'm still working on a plan to get rid of my powers, I still have access to magic if we absolutely need it."

Elior's eyes widened. "Please consider that a last resort. I don't want Taariq to sense you here."

Their father said, "Yes, considering how I got them and the ties I have with the other Circle members, I'll consider it a last resort, only to be used in the most dire of circumstances."

"Melanie and I will be here to help, too," said Eliam. "She might have magitechnology that can help us, too."

"Melanie and I?" repeated Elior. "When did that happen?"

Eliam blushed. "She came by the room this morning after you'd left to meet Nereza. She told me she thought I was cute and wanted to get to know me."

"And?" prodded Neander.

"And," said Eliam, "After seeing how happy Elior and Nereza are, I want the same thing. After being almost eaten by an ancient dragon,

I think I deserve a little happiness."

"Just take it slow," said Elior. "We just met her, and while I trust Nereza's judgement and taste in friends, this whole spy thing has me on edge."

Eliam scoffed. "Don't even sweat it, bro. Melanie has been with Eternity's Refuge practically since they started it. She's legit."

"If you say so," said Elior.

Neander checked his watch. "What time was the envoy leaving for Registaan, Elior?"

"At noon. Why?" Elior asked.

Neander sighed. "You'd better make your way there. I don't want them to have to wait for you."

"Bring it in for once last hug," said Eliam.

The three embraced. A sense of wholeness, family, and belonging washed over them. *We belong to each other.* The only missing member of their family was Emily. Still, if she could see them now, Neander was sure that she would be overjoyed to see the three people she had loved most together at last. The phrase she always said to him she had passed on to their boys. It was a promise, and in that moment, he felt it was a promise fulfilled and overflowing.

Chapter 12
Arrivals

ELIAM SAT DOWN BESIDE MELANIE at the table the fairies had set up for them to eat at when they needed privacy. "I don't think I'll ever get enough of fairy food."

"Really?" asked Melanie. "I can't believe it's already lunchtime, personally. I still feel like I just ate."

Eliam's eyes widened with his mouth full of food. "You hardly ate at breakfast, though!"

Melanie flipped her hair back. "Well, I don't want to balloon up. Taking care of my body is important to me." She slid her hand from her shoulder down to her waist.

Eliam couldn't help but watch as she traced the subtle curves of her body, but he was brought back into focus when Neander came in.

"We need a plan about what we're going to do to catch the spy," he said. "Does anyone have any ideas?"

"Can't we just watch for a while and hope we see something suspicious?" asked Melanie. "I mean, Demetri tried to murder Elior. Wouldn't something similar happen here?"

Neander leaned back and squinted at the sky above. "I don't think Taariq would be foolish enough to try something like that again so quickly. Even if he would, we don't have Opal with us right now. Even if she has a dream or a vision, she might not warn us quickly enough to keep one of us from being assassinated or captured."

"Then we need a different approach," said Eliam. "Have you ever had to catch a djinn or djinn sympathizer, dad?"

A dark shadow passed over Neander's face. "Catching a spy would be nothing like catching a djinn, son."

"He's right," said Melanie. "Even if someone could catch a djinn without another djinn helping them, we aren't looking for a djinn here. We're looking for someone with djinn magic imprinted on them, right?"

"Yeah," said Eliam. "Demetri had that tattoo on his neck. I'm assuming that all the spies have something like that. But would that be djinn magic?"

Melanie and Eliam turned to Neander, who had a coffee cup poised to his lips.

"What?" he asked, setting the cup down on the table.

"Well," said Melanie, "weren't you trained by Taariq, Neander? You have to know something about how this all works. Was that tattoo djinn magic? It did burn Nereza."

Neander leaned forward on the table and thought for several minutes. "It's definitely possible that a certain type of binding spell was used on the spies. It would have to have been a way for them to communicate or sense Taariq's and Ibis's intentions or orders. Why?"

Melanie tossed a golden lock of hair behind her. "I was just thinking that if you know the magic, you might find it using magic."

Eliam laughed and put a hand on Melanie's shoulder. "He can't use his magic, Melanie! That was one thing Opal told him when he was healed. Can't you do something with magitechnology?"

"It's a long shot," said Melanie, a barely perceptible spark of annoyance in her voice, "but I may be able to develop a device that could sense that kind of magic."

"That would be awesome, Melanie!" said Eliam. "Then all we'd have to do is to get together all the leaders in once place. After that, we can use whatever you make to figure out who the spy is."

"And I know the perfect way to get them together," said Neander. "We'll host a dinner to thank them for their hospitality."

Melanie crossed her legs and leaned back. "Do you really think that will work, Neander?"

"I do. Fairies love being hospitable hosts, but they also appreciate being hosted. If we invite the leadership council, we're going to endear them to us and be able to look for the spy at the same time."

"If you say so, I'll believe you," said Melanie, brushing her hair back. "Eliam, do you want to help me put the device together? I'd love to have an assistant."

Eliam's face glowed into a half smile. "Sure. I'd love to help you out."

"Perfect," she said. "I'll meet you down in my room."

"See you down there," Eliam said, standing up and descending to the levels below them.

Melanie leaned forward. "Neander, I really hate to ask, but I do really need a sample of djinn magic in order to create a device that can detect it. Do you think you could—"

"Absolutely not!" he said, standing up and almost knocking down the table. "If I use my magic, I'm opening us up to an angry djinn who's probably hell-bent on finding me and killing me. Because my magic is bound in a circle, he can track me with its use. Believe me, Taariq seems well put together on TV, but he is a monster with a deadly temper."

Melanie pursed her lips. "That may be, but I can't create a device that can detect djinn magic if I don't have any to calibrate it with, can I? Our entire plan hinges on this dinner and finding the spy. Don't you want it to succeed?"

Neander paced back and forth for a minute, bathed in silence before answering. "Of course I want the plan to succeed, but I don't want to put us in danger. Taariq made the Dark Circle bind our powers in a fire oath ceremony. Since I haven't yet rid myself of magic, I can still feel the others using their powers all the time. If I use mine, they'll be able to feel me and know where I am too. It's how djinn find each other."

"Don't you think," she said, "that if a spy is here, they've already reported your presence? If they haven't, we risk them telling Iblis and Taariq at any moment. At least if you help me with this, we'll be able to defend ourselves from an attack we know is coming. But if you choose to stay stubborn in this, we won't know when or how they'll find out you're here."

Neander sank back into a seat. "I hadn't thought about that possibility, that they might already know where I am."

Melanie circled the table and sat beside him. "Look, I only need a tiny sample of magic. A super small, itsy-bitsy spell will probably be enough to help the device I'll create learn what djinn magic feels like. Whaddya say?"

Neander stared intently at the wood grain before pulling a pen out of his pocket. "Do you have any paper?"

Melanie reached into her purse and pulled out a pad of sticky notes. She handed the pad to Neander.

"If all you need is a minor spell," said Neander, "then a written charm might do the trick. As a bonus, it's small enough that when you activate it, the others probably won't notice. It's basically the magical equivalent of tying your shoe on a bench in a crowded park."

When Neander had finished writing the words in djinni script, he handed it to Melanie.

Taking it with a wide grin on her face, she said. "Thank you so much for your help."

Opal put her hand on the window as the mountain roads opened into a valley in the northern territory of Nanony. There, even in the spring and early summer, snow capped the peaks above them. A tingling sensation ran up her arm to her spine. "We're home."

Her mother patted her leg. "By Aelon's grace, my dear."

"I've never seen mountains so high!" said Allura, pressing her face to the window. "Are there cities inside every mountain, your eminence?"

"No," said Opal. "Only the largest mountains host cities. Here in the northern territory, the mountains are high but narrow. The towns here are small and nestled into the valleys between, much like the refuge."

"I was talking with a fairy last night," said Ruby. "He said that the refuge location here *is* a town. The population is loyal to you, and since you're loyal to Michael, the entire town decided they were going to follow your example. Others joined them from outside, of course."

"It's amazing to think that a whole town joined the cause," said Allura. "I'm the only priestess to join the cause from my hometown."

Saphira took a sip of water from a plastic bottle. "Ruby, how much longer until we reach Nanony's refuge?"

"We should reach them fairly soon," said Ruby, scanning the surrounding valley. "I don't understand why we don't see anything yet."

Then, as if responding to Ruby's wonderings, a gate appeared in front of them. A guard clad in all white stood with a silver rifle aimed at their car. "Get out of the vehicle and state your business."

"I guess we were closer than I thought," said Ruby.

Opal opened her door. "Let me take care of this, then." She swung her legs up and stood. "I, and those traveling with me, are strangers who are friends. Do you understand?"

The dwarf's stern features relaxed, and joy painted his face as he recognized Opal. "Your majesty! You're here!"

"Peace, sir," she said. "In this new reality, I'm only a priestess to you now. There's no need to bow. Do you understand what I said?"

"Yes, your eminence," he said, standing straight. "This is Nanony's refuge. I'll open the gate straight away!"

As she got back into the car, Opal said, "Thank you."

The gate slid open, and Ruby glided the car through the gates. As they passed, the air rippled around them and the town behind the veil was revealed. Dwarves lined the streets, watching their car. Those that saw Opal pointed excitedly and called out the news of her arrival.

"If the whole town is the refuge," said Allura, "I'm guessing the main offices will be in the town hall?"

"That's logical," said Opal. "Let's head there."

The town was small, so they arrived at the town hall in about five minutes. It was a stout, domed structure carved in the side of a mountain from the granite. Outside, a small collection of dwarves had formed around a tall dwarfess. When Opal, her mother and aunt, and Allura exited the vehicle, the dwarfess came forward and shook Opal's hand. "I'd always hoped to meet you, majesty. Oh! I suppose it's *your eminence,* now."

"I assure you," said Opal, "the pleasure is all mine. I didn't catch your name, ma'am."

"In the excitement, I forgot to introduce myself," she said. "I'm Mica. I'm the mayor of Granite Valley and the leader of Eternity's Refuge in Nanony."

"It's wonderful to meet you," said Opal. "Do you have some place we can talk in private? There's a very specific reason we've come here now."

Mica turned and motioned with her arm. "My office is available. We can go now."

A few moments later, they were all gathered around a small conference table in Mica's office.

"So," said the mayor and leader, "what is it that made it so important for you to meet with me in private, your eminence?"

Opal adjusted her skirts and folded her hands in front of her body.

"A couple days ago, I was given a vision that revealed that there are people in leadership in each refuge spread throughout Lux Terra that are plants from Taariq's regime."

"My word! Are you sure?" Mica's eyes shifted warily toward the door.

"She's positive," said Allura. "The Vidanian spy nearly assassinated Elior BarVidania, and our friends are already searching for the other spies in the other refuges."

"Is there anything you need from me to ensure they are found as quickly as possible, Opal?" asked Mica, leaning forward with sincerity in her eyes.

Opal held up her hand. "Nothing beyond what you were already planning. I'll hold court and commune with the local priesthood as I would have, anyway. Of course, each of the leaders should be in attendance. If you'll only make sure of that, I'll be able to fulfill my duty here quickly and with relative ease."

"That won't be a problem," Mica assured her. "I'll introduce you to the other priests and our leadership team tonight."

"It goes without saying," said Saphira, "that this is to be kept highly secret. No one must know her true mission here. She would be in danger if the plant knew he or she was going to be found out in the next few days."

Mica smiled and bowed her head. "Of course. I won't breathe a word of this conversation to anyone. You have my word."

Nereza sighed in relaxation as they drove between trees and their shadows. The ride to Arborria with Aspen was quiet. She'd expected as much. It hadn't been long since he'd lost his daughter. He had even insisted on coming separately from the rest of their group because he couldn't be in the same room as Neander. Nereza understood. You could forgive someone and still not be able to look them in the eye.

The Arborrian refuge was not located anywhere close to the spiritual capital, High Hills City. Instead, it was close to the commercial capital, Aelvby. The elves had constructed graceful silver buildings that stretched with the trees up into the sky. Nereza could have sworn they grew out of the ground instead of being built. City and forest melded into one like a marriage that was always meant to be.

When they reached the other side of the city, Aspen pointed out the window. "There, that gate, is the entrance to the botanical gardens. The refuge received special permissions from a sympathetic city council member to set up a village within it."

"So we're going to be staying in botanical gardens? I didn't bring a tent." Nereza hugged her backpack to herself, unsure if she'd be able to make any progress on her portal project while they were here.

"There's nothing to worry about," said Aspen, reading her expression. "There's electricity and all that. You wouldn't know that the village was there because it's deep in the grove of Elven Oaks on the other side of the gardens. The legend is that it was the grove that Aelon sung the first elves from."

Nereza relaxed slightly. "So it's hidden from sight, but not at all roughing it?"

The car rolled to a stop as Aspen chuckled. "We may be connected to the trees and enjoy nature, but elves do not 'rough it.' We're experts at manipulating nature to make it comfortable."

He rounded the car to Nereza's door and opened it for her. She took his extended hand, and they walked through the wrought-iron gates of the gardens together. The clouds overhead cast swimming shadows across the foliage overhead as they rolled by. The flowers swayed as if blown, but there was no wind.

Nereza took a single step closer to a bed of Blue Eyed Jewels, a large white flower with an inner center that looked like a bright blue eye, and a surge of perfume wafted over her, tingling at the edge of her senses. This was the most *alive* garden she'd ever been in.

They walked past so many flowerbeds that Nereza marveled that so many varieties existed in the world. Then, when they had reached the end of the path where it looped back in the other direction, she noticed where all the branches that grew over the garden came from. The grove of Elven Oaks was enormous. It stretched as far to the left and right as she could see and virtually no light could be seen through the density of the trunks.

"This is the entrance to the Arborrian refuge," said Aspen. "My daughter was the founding member. I wonder who replaced her…"

Nereza placed a hand on his shoulder. "Do you know how to get inside?"

He sighed. "Of course. Follow me."

Nereza followed as Aspen stepped over the small fence beside the path and walked over the grass to the edge of the grove. He leaned forward and whispered something into a knothole on one trunk. When he stood back up, the trees immediately around him moved aside as if wading in water.

"Come," he said, motioning with his hand. "The path won't stay open for long."

Nereza jogged forward through the trees, joining Aspen as he began walking through the narrow avenue the trees had opened to them. As they continued, the trees continued to move and make way for them as they traveled deeper into the grove. A short while later, soft music reached the borders of Nereza's hearing. The trees moved out of the way one last time and they were inside a clearing at least a mile in diameter.

Dozens of buildings were scattered throughout the grassy area woven from the interlocked branches and trunks of young saplings. Elf children ran while attended by their mothers and fathers. Some elves sang at the edge of the clearing, coaxing new trees to grow together for their purposes.

An elf woman sprinted forward. "Aspen! We thought you'd died when they executed Elowynn. I'm so glad to see you. Who is this?"

"Linewa," said Aspen, "this is Nereza Kahn. She is close with Elior, Nyx, and Opal. My daughter and I hosted them and Michael several months ago."

Linewa extended her hand. "It's a pleasure to meet you, Nereza. What brings you to Arborria?"

"It's nice to meet you too," said Nereza. "I actually have something urgent to discuss with whoever is in charge now."

"Actually," said Linewa, "after we lost Elowynn, the council of elders ran our refuge like a democracy. I'm as much in charge as anyone else who is of age here."

"So my daughter didn't have a successor?" Aspen bit his lip and squinted his eyes a bit.

"If it's something important," said Linewa, "we can always call a council meeting tonight for you to tell us what you were going to tell a single leader."

"Actually," said Nereza, "since it's run as a democracy, it would be better not to say anything to anyone. At least until we're sure it's a problem here."

Linewa looked as if she was about to argue, but decided against it. "I'm sure you have your reasons. Let me show you to where your house is now, Aspen. We moved it out of the center when Elowynn died. You actually arrived just in time."

"In time for what?" he asked.

"We have been planning a memorial service for Elowynn. Now, you get to celebrate her life and the legacy she left with us. It seems fitting that you should arrive on this day."

Aspen hung his head for the rest of the walk. They stopped in front of a largish home built in the same style as the others, though this one had golden flowers sprouting from patches of moss all over the shaded side.

"Butter Lilies," said Aspen. "They were her favorite."

Without another word, they went inside.

Elior's phone rang, and he answered it as he rose over the crest of a ridge in the desert mountains. What he saw sent him into shock and awe.

Heat rose off the dunes beyond the peaks. Even on his last visit, he hadn't realized how enormous the deserts of Registaan were. Elior gazed out onto the vast expanse of sand below the outer mountain range of Registaan. The air shimmered and sizzled. The only reason he wasn't blistering was because of the altitude in the peaks.

"Elior?" Nereza's voice echoed from his phone.

He cleared his throat, suddenly aware of himself again. "Sorry," he said. "Registaan has a strange beauty to it when you're looking out from the mountains like this."

"I thought the same thing when we drove through it on the way to the Mirror. But you still haven't answered my question. Are you alright?"

Elior crunched a few flakes of mica under his heel, spreading the sparkling mineral across the stone at his feet. "I'm about to enter a place completely full of djinn. I know it made the most sense for me to come because of the gift Aelon gave me, but I'm terrified. What if one of them casts a spell that I don't have time to deflect or they attack me while I'm asleep or while I'm incapacitated?"

The line was silent. Elior waited and was about to call out to Nereza when she said, "I don't blame you for being scared. I would be, too. I wish I could send you some sort of protective charm or device that will alert you when you needed to act."

"I'll be in a refuge made of djinn. Magic won't be in short supply, and I'm sure I'll be able to trust someone there to help me."

"That's true. Stay safe. I don't want to lose you," she said, a hint of fear in the back of her throat.

"Don't worry," said Elior. "I have more than Aelon's gift, I have Aelon. I'll be fine."

She groaned, "All the same, I might do some research to see if I can help you with a new charm or something. See you soon, I love you."

He smiled, the words erupting like liquid joy, "Only if you can. You just got to Arborria, after all. I love you, too."

Elior shoved the phone back into his pocket and walked between two pillars carved from the rock into a long hallway descending below the mountain. As he walked into the depths of the hallway, the air didn't cool as you'd expect. The air became hotter the deeper he went.

Elior rounded a corner and was suddenly in front of flaming chains. The white hot metal singed the air, sending waves of heat hurtling in every direction.

Elior tried to take a deep breath, but the heat made him choke. He covered his face to breathe in the relatively cool air and screamed, "The way opens to strangers who are friends!"

As if on cue, the flaming chains cooled to a dull gray and retracted, opening the way into the Registaanian refuge. When he passed through the opening, the flames returned, but thankfully the other side of the passage was cooler.

The way down was steep and narrow. Elior had to put his hands on either side of the tunnel to keep himself from tumbling down. "This would be so much easier if I could travel by smoke."

By the time he reached the bottom of the tunnel, his legs were shaky from overuse. He slumped to the floor, desperate for rest. He reached for his canteen that the travel party had left him and drank deeply. As he breathed and replaced the cap, a shadowy figure formed in front of him.

As the smoke cleared, a djinn with shock white hair in priest's robes stood before him and bowed. "Elior BarVidania, I am Methuselah, the eldest of the djinn, and before the war, first of the dragons."

"Please, don't bow, sir. Clearly, I should be the one bowing to you," Elior said, standing up.

"By the Great Spirit, no! You're a prince and you drank from the Well."

Elior examined Methuselah again. "Judging by your robes, you're a high priest. You drank from the Well, too."

Methuselah groaned, stroking his beard alive with white flames. "Maybe so, but that was eons ago. I am both the leader and the spiritual guide for the djinn here in our refuge. Walk with me into our underground city."

Elior's legs felt like jelly with every step, so he was glad that Methuselah moved slowly. "I thought Solarium was the first of the dragons to be made into a djinn. How are you the eldest?"

Methuselah chuckled. "Don't you know that there were those of us dragons who were loyal to Aelon? Solarium thought of himself as a king, of course Taariq still does, but many of us didn't see it that way. He was a pompous blowhard and heir to the throne but he was too eager to lead. When Aelon had decided he had to end the terrors the dragons had inflicted on the world, he came to those who were loyal to him and asked wether they would rather Solarium and his followers be put to death or be changed into something else."

"What did you all say?"

"Well, we agreed with Aelon. They wanted the evil dragons to have a chance at redemption. Some of Solarium's servants took that chance after becoming djinn and are among our number here. But we didn't want to foster jealousy in the hearts of the djinn if we were still dragons, so we offered to change as well. That's why I'm the eldest. I was the first male dragon Aelon created and was the first to volunteer to be remade."

Elior narrowed his eyes as he thought about the implications of what Methuselah had said. "You were the first dragon? Wouldn't that have made you king?"

The old djinn groaned. "In a manner of speaking, but I never cared much for that title."

"But you said that Solarium was the heir to the throne. Doesn't that mean that—"

"That Solarium—that Taariq—is my son?" Methuselah stopped and turned to Elior. "Yes, Taariq is my son. It is both my greatest shame and my deepest pain. I love him, and yet my life is devoted to thwarting him."

"Sorry," Elior said. "I didn't mean to upset you."

Methuselah started walking again. "Don't worry about it. Everyone here knows about it. Leonis filled me in on why you're here, so I didn't want to give the spy any way of getting to you by using that piece of information. After all, they could have convinced you I was the spy. Of course, that would be something since I've been a priest since the order was formed."

The tunnels soon opened up into a grand underground city. Rows of buildings made of polished sandstone lined the avenues and streets. Green grass grew under the light of a miniature sun high in the peak of the hollow mountain. Hundreds of djinn bustled and went about their business around the city.

"Welcome to the Registaanian refuge," said Methuselah. "I suspect you're more exhausted than anything. Shall I show you to where you'll be staying during your time with us?"

"As long of a journey as that was," said Elior, "that sounds absolutely perfect."

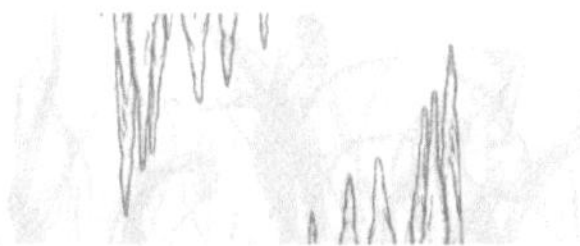

As the fresh water turned to salt water around them, Nyx felt an overwhelming sense of well-being. It had been so many months since he'd been forced out of the sea. Now he was returning alongside Mason.

Mason, his best friend, had survived, but this wasn't the Mason he remembered. It had taken them all day to swim down the river from Faeland all the way to the waters of the brackish delta and now out to the sea. In all that time, Mason hadn't made a single joke. His usual lively banter had been replaced by a series of grunts and terse replies to Nyx. Of course, Mason had been through literal torture. How could Nyx blame him for that?

Finally, they were in the open ocean. For the first time in what felt like forever, Nyx felt like he was taking a breath of fresh air. Yet there was a pang that hadn't been there before.

Mason broke the silence. "The Aquarian Refuge isn't far from here. There's a small reef to the east with a series of sea caves underneath it. That's where we're all living."

"Lead the way," Nyx said.

The current alternated between cool and warmed waters, churning water from the deep and mixing in the sun-warmed waters above. Nyx savored the sensations against his skin, reaching and pulling himself through the water, finally remembering what the webbing between his fingers was for. His tail articulated with more dexterity than his legs ever could. Still, a raven-haired beauty was waiting to see if he'd come back. Could he? He was a merman, and this was the sea.

After another hour of swimming beside Mason, they reached the reef. Approaching the sea floor, Nyx asked, "Are there many of us here?"

"Nearly the whole resistance," said Mason. "Once people learned where Commander Cascata's interests laid, what else would they do?"

"Well," said Nyx, "according to Leonis, it's General Cascata now." Nyx winked at Mason, who guffawed and shot ahead towards the reef.

"We're almost there!" Mason rounded an outcropping of rock and stopped in front of a door made entirely of mother-of-pearl as Nyx caught up to him.

He knocked forcefully on the door and said, "The way opens to strangers who are friends."

Without another moment's hesitation, the door opened. Nadine, an old friend of Nyx and Mason, opened the door. She held back a sob as she clapped her hands over her mouth. She embraced them and said, "I never thought I'd see you again! Mason, how did you escape?"

They extricated themselves from her grip and Mason said, "Actually, a friend of Nyx helped me out. One of the other guys who travelled with Michael rescued me."

"That's incredible," said Nadine. "Come inside. We don't want the door to be open too long." They swam through the doorway as she asked, "How did you get back here, Nyx? Does Mason's charm work for more than one person at a time?"

"No," Nyx said. "Another friend of mine is a magitechnician and duplicated his charm so that I could have one. But how have you been? I really want to hear about how everything happened down here and how the refuge is doing."

"Believe me," said Nadine, leading them through winding corridors, deeper into the caves, "you'll hear plenty of stuff once everyone sees you. Everyone is going to be thrilled!"

It took several more minutes to swim through the winding tubes, but when they reached their destination, Nyx's jaw dropped. At the end of the winding tubes was a large open cave filled with a bioluminescent reef. Glowing corals, anemones, fish with neon lines, and merpeople adorned with glowing paint along their tails and arms so they could see each other clearly.

"I never even knew something like this existed," said Nyx. "How did you find this place?"

Mason rummaged in his bag and handed Nyx a pot of blue body paint, saying, "Put this on." He pulled another pot out and smeared a yellow-tinged green paint over his body and explained how they got there. "We were looking for a collection of caves, but every time we settled someplace, Minerva would find us after a couple days. Then, a scouting party happened upon the tunnels we had just gone through. Once they got here, they figured it would be easier to defend even if she found us, so we settled here."

"It's been awesome! Nyx, you're going to flip when you see who's in charge! When she heard you were made a general by Leonis, she was thrilled!"

"Wait, you don't mean who I think you mean, do you? Is it my mother?"

Nadine beamed, her teeth glowing as they reflected the colorful lights. "Of course it's your mother! Who else would the revolution choose but the matriarch of the Cascata clan?"

"Mason, why didn't you tell me?" Nyx punched Mason's shoulder playfully.

"Hey," he said, "you didn't ask."

Nyx hurriedly smeared the blue paint on his body and said, "Where is she? I wanna see her!"

Nadine swam a few strokes ahead and waved Nyx and Mason forward. "Follow me!"

They swam through the reef to the other side of the cave. At that end was a large coral that glowed pink, under which was another mother-of-pearl door. Nadine knocked.

"Mrs. Cascata?" She knocked again. "Nara? Someone arrived today that you should really meet for yourself!"

The door slid open, revealing a mermaid with the same pointed features as Nyx but softened by femininity and age. "Nyx? You made it back!" She threw her arms around him. "I thought you'd never be able to come back after I heard what you were doing up above!"

Nyx buried his face in his mother's embrace and a tear forced its way out, bubbling out and blending in with the salty water. "I didn't think I would either. I haven't even let myself think of home or missing you!"

She pulled back so that she could get a better look at him. "It's no use. It's too dark out here even with all the glowing corals and anemones and the body paint. Come inside!"

She led them into her home. It was warmly lit with spongy couches and the inviting smell of freshly sliced fish seared on hot lava rocks spilling out from the kitchen.

Soon, a plate of food was in each of their hands. They ate while they lounged on the sponge sofas. They talked about Nyx's adventures with Elior, Opal, Nereza, and, of course, Michael. Then they talked about how he'd come back.

"Of course, we'll have to welcome you back this evening with an old-fashioned victory party," said Nyx's mother. "Everyone will be thrilled to see you." She motioned to Nadine. "As soon as you finish eating, I want you to go put everything together. Don't tell anyone else why, though. Nyx's return will be so much more fun as a surprise!"

"Of course, Mrs. Cascata," said Nadine, scarfing down the last bites of her fish before gliding out of Nara's home.

Nyx set his plate down on a coffee table constructed out of smooth stone. "Mom, there's something you should know about my return. There's a reason I came back now, even though my position with the Refuge is so new."

"Well, Nyx," she said, "you know you can confide in me. I helped your father with all of his important issues before he died. You know that."

"Opal, the dwarfess I've been traveling with, became a seer after we drank from Eternity's Well. She had a dream in which the Great Spirit revealed that there is a spy in each of the regional refuges. Someone in leadership here is leaking information and reporting on events here to Iblis and Taariq and using it to thwart Michael and Aelon's plans."

Nara's gaze floated to Mason. "Minerva isn't controlling you again, is she, Mason? Your curse is still broken?"

"Yeah, I'm safe. I haven't been in the same room with Minerva since I left her before she used me to end the rebellion."

"Good," said Nara, putting her plate down and coiling her tail behind her. "Then do you know who the spy is, Nyx?"

Nyx's shoulders slumped, his body feeling especially heavy against the plush sponge beneath him. "I don't know. Unfortunately, we don't have any names or anything. What we're guessing is that the spies have a tattoo of djinni script and dragon wings on their neck behind their ear."

"Here in the darkness, that's going to be hard to see in passing," said Mason. "We're going to need to flush them out."

"We need an investigation," said Nara. "The party to welcome you back can be a good start. Feel people out, especially the high-ranking ones. After all, you're the general of the Refuge! Most people here will be thrilled to meet the newest General Cascata."

Chapter 13

Up the River

"YOU CONVINCED MY DAD TO do what?" Eliam stared at Melanie open mouthed as she sat at the work station she'd set up in her room.

"Relax," she said. "It isn't a big deal. Besides, I don't even know if it's enough magic to work. It's only a little charm, so I'm going to have to activate it in the middle of calibration. I may have to convince him to give me something a little more… impressive."

"Melanie, my dad can't use magic, or Taariq will find him."

She turned the chair to face him and grabbed one of his hands, pulling it onto her left thigh and holding it there. "I'm sorry. I know this must worry you, but I went through all that with him. Besides, if he didn't trust me, would he have even given me the charm in the first place?"

Eliam was drawn in by Melanie's eyes. There was a fiery passion in them, betrayed by the deep tones of her brown irises. When she breathed, there was a softness around her as her chest rose and fell like waves on a shore. Her lips were a sultry pink, pouty, as she met his gaze. Why had he disagreed with her?

"I guess it's ok," he said.

Grazing her hand along his thigh as she let go of his hand, she said, "Of course it is." She winked and turned back to the desk. "Let's get to work, shall we?"

"What do you want me to do?" he asked, saluting like a soldier reporting for duty.

She smiled. A giggle escaped as she said, "Can you hand me those wire cutters?"

He reached for the tool and handed it to her. "So how does magitechnology work? I mean, I know we use it basically every day, but I've never quite gotten what it *is*."

"Well," she began as she tinkered with the parts in front of her, "the world is full of two kinds of energy. The first kind is physical energy. Before the second industrial revolution, we relied on physical energy. Thinks like coal, solar power, and nuclear power all rely on the physical properties of the world to propel things forward. Eighty years ago, we used to use cars that ran on natural gas."

"I think my uncle still had one of those classic cars, but they only used it for extremely special occasions."

"Exactly," she said. She pointed to another tool for Eliam to hand to her. She took it and continued. "We use physical energy for the regular kinds of technology like cars and cell phones and anything that relies on electricity. The second energy is magical energy. It's what keeps fairies in the air when they fly, helps elves garden so well, and what the djinn channel when they use their powers. It's also what enables ancient artifacts like the Mirror of Eternity and the Well of Eternity to work the way they do."

"Oh, ok. So it's like a weird form of energy that's harder to nail down."

"Yeah," she said. "Basically, magical energy is all around us, except it isn't tied to anything physical to make it work. It exists in the world, but it isn't exactly part of it. The closest we've gotten to understanding it is studying the way it exists in the ether's space that surrounds our world. Huge unpredictable waves of it exist out there. Occasionally there's a magic storm, and that's how we got things like enchanted forests or enchanted reefs or anything that isn't usually magical, that is."

Eliam held a wire taught that Melanie handed him. "That makes sense. So how do you get stuff that uses both magical and physical energy?"

"About sixty years ago, we started our second industrial revolution when a magician and a scientist got together and discovered that we could get clean, renewable energy from magic. Because it never runs out, you only need like an ounce of enchanted soil to power the world forever if you have the right set up, which we do. An ounce of enchanted soil or sand supplies power to each region of the world."

Melanie wrapped a few wires in electrical tape. "For product development, we use sand since it's less messy. I always keep a small, plastic zip bag of sand with me so I can use it. The great thing is that the enchanted sand doesn't just help to generate electricity. It also helps us harness other kinds of magic. When we discovered that, magitechnology was born."

Eliam raised an eyebrow and smirked. "It's way attractive that you know all that. Smart girls are cute."

Melanie pursed her lips and met Eliam's gaze. "Well, what you do is awesome, too. Pulling people out of dangerous situations?" She sighed and squeezed his left bicep. "A girl could get used to having a guy like you around."

A knot formed in Eliam's throat as Melanie leaned forward. "Is the device ready?" he asked, too nervous to meet her lips.

Her expression drooped a bit as she leaned back. "Yeah, we just have to see if the charm your dad gave me was enough to calibrate it properly."

"How do we activate the charm?" he asked.

"Here," she said. "Hold it and rub your thumb over the words when I press this button. Ready? On three."

"Ok," he said.

She counted to three and Eliam rubbed his thumb over the words Neander had written. A ball of light rose from the paper and hovered in the air as the device gathered data about the magic above it. After about a minute, the light faded.

The device glowed with a purple hue. Without a moment's hesitation, Melanie shut it off, her shoulders tensing and relaxing.

"Did it work?" Eliam asked.

"Yes," said Melanie, handing the device to Eliam. "This will now detect djinn magic. Thanks for your help." She leaned forward and brushed her lips against his cheek. "I'm going to go see how your dad is doing with the dinner plans."

At the reception that night, many people brought Opal gifts and paid their respect to her not only as a high priestess but as a monarch. Here, in Granite Valley, no one accepted that her reign ever really ended. It was such a strange feeling because, almost without realizing it, she had let go of this version of leadership and fulfilling her legacy. Being a queen meant less than sharing who Michael was with people as a priestess, but she also felt close to her father when people called her 'majesty.' Could both the new reality of where Aelon's path had taken her and the old reality of her royal birth coexist in who she was now? Or perhaps the shift in her thinking had more to do with a certain merman than she would have thought possible.

It was a question to ponder another time, though, because as she brooded on it, Mica brought a succession of the various elders and advisors to her. As soon as they had left, each with a blessing on their paths and for Aelon's power to guide them, Mica turned to her.

"So, did any of them stick out as suspicious to you?" She sipped her wine glass delicately as the band continued to play folk songs in the square.

Opal sighed. "I'm afraid not. What's worse is that they're all male."

"Come now," Mica said, surpassing a laugh. "I understand why you might be cross with male dwarves of noble birth after what happened with that traitor, Steelwort, but that doesn't mean every single one of them is bad, does it?"

Opal stood, the wind sweeping and catching her skirts, rippling them as she walked, motioning for Mica to follow. "It isn't their gender," she said, stopping in a shadowed area. "I could see their necks as they walked away. The spy we've already discovered had a tattoo of djinni text flanked by wings behind his ear. None of the elders and advisors you brought to me had that."

"Truly? Do you think the mark is truly significant?"

Opal crossed her arms, knitting her brow. "Yes. For my peace of mind, would you mind pulling your hair back so I can confirm you don't have the tattoo?"

Mica handed Opal her wine glass and pulled her hair back, and turned around so that the priestess could see. "Any tattoos I didn't know about?" she asked, releasing her dirty blond mane once more.

Sighing, Opal handed the glass back to Mica and said, "No. Though I didn't truly suspect you, anyway."

Mica leaned in as if about to share a grand conspiracy. "There is always the possibility that we don't have any spies among us in Granite Valley. This might be the most secure refuge. I mean, the dwarves even still think of you as their queen here."

Opal turned back towards the festivities. She glimpsed her mother among some elderly dwarven women, laughing. The expression on her mother's face was the one she always wore when she remembered happy memories of her father. It was true. The dwarves here remembered who her family was, remembered her father, and still thought of her as Opal Stronghold IV, Queen of Nanony. But her dream had specifically said that there was a spy in each refuge. Hadn't it?

Opal reached up to rub her temples.

"Are you alright, Opal?" Mica asked, placing a warm hand on Opal's shoulder.

Opal mustered a smile. "I'm just overtired. We had a long journey, and this has been a lovely evening, but it's also been exhausting. I'm afraid thinking about all this has brought on a headache. Could you have one of your people show me where I'm staying?"

Mica smiled broadly and inclined her head. "Of course, your eminence. I'll have a guard escort you right away. I'd hate for you to be uncomfortable and have the festivities ruined for you."

Mica snapped, and a guard came over. After receiving his orders from Mica, he led her to the small temple where there were rooms for the priests. Hers was specifically set apart for visits from a high priest, which still felt like a foreign title to her. She sat on the bed when there was a knock at the door.

"Who is it?" she asked.

"It's Allura. May I come in?"

"Of course, come right in."

Allura opened the door. Her robes were slightly crumpled in places from the car ride and celebration. "It's been a long day, hasn't it?"

Opal took a pin out of her hair, and the dark waves crashed around her shoulders. "Probably the longest I've had in a while, if I'm being honest."

"I'm sorry to hear that," said Allura. "Did any of the leaders give you a bad feeling or anything?"

Opal crossed her legs and motioned for Allura to sit as she said, "No, and that's what's strange. The vision I had told me that there was a spy or a mole in every refuge. Mica seemed to think that it's possible that there isn't one here."

Allura puckered her lips, obviously deep in thought. "That is a puzzler. Have you used your prayer alcove yet?"

"What do you mean?"

Allura pointed to a small fountain on the far wall with unlit candles surrounding it and a padded step in front of it. "That's a prayer alcove. They're always in priests' private chambers in the temples."

Opal tilted her head and moved over to the fountain to examine it. "Do you light the candles and then pray on the step?"

Allura joined her beside the fountain. "You never light the candles. You kneel on the step, dip your finger in the water and place a drop on your heart, and meditate while talking to Aelon. Ask him to help you discern who the spy is. If it is within his will to grant your request, he'll light the candles. Then you can sleep soundly knowing that the answer is coming."

"Thank you," said Opal, hugging Allura around the waist since the other priestess was much taller. "I'm so glad you're sticking with me to teach me how all this works."

Allura returned the hug. "It's my pleasure, your eminence. I'm going to my room, so I'll leave you to it."

She turned to go. When the door had latched behind and Opal was alone again, she kneeled and followed Allura's instructions. As she kneeled, she noticed a light mist coming off the splashing of the water in the basin. She dipped her finger in and placed a drop over her heart as she closed her eyes. The gurgling of the fountain in the prayer alcove calmed her and focused her thoughts.

"Michael," she began, "I'm so lost. I know I heard your message correctly. I know your people are in danger from the attacks of Iblis and Taariq, but I'm lost. Even with the gift of sight you gave me, I can't see our way forward here. None of the leaders had a tattoo. I don't know if they hid it or I missed something or if the spy here hasn't broken into leadership yet, but I know that the Great Spirit sees all. You didn't give me that message or instigate our goals in vain. Help me see what you would have me see here. Reveal the identity of the spy so that I can protect my people here. Help me protect Eternity's Refuge."

As she opened her eyes, the seven candles surrounding the alcove were lit with blue flames that gave off no heat.

"I suppose I should sleep on it," said Opal. She slipped off her robes and climbed into bed, sure that Aelon would give her a dream that would help her figure out what was going on.

Despite not knowing Elowynn in life, the service had brought Nereza to tears. Her friends had said beautiful things about her, and her father had sung the song that had given her courage through her last moments. The reception was lit by lanterns hovering below seedling propellers. Various foods were spread out among tables. Exotic spiced vegetables on one table, salted fish and cheese on another, and creamy fruit tarts of every flavor imaginable on another.

Aspen sat down next to Nereza. "Have you had any luck finding the spy?"

"Not yet," she said, fiddling with a bracelet on her wrist. "I didn't want to be too obvious trying to look at a bunch of people's necks. At least I've ruled out most of the men since they either have short hair or have it braided and tied up."

"I'm sure you'll be able to fulfill your mission," said Aspen, standing up again. "I'm going to retire to the house. Stay and socialize."

"No, I think that the long journey and the emotional pull of the memorial have drained me enough. Besides, I told Elior I'd call him when I was settled. He's probably getting acquainted with the Registaan refuge by now. I'd like to catch him before he gets too busy."

Aspen extended his arm. "Then allow me to escort you back personally."

When Nereza was showered, changed, and settled into the room Aspen gave her to sleep in, she pulled out her phone and called Elior. It rang only once before he picked up.

"I was wondering when you were gonna call," he said, a yawn threatening behind his voice.

She sucked air in through her teeth. "Oh, no! Did I wake you? I can let you sleep."

"Not at all, I've been waiting for your call. Don't worry."

She leaned back into her pillows. "Did you get into the refuge safely?"

"I did. I met the priest here, and I'm staying with him. I'll probably set out and do some exploring tomorrow. Start finding the spy here. Have you made any progress?"

"Not yet. We went to Elowynn's funeral today." Nereza groaned and said, "I know it made the most sense to send you to Registaan, but I'm still scared for you. Even the djinn on our side have magic."

He chuckled. "That should even the scales for me. There's only one spy and dozens, if not hundreds, of other djinn who serve our cause and are loyal to Aelon."

She closed her eyes and breathed deeply. "I suppose you're right. Just be careful."

"I will," he said. "How is the Arborrian refuge?"

"It's beautiful, Elior. The elves have such an interesting way of building. Nothing feels at odds with nature, which is cool to me since so much of my life has been focused on technology and moving magic to work against it."

"The elves certainly have a very gentle form of magic. What's keeping you from being able to find the spy there?"

She groaned.

"Did I hit a sore spot?" he asked.

Nereza sat up in bed and let her feet dangle over the edge. "They don't have the same leadership system that we've seen in the other refuges. After Elowynn died, they didn't replace her, and now they function as a democracy. That means that literally everyone here could be a suspect."

"Yikes," he said. "And you haven't run across any tattoos yet?"

She sighed. "No. Could it be that there are spies that don't have the tattoo? I mean, we assume they do, but what if there are djinn in glamours doing the spying, too?"

"Or," said Elior, "maybe the spy is a priest or priestess? High Priest Loki is the leader of Arborria. Maybe he helped Iblis with the placement."

Nereza tutted. "I don't know. I feel like it would be hard to convince other priests you weren't totally loyal if you were constantly doing ceremonies and services together."

"Loki seems to have managed alright."

"That's different," said Nereza. "He's the High Priest of Arborria. No one is going to question him. Plus, I'm sure he doesn't actually take care of a lot of day-to-day business."

"It's just a theory. Take it or leave it. I'm going to have to sort through a bunch of djinn anyway, so I won't tell you how to find your guy when I don't know where to start with mine."

"You're going to be fine, Elior. I know it."

He huffed a bit. "Thank's Reza." He paused, the sound of his breathing heavy like fog on the other end. "Hey, I love you."

Her heart swelled, and a smile painted itself across her face. "I love you, too. Now don't die over there!"

"You either!"

She hung up and shut off the lights, unsure of what the next day would bring.

Smoky figures danced at the edge of Opal's vision as the dream came into focus. Muffled words became clearer as her dream self floated into a room lit by a harsh fire in the corner and oil lamps overhead.

"No, I cannot recruit one of their own for those places," said a djinn with shiny black skin, almost as polished as glass.

"Then," replied a female djinn, "what exactly are you asking of us, Iblis?"

"Lilith, I'm so glad you asked. You three are going to infiltrate the underground." Gesturing to another djinn, Iblis said, "For you, it won't even require a glamour since you'll be infiltrating the underground within our own borders."

One of them asked, "But you've already recruited others to be spies and marked them for the cause. Why do you need any djinn to do your dirty work?"

Iblis growled and puffed smoke out of his nostrils. "Because some of these communities are more tightly knit and *faithful* to the Sky Demon than I had expected. If I can't convert a leader or put someone in to climb the ranks that will convince them, then I'll just have to replace some, but I can't go because of my station with Taariq. No, I need you three to go for me."

Lilith rolled her eyes "But—"

Iblis held up a hand and silenced her. "Not another word of argument. Lilith, Amana, and Kell, you were some of the best dragons to fight in my legion in the war. I hope you haven't gone soft."

Fire flashed as the three djinn facing Iblis grew angrier.

"Then you haven't lost your fire," said the black djinn. "Good. Then you can do the job without more argument." He slid files across to each of them. "There are your assignments. Now, go!"

The two male djinn disappeared in puffs of smoke.

Lilith stood. "I don't like it, but I'll obey. Can you at least make sure I get this glamour right? I haven't done one in so long."

Iblis waved his hand as if to encourage her to try it. Smoke washed over her. When it had dissipated, a much shorter form was standing where Lilith had been.

"It's perfect," said Iblis. "Now do as you're told."

Lilith turned, and if Opal could have gasped in the dream, she would have. The sharp features of a djinn had been replaced with the soft, dwarven beauty of Mica.

Chapter 14
Into the Throng

OPAL'S EYES FLUTTERED OPEN AS the morning sun washed the room in a soft glow. The blue heatless fire still burned from the candles by the prayer alcove from the night before, and a figure was kneeling on the padded step. He stood and turned to her.

"Michael? What are you doing here?"

"Good morning, Opal. I hope you slept well."

She sat up in bed, grabbing a robe the attendant had placed on the hook on the bedpost. She slipped it on as she said, "I've slept better. Of course, you know what I saw. How do I even approach Mica now that I know she's a djinn?"

"Well," said Michael, "Mica is a real dwarf, but the one you met with yesterday is a djinn pretending to be her."

Opal combed her fingers through her hair absentmindedly. "Will we be in danger if I reveal who she is, Michael? I don't want anyone to be hurt."

"Opal," Michael said, "have I ever put you in danger without also protecting you from that very danger?"

She sighed, remembering the dangerous path she'd walked since leaving her palace the morning after she met Michael. She hadn't known what would happen all these months later, but every step had been guarded by this man.

"I trust you. Is there anything I should do to make sure I'm safe?"

Michael pointed to the prayer alcove and the fountain that flowed within it. "Take a bottle of that water. When Lilith reveals herself, douse her with water. If the flames on her skin go out, she can't use her powers for long enough that you can have her arrested."

"I understand, Michael. I have one more question."

He smiled, giving her a knowing look that beckoned her to go on.

"What should I do about Nyx and all these feelings about my destiny changing?"

"Opal, it's easy for a seer to get caught up in things like destiny, especially when she grew up as a princess with a pre-described future from the day she was born, but life changes in beautiful and unexpected ways all the time."

She laughed, pushing herself out of bed. "That isn't really an answer, Michael."

He started fading as he said, "If I gave you all the answers, what choices would be left for you to claim?"

With that, he was gone. She pulled a used water bottle out of her backpack and filled it with water from the alcove. There wasn't any time to waste. She had to act quickly if she was going to catch Mica and apprehend her all at once.

The morning in Registaan had been productive. Elior and Methuselah had talked at length about Taariq's history and the spy here. When Elior's stomach growled, Methuselah suggested a restaurant he might enjoy while the old djinn met with the other djinni priests.

When they arrived, Methuselah said, "Don't leave the restaurant until I come to collect you. Shama is a good friend, and he'll make sure you're safe, but until we know who the spy is, I don't want you wandering around unaccompanied. Do you understand?"

Elior smiled, examining the way the white flames on Methuselah's eyebrows flickered when he was worried. "Don't worry," Elior said. "I have powers, too, remember? If I'm in danger, I'll protect myself."

"No, never forget that protection comes from Aelon, child." Methuselah breathed out cool, blue smoke. "Just don't do anything stupid. We don't know who the spy could be."

"In all likelihood," said Elior, "the spy is someone in leadership."

"That's extremely unlikely because we run this refuge as a theocracy. The priesthood is in charge here and I've known the priests I serve with for a very long time. A few decades at least, and several centuries at most."

Elior's stomach growled audibly, insisting on food.

Methuselah smiled. "Eat. We can discuss this later. I'll gather the priesthood and I'll collect you for our meeting this evening."

"Thank you, Methuselah."

The ancient djinn turned to go, and Elior stepped inside. The aroma was deeply smoky, though not in the magical way. The scents of fire-grilled meats, spices, and rich broth perfumed the air. A lithe djinn with red hair stood behind the counter. Elior approached the counter and said, "Shama, I presume?"

"You presume correctly," he said, labeling broth into a bowl. "How can I help you?"

"Methuselah said that you make the best food in the Refuge. I just happen to be hungry."

"Are you now?" Red flames flickered at the corners of Shama's eyes. "Methuselah is a good djinn. He brought me down here because my whole family believes in Aelon. We lost our business in Sumara because Taariq doesn't exactly treat Great Spirit sympathizers kindly. What's your story?" Shama handed the bowl he'd assembled to a waiter and motioned to a stool in front of him.

Elior sat at the counter. "My name is Elior. I traveled with Michael and drank from the Well with his help."

"Wow!" Shama's eyes widened, and he whistled. "There's got to be more to it than that, but even that's loaded. What brought you to Registaan?"

While not too busy, the restaurant was not empty. Elior felt the eyes of others on him. Any djinn Methuselah didn't implicitly trust could be a threat. "I'm here at Leonis's request. I've done some work for the refuge in Vidania, so I thought I could be of service here too."

Shama put a finger on the side of his nose and dipped his head, a smile spreading across his face. "Some of your business stays your business until you're comfortable to share. I respect that." He pulled a bowl down from a high cabinet. "Look, I can tell from the way you sat down that you're exhausted. Let me fix you something that will put the strength back in your legs."

A few minutes later, Elior was inhaling a bowl filled with a savory spiced broth; flat, square dumplings; grilled chicken with a spicy-sweet glaze, and fresh herbs. The effect was overwhelmingly warm and hearty. Each bite simply burst with flavor and was as warm and comforting as a full night's sleep. Without even realizing it, Elior had moaned audibly as he enjoyed his meal.

"I swear Shama works magic with his soups. The first time I ate here, I moaned too." A male djinn with jet-black hair and icy blue eyes sat next to Elior. "I'm Kell. I don't think I've seen you around."

Elior wiped his mouth on his sleeve. "I just got here yesterday afternoon."

"Then you got an extremely hot tip to come here," said Kell, leaning on the counter in front of him.

"Methuselah brought him by," said Shama.

Kell smiled. "So you're the guy I heard was coming! The one from the Vidanian refuge?"

Shama laughed. "Kell, you know as well as I do you can't believe everything you hear! Besides, for the western quarter of Vidania, we're the closest refuge to them unless they want to go underwater."

"That's true, I suppose," said Kell, smirking. "I won't pry. I was just trying to make conversation. I was just heading out, anyway. Thanks for the soup, Shama."

When the door had closed behind him, Elior asked, "What was with him?"

"Kell is relatively new. He's been here about a month. I mean, other people are newer, but I don't know what you're doing here, but I know one thing. A few weeks back, Methuselah stopped coming in every other day. He hasn't been in at all, and that means something big is going on. Just don't trust anyone that wasn't a founding member of the Registaanian refuge. I don't know what's going on, but being careful doesn't hurt."

"Thanks for the advice," said Elior, pulling out his wallet to pay for the meal.

"Don't worry about that," said Shama. "It was a pleasure to serve you, Elior."

Opal opened the door to Mica's office, dwarven guards trailing behind her. Mica, or the djinn pretending to be Mica, stood and walked around her desk to greet her.

"Goodness! I know I like to be at work early, but I didn't think I'd see you until after breakfast time. Has something happened?"

Opal clenched her jaw momentarily, but forced herself to exhale and approach the situation calmly. "I know who you really are."

"Your eminence, did you sleep alright? You sound delusional or overtired." Mica's lips pulled up into a condescending smile. "The gurgling fountain in your chambers must have kept you up half the night. Honestly, I'd be up to the bathroom every twenty minutes if that was in my room. You can sleep in my house, if you'd rather."

Opal squeezed the water bottle filled with the fountain's water tightly behind her back. "No, Lilith, I know who and *what* you are. You're a djinn."

"And here I thought I had maintained the glamour spell so well." The guards aimed their weapons at Mica as her face melted, revealing the sharp-featured djinn underneath.

Opal's muscles tensed, watching for the moment to strike. "I was convinced but the spell, but being able to see things revealed by

Aelon, is quite the gift. I saw who you are in my dreams."

"Too bad that won't save you," said Lilith. Fire rose along her back and in her eyes as she lunged forward at Opal.

If Opal had launched the uncapped bottle a moment later, she would have lost an eye on the outstretched talon-like nails of Lilith's hand. However, just as the djinn was about to sink her claws in, the water drenched her fire and she fell out of the air, steaming, onto the floor. The guards seized the opportunity and restrained her.

"Take her to the clinic," said Opal. "She needs to be sedated or she'll be a threat to us all."

The guards dragged Lilith out, leaving Opal alone. She slipped out her modified phone and set up a video call with her friends. Everyone picked up on the first ring and she saw the smiling faces of Elior, Nereza, and Nyx.

"Hey, Opal. What's up?" asked Elior.

Opal smoothed back her hair as she answered. "I have some news. It's a pretty interesting development, actually."

"Well, tell us," said Nereza.

Nyx gave a thumbs up. "Anything that will help us find these spies quickly would be awesome."

Opal breathed deeply. "Not all the spies have tattoos. I had a dream last night. Aelon showed me that three of the spies are djinn in disguise. Look for either a djinn or a tattoo. Be careful and suspect everyone you didn't arrive with."

"Oh," said Elior, "I don't think I'll have any issue finding a djinn in *Registaan*!"

"Fair point," said Opal, "but the information is useful to everyone else."

He laughed. "I'm sure it is. I just hope we're able to find who we're looking for."

"I think you have the most difficult job," said Nyx.

"Do you have any idea who is where?" asked Neander.

"Melanie made a device that can detect djinn magic. That might help everyone, right?"

Melanie winced. "Not unless I can get more magic from Neander. I don't have any magic left to calibrate another device."

"Oh, well, that can't be helped. In any case," said Opal, "don't hang your hopes on the tattoos. If your area was one that had a djinn covering it, you won't find a tattoo on anyone."

"Good to know," said Nereza. "Let's stay sharp, everyone. I'm gonna let you guys go. I have some more exploring and talking to do around the Arborrian refuge."

"Be safe," said Elior. "Are we still talking tonight?"

"You bet," said Nereza, before hanging up.

Elior left too, and for a moment, Opal looked into Nyx's eyes, saying nothing.

He smiled. "Ill see you when we all get back, right?"

Michael's reminder that she could get too caught up in destiny surfaced. If there was anyone pulling the strings of fate, would they ever have planted a seed like this for Nyx in her heart, or was this the first thing that she was choosing for herself? It wasn't worth thinking about if he stayed in his home, far away from her.

"Yeah," she said, smiling back at him. "*If* you come back, I'll be there waiting for you."

He winked boyishly and hung up. The call was over.

Melanie jumped in her seat as Eliam knocked on the doorpost of her room.

"Dinner starts in five minutes, Melanie," said Eliam. "Why aren't you ready?"

She sat precariously on the edge of her seat, staring unblinkingly at her computer screen. "If I don't monitor the data coming from the device, we won't be able to catch the spy. I need to stay here."

Neander, coming up from behind, put his hand on his son's shoulder. "Don't worry, Eliam. If she's here monitoring the data, we're going to be perfectly sure when we capture whoever the spy is."

Melanie turned around and smiled. "I'll miss you at dinner, but seeing you make all our hard work mean something is enough for me. Bring me a plate back?"

"Of course," said Eliam, returning her smile. "I guess I'll see you in a little while."

Neander pulled his son along with him as he walked out of Melanie's room. He'd hosted the dinner in the same area where the fairies had been hosting them so far. As they ascended to the top deck over their quarters, the sound of a few dozen fairies hovering, chatting, and laughing took over the silence of the woods.

Moretta, the leader of the Faeland refuge, emerged from the crowd to greet them as they reached the wooden overhang. "Neander and Eliam! Thank you so much for this. It has been a pleasure having you all here and I'm so glad that you have enjoyed our hospitality enough to take part in showing it yourself."

"Of course, Moretta," said Neander, reaching out to shake her hand. "As one of Leonis's advisors, I couldn't in good conscience receive without giving back. However, I must tell you that there is another reason we hosted this little party."

"Oh? What is that?"

Eliam opened his jacket to show her the device. "Opal, the high priestess and seer, was told that there is a spy in the leadership of each region's refuge. This device will help us find them."

Moretta turned back to Neander. "Is this true? What will we do when we find them?"

"Let's not worry about that just now," said Neander. "For the moment, our job is to enjoy this dinner and behave normally. Everyone is innocent until proven guilty."

Moretta gave a curt nod. "Let me introduce you so that the festivities can begin, then."

The fairy flew over the heads of all the others and clapped her hands. The buzz of activity relaxed to a hum as she hovered. "Everyone, I would like to introduce you to our host this evening. Neander Novak, who the world knew until a few short weeks ago as Yrahkaz Almasi, has transformed from an enemy of Eternity's Refuge into one of its most vehement supporters. Tonight, he hosts us in gratitude for our hospitality and in eagerness to be a part of our community. With him tonight is his son, Eliam BarVidania, a prince of the former kingdom of Vidania whose mother was Princess Emily. Please welcome them with a hearty round of applause!

A roar of applause greeted them as they walked in among the fairies. Conversations were made and plenty of food was eaten. Eliam tried to keep moving among the leaders, but it was difficult to figure out who was who. Of the large council that made up the leadership of the Faeland refuge, many had brought their families, and navigating through the endless string of conversations meant that there might not be enough time to find the traitor.

After nearly half an hour, he sat down to rest his feet for a moment when a fairy landed next to him on the bench. "These kinds of parties can be so exhausting, can't they?"

"I'm afraid I haven't been too many," Eliam said. "Even though I'm a prince, we never went to the parties and dinners with dignitaries."

"I don't suppose you would have," said the fairy. "I'm Bashera, by the way." She held out her hand, and Eliam shook it.

About two seconds later, Eliam got a notification on his watch.

Message from Melanie: Keep talking to her. I'm getting an interesting reading on the monitor.

Eliam swallowed and asked, "So what exactly is it you do here, Bashera?"

"I'm in charge of our communications department," she said. "I make sure all our correspondence goes to the right places."

Internally, Eliam wondered what she considered the right places to be. "Wow, that's a really important job. Then you were the first one who knew that we were coming?"

She chuckled. "I'm not in charge of reading communications, just delivering them and maintaining our system of electronic and magical communications."

"Then did you study to be a magitechnician?"

As she answered, Melanie sent him another message.

Message from Melanie: Check the device. Is it glowing?

Covertly checking by reaching for his phone in his jacket, Elior saw the device was indeed glowing a deep, shadowy red. He typed in 'yes' into the message box and replied to Melanie as he half listened to Bashera's entire story about how she became a magitechnician and how wildly different her university days were from what life was like for her now. He continued to nod along as he waited.

After a few more minutes of conversation with Bashera, Neander and Moretta strolled over. Moretta leaned over and whispered. "Bashera, will you please accompany us to the communications hub? There's something urgent we have to discuss."

A nearly imperceptible quiver washed over Bashera's face, but she stood and rose a few inches in the air as her wings beat again. "Of course. I'll lead the way."

They went all the way to the ground from their high position in the trees to a metal bunker where all the wires and magic conduits connected to. Bashera unlocked the door and ushered everyone inside.

"What's the matter, Moretta?" she asked.

Moretta's features pinched with effort. "Will you please lift your hair, please?"

"Excuse me?"

Neander sighed. "We weren't going to announce it, but we're looking for a spy of Taariq and Iblis. They seem to all be wearing a tattoo on their necks."

"I don't suppose I can refuse, can I?" Bashera asked, lifting her hair. There, plain and obvious, was the tattoo with djinni script and dragon wings.

"I can't believe this," said Moretta. "We've known each other since we were young! How could you do this to us?"

"I lost everything because of being *loyal* to Aelon, Moretta. My family died at his hands!" She pointed to Neander. "But when Iblis approached me, he explained Taariq's vision for the world. He told me all the gory details of what Aelon did to the dragons and what Michael's role in that was. My heart broke, and I wanted to help bring them down."

Moretta pushed back a tear. "You had a broken heart, like many of us, but we banded together. You sold your soul to a demon of fire, and his brand is on you now."

"What are you going to do with me?" Bashera asked.

Moretta had collapsed into sobbing for her friend. Neander put a hand on the fairy's shoulder and supported her, keeping the inconsolable fairy from falling. "That will be for the other elders to decide."

Chapter 15
On the Brink

IT WAS BARELY THREE IN the morning when Nereza woke up in bed. The chills that ran down her spine were like ice. An idea had come to her as she dreamt and there was no way she could let go of it now.

She set up her workstation, inadvertently dropping heavy equipment on the floor. She cursed under her breath, hoping that the noise hadn't woken Aspen on the floor below.

Unfortunately, as she set up in the corner, there was a knock on her door. "Nereza? Is everything alright?"

She opened the door. Aspen stood there, bleary-eyed with a mossy bathrobe tied round his waist. "I'm sorry," she said. "I had a thought I couldn't ignore, and I dropped my equipment. I didn't mean to wake you."

"That's alright," Aspen said, rubbing his eyes. "I wasn't sleeping all that well, anyway. What was your idea?"

"Well," she said, leading him into her room, "I had a sort of mismatched dream where people were changing faces while a staticky wave went past them. Completely weird, but it got me thinking. What if I could make a bomb that temporarily disabled magic spells? If the spy here was a djinn in disguise, it would reveal them immediately!"

Aspen's gaze grew suddenly sharper. "Is there anything I can do to help?"

"Really?" she said. "You want to help me build a bomb?"

Aspen sat down on Nereza's bed. "I have spent the last several weeks in utter agony after losing my daughter. I can't even really stay angry at the man who killed her because he was forgiven and redeemed by Michael. The only thing I can do is to work against the system that caused her death. If helping you can make even the smallest difference in this war, I want to fight."

"Then let's get to work."

Nereza and Aspen worked on combining electrical components and aligning what she knew about djinn magic to calibrate the detonation exactly right. She rechecked figures, Aspen followed instructions, and when the sun had risen and it was nearly nine in the morning, they stopped.

"The final touch is a grain of enchanted sand from the enchanted reef," said Nereza. "Thankfully, like all magitechnicians who love to create, I keep a bag with me." She went over to the bag that held all her components and parts. She pulled out a small bag of sand and the tiniest tweezers. She took one grain out of the bag and placed it in the reaction chamber in the center of the bomb. While she put the sand back, Aspen sealed the bomb shut and connected the last wire.

In front of them, on the table Nereza had set up, was a small completed bomb. The tension of a waiting explosion hung in the air, keeping both of them from moving for nearly three minutes.

Aspen bit his lip, terrified of breaking the silence. "This won't hurt anyone, will it?" he whispered.

"Not at all," said Nereza. "The only thing it might do is make a few leaves fall off the trees that are magically bent into buildings, but they won't suddenly straighten or hurt any of the elves. If there's a djinn among us, their glamour will fail and they won't be able to travel by smoke or use their powers for at least thirty minutes while the magical energy from the bomb continues to interfere with theirs."

"The perfect place to set it off would probably be breakfast," said Aspen.

"Right! The entire refuge eats together, and that's the only time that ever happens," Nereza said, picking up the bomb and scooping it into a leather satchel.

"I'm nervous," said Aspen.

Nereza yawned. "Me too, but we should try to get some sleep."

A djinn priest and a priestess sat around the table with Elior and Methuselah. The elder djinn called the meeting to order.

"As you both know," he said, "the seer, Opal Stronghand, saw that there were spies among our number. They sent Elior to help us find the djinn and expel them from the refuge."

Rana, the lone priestess, brushed her golden hair back, throwing sparks. "Do you have any leads or ideas, Elior?"

Elior rapped his knuckles on the table. "Unfortunately, I don't. I know that the one in Vidania had a tattoo on his neck, but he was human. I don't know what we're looking for other than a spy. The one in Vidania had infiltrated the leadership system. Is that possible here?"

"I doubt it," said Mobak, the other priest. "We are the leadership for this refuge. When we started this, we knew we could only trust other priests."

"We also put powerful enchantments around the perimeter of the city," said Methuselah. "No one within the borders can perform a glamour spell. Everyone has to be their unique selves here."

"Can you describe the tattoo, Elior?" asked Mobak.

Elior ran his hand through his hair. "Well, it was djinni script flanked by dragon wings, and when it's touched by someone else, it burns their hand."

"A binding mark," sighed Rana. "That's a difficult enchantment."

Methuselah groaned as he sat taller in his chair. "And not something a djinn can be subject to."

"So we have no way of identifying the spy? We can't disable glamours that are already disabled, and we can't look for a tattoo. What can we do?" Elior asked.

"There's always the local rumor mill," said Mobak.

Rana laced her fingers together. "What are you thinking, friend?"

"Well," said Mobak, leaning forward and lowering his voice, "what if we started a rumor that would draw the spy out of hiding?"

Elior's spine felt as if it had been electrocuted. "Me. I can be the rumor."

Methuselah furrowed his brow. "What do you mean, Elior?"

"Isn't it obvious?" Elior asked. "Taariq and Iblis have already made one attempt on my life. They want me dead now, so what if we made it look like they could succeed?"

"Elior," said Rana, "what are you suggesting? How can we make it seem like they could kill you? You're a protector and well-guarded here as well."

"We can tell everyone my powers haven't worked since entering the refuge. They'll just assume that my powers were disabled by the enchantments placed over our borders and walls."

"They haven't actually stopped working though, have they?" asked Mobak.

"Of course not," said Elior. "I just think that offering them a tiny glimmer of hope for their cause might work better than pulling every individual djinn in for questioning. After all, that would be the alternative, wouldn't it?"

Methuselah leaned back in his chair again. "That's accurate enough. Though there are several newer djinn that I don't know as well as I would prefer, there are just as many people that have been coming to services since before we went into hiding."

Elior rapped his knuckles on the table, punctuating a moment of silence. "Then it's decided? We'll let a rumor leak that I've lost my powers?"

"If we do this," said Rana, "I want guards watching him at all times, even closer than we already do. I won't have a prince's blood on our hands."

"That goes without saying," said Methuselah. "This is an anointed servant of Aelon, and he's under our protection."

The party was everything Nyx had missed about his home. All his favorite foods were served, dozens of friends greeted him. He was saluted with military precision just like his father had been. Yet after months of being with everyone, after being with Opal for so long, he felt almost naked, like his armor had been taken away. Even with all the comforts of home, there was an ache for the world and friends that he'd made a new home with.

Still, it was good to feel the water against his skin again. Even more, the dozens of embraces his friends drew him into were warmer and deeper than he'd remembered them being before.

After the party, Nyx nestled himself into the cradle of a sponge mattress, but no matter which position he moved into, he just couldn't seem to get comfortable. His mind drifted to the receiving line again, and something struck him as odd about the way Nadine had hugged him. While their initial meeting had been joyful, there was something stiff and scripted about the way she had acted when she welcomed him home publicly. Hope rang in his heart that he was imagining it, nevertheless, there was a spy here, and if Minerva had got to *Mason*—of all people—could he rule anyone out?

He allowed himself to float up off his bed and glided over to the corner of the room where he'd stored his bag. He retrieved the special communication device that Nereza had given him and dialed.

He hoped Opal would still be awake. It rang once, twice. After the third, he thought he should just give up and let her sleep, but she picked up.

"Nyx? Are you ok? It's so late!"

He breathed, not realizing he'd been holding it in. "I'm ok. I just can't seem to fall asleep."

"I'm actually having the same issue," she said with a sigh. "I've been trying to meditate, and I thought the ringing was a hallucination until I opened my eyes and saw your name on my phone beside me."

Nyx chuckled. "I'm just glad I didn't wake you."

"Something is bothering you, isn't it? You usually go to sleep so easily."

Nyx bit his lip. She knew him so well. "Yeah. Something weird happened tonight. My mom, who's the leader of the Aquarian refuge, threw a welcome home party for me. Most of the merpeople who were part of the rebellion are part of the Refuge too, so I saw a lot of my old friends."

Opal hesitated for a moment. "That's a good thing, right?"

"Of course! I'm thrilled to see all my friends again, but there's something I just can't put my finger on that really bothers me about it all."

"Do you wanna talk it out? Maybe I can help."

Nyx floated back to his bed and laid down while he talked. "I was so happy to see everyone. I mean, it's been over six months since I've been back, of course I should be happy to see them. But with one of my friends, it almost seemed cold. I don't know if I gave them a funny look or something, but they seemed to back away when I hugged them just a little faster. I don't know, I may be reading too much into it."

Opal groaned on the other side of the line. "I don't know Nyx. I mean, you know these people, but there's still a spy there. If one of your friends was acting weird, maybe there's a reason."

"Yeah," said Nyx, biting his lip. "That's what I was afraid you'd say. I just don't want to believe that."

"Did you see a tattoo on their neck?" asked Opal.

"That's just it," Nyx said, sitting up. "The whole refuge is in a dark cave. I can't see anything that doesn't already glow in the dark."

"You need another way of ruling it out then," said Opal. She yawned. "You know what, I'm suddenly sleepy. Can we talk later?"

Nyx frowned but said, "Sure. I know it's late. Bye, Opal."

"Bye Nyx."

The line went silent. While he didn't want to believe it, he knew what he had to do. He had to send Nadine on a mission that would test her and prove that she was as loyal as he'd hoped. While she initially seemed happy to see him, there was something odd about the way she interacted with him in front of other people. He had to be sure.

Elves meandered along winding buffet tables taking their time to gather the various components of their morning meal. Teas brewed from the needles and leaves of various trees, a shocking array of fresh fruits glistening with a sheen of morning dew, bowls of porridge adorned with sweetened nuts or dried wild game and poached eggs, and velvety-soft pastries filled with floral jellies and iced with citrus icing adorned the spread the elves had set out.

Nereza's stomach groaned reminding her how much energy she had expelled worrying about this meal since she woke up. She whispered out of the side of her mouth to Aspen, "Would it be better to eat and then set the bomb off or set the bomb off and then eat?"

He raised one eyebrow at her. "I think that since we don't know who the dangerous one is, we should prioritize protecting the elves here rather than play with time and risk more information leaking to Taariq and his servants. Besides, I'd hate for you or myself to be the next target of assassination."

It was then that Linewa waved them down. "Come! Come sit at my table!"

Nereza and Aspen pulled up chairs at the table where Linewa was seated. "I pulled all my favorites for you to try," she said. "Have you ever had Arborrian cuisine, Nereza?"

"Nothing as authentic as this," Nereza replied.

Linewa clapped excitedly. "You must try the faro porridge with egg and thinly sliced forest foul!" The elf pulled a small bowl from the center of the table and placed it in front of Nereza.

"Thank you," said Nereza, grabbing a spoon placed to her right. Her eyes lit up as she tasted the porridge. "This is amazing! I've never tasted something so creamy."

"The secret," said Linewa, "is a cream cheese made from sheep's milk. They mix it in at the end and it is the best breakfast food in the world, I'm absolutely convicted about that! Try it with a rhubarb crescent on the side!"

The elf searched the pile of pastries she had placed on the table. "I forgot to grab one! Well, now that everyone is here and has gone through the line, I'll have to go grab you one."

Linewa got up and left in search of the pastry pairing. Aspen rapped his knuckles on the table. "No one is watching, Nereza. Set the bomb off now."

"Are you sure?" she said.

"Yes!" said Aspen. "Linewa just said that everyone is here. It's the perfect time to detonate it. Everyone will see if a djinn is unmasked."

He was right. Nereza withdrew the bomb from her bag and set it up between her and Aspen. "You look over on the left of the banquet area and watch the right."

Aspen grunted in agreement. With no further reason to wait, Nereza pressed a large button on the top of the bomb. A gentle beep sounded growing stronger as the mechanism aligned the catalyst and fuel. A moment later and a wave of green glitter pulsed from the bomb outward. For much of the valley, this was nothing more than a curiosity. But for Nereza's target, this was the end.

Linewa's face melted away, revealing the shocked face of a djinn grasping a platter of rhubarb crescents.

Aspen pointed and raised his voice. "Imposter! That djinn has disposed of the real Linewa and has been sharing our secrets with Iblis and Taariq!"

Every eye turned toward the djinn who had been Linewa.

The djinn snarled and bared her teeth. "That's right, I am the djinn Amana, feared throughout all realms for the burning of Avandor on the northern plains when I flew with Iblis." She took slow, deliberate steps toward Nereza. "Revealing me was a mistake, girl. I'll burn you alive where you stand."

Nereza breathed and pinned her feet in place as she stood. "You have no power here."

"Ha!" screamed Amana. "We'll see about that." With blinding speed, she thrust her hands forward.

Nereza fought the urge to flinch, hoping to watch Amana's face when she realized her powers were disabled. She was not disappointed.

"What? What happened to my magic?"

"Simple," said Aspen, "*We* disabled it with our little bomb here."

"That's impossible!" Amana tried to deny it with her words, but she was backing away, attempting to create distance, but the whole throng of elves closed in around her.

"This is the end of the line, Amana," said Nereza. "You can't hurt the Arborrian refuge anymore."

With that ultimate word, two burly elves pushed out of the crowd and slapped iron chains around Amana's arms and neck and carried her off into the forest.

Chapter 16
Of Victory

"I WISH YOU'D CONSULTED WITH me before you sent that search party, Nyx," said Nara. She glowered at his command report on her desk. "This is a dangerous mission that we haven't assigned specifically because the last time we tried, two of our best men were in treatment for two months. What if someone dies or comes back mangled beyond belief?"

Nyx took a deep breath. "I told you why we're here. I have a hunch one person I sent may be the spy. Besides, if there are any injuries, I can heal them. I doubt anyone would die. They are all skilled merpeople."

Mason floated into the room. "I just heard you sent Nadine along with that search party to the lower depths of the caves. Didn't you ask your mother about what happened the last time?"

Nyx huffed. "Stop! Look, I know you guys think you know more about this cave and previous missions, but I did my research. I chose this mission specifically because I had a hunch about Nadine that I needed to prove."

"I don't understand what sending people into sure defeat would even prove," said Nara.

Nyx rubbed his temples. "I was named general by Leonis for a reason. Can you just trust me?"

Just then, a knock sounded on the door, echoing in Nara's office. Nara settled in her seat and called, "Come in!"

A guard entered and saluted them. "General Cascata, I have news concerning the search party you sent out this morning."

"Out with it," said Nara. "Tell me they're safe."

"They returned but are being treated for extensive injuries in the infirmary," said the guard.

Nara shot a look that screamed *I told you so* at Nyx and said, "Let's go see them then, shall we?"

They all swept out of the room and out into the blackness of the reef. They sped past the other merpeople, minding their business and through the buildings until they reached a side cave lit from the inside with soft blue light. On the far side of the smaller cave, the three people Nyx had sent out were strapped to beds and were being gently dabbed with medicinal seaweed.

"I knew something like this would happen," said Nara. "Just look at them!"

It was true. Something dangerous was in that cave, and while it left them alone as long as they left *it* alone, Nyx's invasion of its sanctum had caused these three merpeople to be so badly injured as to be utterly unrecognizable. Nyx swam over to the first bed.

"Nigel? I recognize the pattern of your scales. I'm going to heal you now, ok?"

The mangled, bloody merman let out a garbled sigh from where his mouth should have been. Flaps of skin were shredded over his whole torso. Scales were torn out, and his tail fin had a sizeable chunk bitten out of it. A fine mist of blood emerged from every wound, reddening the surrounding water.

Nyx held out his hands to Nigel and closed his eyes, uttering a silent prayer. The water glowed blue around him as skin closed, scales regrew, and every injury set back better than new. When Nyx finished, Nigel opened his eyes and breathed deeply.

"Thank's Nyx," he said. "Did it work?"

"Did what work?" asked Nara.

"Mom, let me handle this, you'll know soon enough," said Nyx, approaching the second bed. "Melodia, I'm going to heal you now."

Her injuries were similar, but Nyx healed her just as easily. When she was recovered and sleeping peacefully, he moved to the last bed.

"Nadine," he said. "It's your turn."

He held his hands over her body, doing the same thing he'd done for his other two friends. Most of her injuries healed easily, but her neck remained bloody behind her ear and the skin would not knit back together.

Her body was completely polished and whole, except for that one spot. Nyx sighed and asked, "Why won't your neck heal, Nadine?"

She turned away from him to stare at the wall. "Since you're here to find a spy, I expect you know why my neck won't heal," she said, motioning to a nurse. "Hand me that wipe, please."

The nurse complied, and Nadine wiped her neck, displacing the blood that had disguised her tattoo. There, cut up in a few places, but now obvious, was a tattoo of djinni script and dragon wings.

"Why did you decide to serve Taariq and Iblis, Nadine?" asked Nyx.

Nara and Mason covered their mouths with their hands, shocked at the turn of events.

"I saw what they did to Mason to take down the rebellion. I didn't want to see our people suffer any more than necessary, and I don't really have that much faith in you or the man you followed. The Cascata legacy failed us, and it was time to embrace the new world order."

Nara choked back a sob. "My family's legacy never failed, dear girl, it just changed hands."

"Whatever," said Nadine. "I love you and all that, but I just can't get behind anything that's happened. I don't want to be a part of this. I want peace, and Eternity's Refuge is keeping that from happening."

Nyx blinked as tears floated out of his eyes. "If only you knew just how deeply wrong you were."

Iblis strolled through the gardens outside the palace. Jasmine and rose perfumed the hot air. Taariq lounged in the shade of a rose bush so large and dense that its branches had been woven into a sort of trunk, allowing it to grow like a tree.

"Master?" Iblis sat on a bench and waited for Taariq to acknowledge him.

Taariq opened a single eye and glared at his friend. "Can you not see I'm trying to relax, Iblis? What is so important that you feel you need to bother me?"

Iblis leaned forward. "I have a report from Kell, the djinn I stationed in the Registaan underground. He says that Elior BarVidania is there."

"Is that so?" Taariq opened his other eye and sat up. "Is anyone else with him?"

Iblis smiled, his white teeth sparkling as he parted his dark mouth. "He came by himself, apparently. However, there's something even better that you're going to love hearing."

"After the bad news you've brought me of late, I could use some cheering up," said Taariq. "So, out with it. What is even better than him being there alone?"

Iblis moved from his bench to kneel before Taariq. "Ever since he came within our borders, Elior's powers have left him. Apparently, the blessing of Aelon does not extend to our lands."

For a moment, Iblis was not sure if Taariq had heard him. His master stared forward, unblinking and blank. In an instant, the fire in his eyes intensified and his lips curled in a cruel smile. "Then we have a second chance of ending his life, once and for all." Taariq stood and snapped, commanding Iblis to do the same. "Command your spy to dispatch him. I want the BarVidanian thorn in my side to be gone for good."

Iblis stayed put as Taariq walked away, leaving him in the garden. He pulled out a black orb that shifted and changed like smoke inside. Warmth filled him and pleasure surged through his veins at the thought of ending the boy's life. The little bastard had killed his dragon form and foiled his plan. Now his spy would dispatch him. His only regret was that he would not tear Elior's throat from his body himself.

Softly, Iblis spoke into the orb. "Taariq has commanded that Elior be killed. Act swiftly and end his life within the next day. Contact me when it is finished."

"I don't know when it's going to happen, but I'm expecting it any time," said Elior.

On the screen, Nereza put her head in her hands and pushed her curls back. "I wish you'd have called me before you and the priests there came up with this scheme, Elior."

"You would have told me not to do it!" he retorted, pulling a pillow from his side and pushing it behind him. "How else were we supposed to flush the spy out?"

Nereza closed her eyes. "I don't know. I don't know how you were supposed to do that, but c'mon, Elior! They already tried to kill you once, and they had no supposition that your powers were gone."

"But they aren't gone, Reza. Nothing's changed!"

He could hear her breathing get heavier. "Nothing except they're going to be more determined to kill you. I saw how Taariq looked at you on the ship when we left Vidania. He won't stop until he sees you dead, and you've given him the perfect reason to try again. What if he succeeds?"

Elior's stomach twisted. He hadn't thought of how Nereza would feel, thousands of miles away, worrying about him as they tried to find the spy. "I'm sorry, Reza. If it makes you feel any better, Rana insisted that guards watch me round the clock. I have two big, bulky djinn outside my door right now."

"Yeah," said Nereza, "but what if a guard is the spy? Doesn't that mean that they'll have perfect access to off you?"

Elior's eyes fell away from the screen. "I hadn't thought of that."

"Maybe the bomb I made to disable djinn powers would help you. I made a spare, just in case. I just don't know how I would get it to you."

"Maybe Methuselah can help?"

"The priest you were telling me about?" Nereza asked.

"Yeah," said Elior.

She chuckled. "I can't believe that Taariq's father is the leader of the refuge in Registaan. I guess family values don't always transfer between generations."

"Yeah, I mean, Taariq is so unhinged, but Methuselah is perfectly composed. He's warm and genuine, which is weird considering he's a djinn, though I guess most of the djinn I've met here have been nice enough."

Nereza breathed deeply, her shoulders slumping as she tried to release tension. "Ok, but if he's going to help, we should do it now. I want you to have this backup plan just in case you're not able to summon a force field or anything when you need to. Where is he?"

"He's probably in his study," said Elior. "I'll go check."

Elior swung his legs over the edge of the bed and stood. As he walked out of the room, the two djinn guards that had been assigned to him followed him out down the hallway to the corner room Methuselah used as his office.

Elior knocked. "Methuselah? Are you in there? I have something I could use your help with."

"Come in Elior!" he called from the inside of the room.

Elior opened the door and approached Methuselah. He was seated behind a black marble desk stacked high with papers and books and all kinds of little stones.

"What can I help you with?"

Elior turned his phone so Methuselah could see. "This is my girlfriend, Nereza. She's a magitechnician, and she's created a device that can temporarily disable a djinn's powers. She wants me to have it as a backup in case of an attack. We were wondering if you could magically transport it here."

Nereza held up the bomb, a miniature version of the one she'd used to reveal the spy in Arborria. "It's this. I made it small so that it could be more easily mailed, but I don't think the postage system would get it close enough to you quickly enough for it to be useful."

Methuselah slid on his glasses. "I don't think it would be a problem for me to pop in and get that," he said. "I'll be right there."

The elder djinn disappeared in a misty cloud of white smoke and reappeared on the other side of the phone screen a matter of moments later. "Here," he said, "I'll take it back with me."

Nereza handed him the device, and he dissolved into smoke again, reappearing in his chair once again.

"That was impressive!" said Elior. "I didn't know smoke travel was so fast."

"Fast because our refuges are magically linked. It can take a while if you're traveling in the wide open world, but each of our outposts has an intimate connection to the others." Methuselah held out his hand and motioned for Elior to hold his out.

The little round ball dropped into Elior's hand. "Thanks for your help, Methuselah."

"Yes," said Nereza, "thank you. I feel better knowing he has that."

Methuselah dipped his head. "I just hope that we did the right thing in spreading those rumors. We're doing the best we can, but I don't know what those spies might be capable of. Maybe they even went under a Fire Oath and have the power of ten djinn behind them. We don't know."

"Even if they did," said Elior, "now I have Nereza's gift. I'm going to be fine, so you can both stop worrying."

Nereza sighed, picking up her phone and bringing it close to her face. "Elior, I hope you're right because I can't lose you."

His heart ached. "Nereza, I'll be fine."

She pouted.

"I promise, Reza, you'll never lose me."

Elior woke from a deep slumber as the sound of an explosion shook the temple. He leaped out of bed and ran to the window. The miniature sun in the hollow peak of the mountain was spitting streams of fire down. Screaming djinn women and children rushed inside while djinn men blasted magic up, trying to contain and stabilize the explosion.

Methuselah burst into his room. "I don't know what happened to the sun, Elior, but stay inside until we have it fixed. The temple staff cast that spell together, so if we all go, we should be able to fix this before any damage is done. Unfortunately, that means I have to take your guards, which is why you must stay inside. Don't stand by windows, don't open the temple door, don't leave. I won't have you caught unawares and killed while no one is there to help you!"

Elior backed away from the window and sat on the edge of the bed. "I understand. I'll wait here."

"Good." Methuselah rushed out, motioning for Elior's guards to follow.

Elior was alone in the relative silence of his room in the temple. He could see a bit from the window, and it looked like the combined magic of those in the temple was helping to force the little star to cooperate.

His attention was jerked to his door as a djinn with black, slicked back hair burst in, huffing, slamming the door behind him, and slumping to the floor.

"What are you doing here?" asked Elior, mentally measuring how many steps he was from his sword.

The djinn opened his eyes and stood up. "I'm sorry. I thought this room was unoccupied. I ran into the temple to get away from the explosion, and this was the first unlocked door I found."

Recognition washed over Elior. "You're Kell! You're the djinn I met at Shama's restaurant on my first day here."

Kell smiled, showing all his teeth as he said, "Oh! Yeah, you're the new guy. Elior, right? You're staying in the temple?"

"Yeah," said Elior. "Methuselah put me up here."

"Gotta stay safe, right? I heard about the effect the desert had on you."

Elior edged his way to his sword, trying not to appear too obvious. "Yeah, Methuselah thought this was the best place for me."

"I agree with him," said Kell. "When I heard you were here, the guy who travelled with Michael and drank from the Well? I was so stoked. I actually always wanted to meet you."

Elior relaxed slightly. "Really? Why?"

"Isn't it obvious?" asked Kell. "You rescued all those people that Taariq's regime would have killed without you. I really hope your powers come back. Maybe when you leave?"

"Thanks, I appreciate it."

Kell's eyes fell to Elior's locket. "Hey! Is that the Vidanian Royal Crest? Can I see?"

Before Elior knew what was happening, Kell had swept over to him and was intimately close, examining his locket. "Yeah," he croaked. "My mother gave it to me."

"I didn't know you were a prince, too!" said Kell. "The crowned eagle, the scroll, and the olive branch, all carved in amazing detail. The Vidanian Royal crest always fascinated me. So much symbolism packed into a small space."

"I guess I never thought about it that way," said Elior, meeting Kell's eyes. Time slowed down for several moments as Kell continued to smile and the locket heated until it was glowing red.

As soon as the fire reached Elior's neck, his instincts took over. He raised his hand and a blast of blue energy forced Kell back against the wall.

Kell fell to the ground. He spit blood and snarled at Elior. "It was a trick! Your powers work!"

"What?" taunted Elior. "Upset that the other side can be clever too? What are you gonna do about it?"

"Guess I'm just gonna have to be faster than you." Kell summoned flaming dual scimitars and charged at Elior.

Elior rolled, grabbing his sword and flinging the scabbard away. He raised it just in time to block Kell's blow. He pushed the djinn away and summoned a shield, scanning his dresser for where he'd left Nereza's device.

Kell struck again and again, flurries of blows heating the air with an intensity Elior had never seen. He flicked his sword sharply up as he parried and flung one scimitar out of Kell's grasp, causing it to disappear as he nursed a sweltering cut on his wrist.

Elior took the chance and lunged sideways to scoop Nereza's bomb off his dresser. He turned back to Kell as the djinn lifted his hands, summoning an enormous fireball. All at once, Elior pressed the button and raised a force-field around himself. He closed his eyes, bracing for impact, but none came.

"What did you do?" screamed Kell.

Elior opened his eyes, and the force-field dropped. No flames licked over Kell's arms. The fire in his eyes was dead. No matter how he flailed his arms, no fire was thrown.

"I've disabled your powers, Kell, if that's your real name."

Kell went white as paper. "I didn't even know that could be done."

"Well," said Elior, "it can. Now, let's go talk to Methuselah."

Elior grabbed Kell's wrists and pinned them behind his back as he forced the traitorous djinn out of his room and out of the temple.

Chapter 17
Vengeance

THE WARM, SUMMER WIND WHIPPED through the trees of the
Faeland refuge, spreading the fragrances of northern pine flowers and
mountain cherry blossoms through the air. Birds chirped as if nothing
had happened, but as Elior watched the blood pool underneath the six
bodies in the clearing, he couldn't help but feel sick to his stomach.

Elior stood, glancing around at all those who had gathered there.
Leonis, who came and helped interrogate the prisoners and finally
ordered their execution, stood stony faced, leaning against a tree.
Eliam sat on a fallen log with Melanie. Neander crouched, his back
turned away from the growing pool of blood. Opal swayed in the
breeze, her skirts brushing against Nyx next to her, and Nereza inched
closer to him, heavy with the weight of what had happened.

Nereza coiled her fingers with his and lay her head on his
shoulder. "I wish that they would have recanted. It feels dirty putting

them to death like this."

"I know," said Elior, laying his head on hers. "They didn't recant after four days of interrogation and pleading, though."

Neander cleared his throat. "We couldn't exactly let them go, and keeping them around would have put everyone in danger."

"That doesn't mean this was any easier," said Opal, brushing a piece of hair behind her ear.

Nyx wiped a tear from his cheek. "I'll never be able to wipe the image of one of my oldest friends dying out of my mind. This whole situation sucks. That's just the long and short of it."

Eliam stood from where he and Melanie had been sitting. "What do we do from here, though? We can't dwell on this forever."

"We have to burn the bodies," said Leonis, "and then we have to figure out what's next. You can bet that Taariq will figure out that his spies are dead, and he's going to come for our throats."

"Let's let them all gather their thoughts first," said Neander. "This wasn't easy to for anyone."

Leonis stood tall as he walked away from where he was leaning. "That's true. Let's all meet after sunset then. I'll go find someone to do something about the bodies as soon as possible."

Leaves crunched, deafening against the silence, as Leonis left. Neander followed him out of the clearing.

"I don't want Nadine to be disposed of with the rest of them, guys," said Nyx. "Will you guys help me take her body to the river? Even after all she did, she's still one of my oldest friends."

Opal gently took Nyx's hand. "Of course we'll help you."

The six of them pulled her body onto a tarp that had covered a small pile of firewood and lifted her off the ground. Nadine's body was pale and clammy. The half dried sweat betrayed the fear she must have felt before her death.

"Do you think those tattoos made them stay true to Iblis and Taariq by magic?" Elior asked.

Melanie chortled. "Of course they did! I know enough about djinn magic to know that any marking on the body, especially one with text, was the binding of a magical oath. You can't break an oath sealed with magic."

"Then they might have wanted to repent?" asked Opal. "Nadine might have wanted to…"

Nereza sighed and said, "It doesn't really matter, now, does it?"

"She's still responsible for the vows she made," said Melanie, "so I don't think it matters at all. Aelon punished the dragons for staying true to what they believed, too."

Nyx growled and stamped his foot. "Stop! Regardless of the vows she made, whether she could break them, she was a real person. I went through training with her, I knew her family, I ate meals with her." He stopped, tears on the edge of his voice. "She was my friend. All the people we just *killed* were real people with real lives. Just because we couldn't let her, or any of them, live because Eternity's Refuge has to be protected, doesn't mean that they deserve any less respect."

That ended any further conversation as they walked to the river. When they reached the bank and the sound of the rapids a mile upstream whispered in their ears, Elior and his friends set Nadine's body down and used the tarp to roll her into the river.

As her body hit the water, she dissolved into sea foam and flowed down the river towards the sea and her people. Nyx swayed back and forth and started to half sing, half whisper a little song.

Flow away, flow away!
Don't mind where.
Your time in waves
Has ended, but don't despair.

You swam with me,
And I with you.
Your time in waves
Has ended, but don't despair.

The Spirit has a way
To bring you back to me.
Your time in waves
Has ended, but don't despair.

They stayed quiet for a long time after that, only stirring when the sun finally dipped below the horizon and the forest cooled. Slowly, the six of them turned from the river and returned to the warmth of the refuge.

Taariq stoked the fire in his office, lovingly coaxing the embers to brighten and shine in his darkened office. The smell of smoke filled the room and chills rolled down his spine in a delicious tingle as he inhaled as deeply as he could. Burning. The scent of anything burning drove him to wake in these tumultuous times.

A knock on his door made him tighten his mouth into a tiny

pucker, the blood red of his lips whitening as he clenched. He forced his tightened jaw open to say, "Come in."

The door swayed open and Iblis, tall and regal with his obsidian form, stood there, his brow knit.

"What bad news do you bring me now, Iblis?" said Taariq, standing from the fire and sauntering over to his desk. "I'm thinking that just because someone is a magnificent dragon doesn't mean they can be a competent djinn."

Iblis simply bowed and said, "Master, I haven't heard from any of the spies placed within the Refuge in several weeks. I'm concerned something may be wrong."

Taariq rolled his eyes and sat in the large leather armchair behind his desk. "That's not news, Iblis. That's you worrying."

"Sir?" questioned Iblis as he sat across from Taariq.

"It's possible that there's just nothing to report, right? Why should it concern me that there isn't any news? As annoying as they are, I don't expect the underground to always be active."

"That's just the thing," said Iblis, "I don't either, but I told them to check in with me once a week, regardless. After all, they are in enemy territory."

Taariq wished he could smack Iblis on the face and throw him out, but the poor djinn was still adjusting to losing his dragon form. Perhaps he could extend some grace. After all, it had taken Taariq hundreds of years to even fully remember who he was.

"Would it make you feel better if I summoned the Dark Circle to perform a location spell? I'd need you to stand in for Yrahkaz since he's still behind enemy lines, too."

Iblis sighed, black smoke dropping from his skin. "I would like the reassurance that they aren't dead."

Taariq snapped and called to his Circle in his mind. Purple, green, gold, and red smoke columns all appeared in his office and solidified into Minerva, Loki, Swiftwing, and Steelwort.

Bowing, his hands buried in his robes, Loki said, "It has been quite a while since our last meeting. Are things not going as smoothly as we'd hoped?"

"There's a problem with our spies behind enemy lines," said Iblis.

Taariq stood. "I called you all here to perform a location spell. We're just going to check in to make sure they're all ok for Iblis."

Minerva tutted and rubbed a hand over Iblis's shoulders. "Worried, are you?"

"Now is not the time to flirt, Minerva," said Loki. "Tell us, Taariq, what do we have to do?"

"And let's make it snappy," said Steelwort. "I have a slope ball game. I'm supposed to be the honored guest tonight."

Swiftwing's eyes widened. "Do you have boxed seats? Take me with you!"

"ENOUGH!" Taariq screamed, the fireplace spitting sparks. "It won't take long, but you all have to shut up." Taariq waved his hand and a basin of silver liquid appeared in the center of his office. "Everyone stand around the basin and hold hands. Iblis is filling in for Yrahkaz."

They followed his instructions. As they held hands, Loki asked, "Now what do we do?"

"We chant '*aeadu sihri lilaya, wa'ulqi taewidhat aleawdati*' until the silver liquid in that basin forms a map with the locations of the spies lit up with points of light. It interacts with magical oaths we

surprised Iblis was that Taariq did not stay to eat his kill. But perhaps djinn did not need to eat as much meat as dragons did.

The door opened and Taariq strolled in, his blood-red lips framing impossibly white teeth. "Good morning everyone, I'm glad you all could make it!"

"Good morning," they chorused.

"You might want to brainstorm later, so I brought these." Taariq passed around pads of paper and pens. "As you know, our spies are dead. This poses a serious problem."

He paused, as if waiting for someone to speak. When no one did, he continued. "We have to strike back. We can't let the underground go unpunished for killing our trusted allies within their little hideaways. So, what are we going to do about it?"

Minerva shakily rose her hand.

"Go ahead, Minerva," said Taariq.

Minerva stood, pushing back her chair, and said, "If taking them down from the inside didn't work, why don't we take them down by ruining their reputation?"

"Oh, I like this idea," said Taariq. "Go on. How would we do this?"

"If we can make people around their base of operations believe they are evil and have nothing good to add to the world, I'll bet anything that they'd burn them to the ground themselves."

"I see what you're saying," said Loki, smirking. "If we sell the right story, the general population will tear them down for us."

Chapter 18
Propaganda

"Are you sure we should go out into the town so openly?" Elior asked.

The sunlight filtered through the thinning trees as he and Eliam reached the edge of the forest. Already the bustling of townsfolk in Wick's Flight, the town closest to the Faeland refuge, echoed around them.

Eliam tutted and laughed off his brother's worry. "I've been into town loads of times since you left for Registaan. In fact, most of the town is tolerant of or interested in what the Refuge stands for."

"The townsfolk know what we are?" Elior's stomach clenched.

"Dude," said Eliam, "relax. We have to get our supplies from somewhere. Wick's Flight is safe, and even if it wasn't, we only have to get one thing today. If you're really worried, we still have those watches Nereza made for us, so we can go into stealth mode if it gets dicey, but it won't."

Elior let his worry go. His brother was convinced it was safe, and Eliam had been more skittish than he'd been before he'd been trapped in Lux Terra.

Fairies walked about and flitted jovially around Wick's Flight. The town was small in that it was crammed into a narrow corridor between mountains where the forest hadn't completely taken over. Cobble stone streets wove through the city, connecting everyone. Brick buildings with quaint storefronts lined the road through the main avenue, and the crinkle of shopping bags punctuated the conversations happening all around them.

They walked to the corner of main and third and entered a little shop specializing in stationery and ink.

Eliam picked up a carton and examined the numbers on it. "Do you remember which size ink cartridge Leonis needed for the printer in his satellite office here?" he asked.

"I think he wanted a 530xt, but I'm not entirely sure." Elior thumbed through stacks of paper, looking for the correct color.

Eliam shook the carton. "Nah, I think you're right. This is the one. If it isn't, we can always come back."

"I suppose it's fine then," said Elior, sliding a stack of cream stationary out of the pile.

They paid for their things and were about to walk out the door when a fairy, harried and flustered, pasted an enormous poster over the window to the left of the exit and left with an entire roll of posters to hang.

"Think he lost his dog?" asked Eliam, opening the door.

Elior followed him and said, "I don't know…" He trailed off as he turned his head. He grimaced, confused, at the poster. Emblazoned across it in red and black ink was a caricature of his face and the phrase *"The Refuge is a place for Criminals."*

"By the Spirit, what is that?" asked Eliam.

Elior turned on the stealth mode on his watch. "Better go back quietly. This is terrible."

"Yeah, but what are we gonna do?" Eliam whispered as he activated his watch. "People from the refuge occasionally come into town, and we get most of our food from here. This is so far beyond not ok!"

Elior checked to be sure no one was watching. When the coast was clear, he reached up and tore the poster down. "Everyone back at the refuge needs to see this. If they're putting posters up, you can bet they have things on TV, radio, and any other method of communication. Taariq couldn't get to us through his spies, so now he's trying to ruin our reputation."

"I don't want to get caught out here," said Eliam. "Let's go back now. Quickly."

Nereza wiped her forearm across her face, leaving a grease stain emblazoned on her forehead. "I think we're ready to run our first test."

The enormous machine that had taken her and Melanie the last several weeks to build after Nereza completed the first round of schematics was finally ready for testing. Nereza took a step back to admire their hard work. If they had been successful, this would be the new link between Lux Terra and Nox Terra. The machine stood eight feet tall and ten feet wide with a large, circular copper arch making up the largest part of it. On either side, two humming conduits held the arch affixed to a steel plate dotted with fibre optic cables created from magical sand.

Melanie glanced up from her computer screen. "Ok, but you should let me do your make-up for the unveiling."

"What?" asked Nereza. She turned to her right where a mirror hung on the bedroom-turned-workshop wall. "Ugh! I can't believe I smeared that stuff all over my face!" She picked up a rag and wiped at the stain.

"Are you sure we're ready to turn this on?" asked Melanie, standing up to examine the arch. Her fingers traced the copper wiring they'd woven together for the arch. "I'm still hesitant to believe the copper wiring will conduct the light coming from the fibre optic cables beneath."

Nereza slid off the gloves she'd been wearing and crouched by the control panel on the right conduit. "We have to test it sometime, Mel. We've been working on it for weeks, and there are people on the other side of the world that need to hear about Michael and the work we're doing here." She stood up and faced her friend. "It's just as much their world as it is ours. Besides, I don't think Taariq will stop until he's able to take over Nox Terra, too."

"I thought he couldn't make the mirror work," said Melanie.

"Sure," said Nereza, "but if this works, then it's technically possible for any magitechnician."

Melanie crouched by the control panel on the left conduit. "Ok, then. Let's run our first test, then."

Both of them entered several commands to the computing units and then their was silence. They looked at each other and silently counted down from three. On one, they both flipped their respective switches and power flowed through the arch.

Heat sizzled in the humid forest air around the copper arch. Underneath, the fibre optic cables glowed in a blaze of colors. Nereza was about to give up hope it would work when a thin veil of light materialized in the arch. Just as the veil became bright and solid, the computers housed in the conduits on either side crashed, the programs they'd built into them stopped responding, and the lights went out.

"The systems overloaded," said Melanie.

Nereza fell back from her crouch onto her back and laughed.

"What's so funny?" asked Melanie. "The test failed."

"Maybe so," said Nereza, the memory of laughter still in her voice, "but did you see what happened? It almost worked. That portal was almost solid, so all we have to do is make a few more tweaks and we'll be there! Nox Terra feels closer than it has in months."

Melanie was about to say something, but Nereza's phone rang.

"Hold on, Mel. It's Elior." She answered the call and held the phone up to her ear. "Hey, Elior! What's going on?"

Elior hung up. "Melanie and Nereza will be here in just a few minutes, Leonis. Is everyone else on their way?"

"Yes. I'm glad I hadn't left yet when you returned. This is going to take a great deal of effort to overcome."

The door swung open and Neander, Opal, and Nyx walked in. Neander's brow was knit. "What's this Leonis said about a UFSS propaganda campaign?"

"We should wait till Melanie gets here," said Eliam.

Elior rose one eyebrow at his brother. "And Nereza?"

"Yeah," said Eliam. "That goes without saying."

"You've got it bad for here!" Elior poked his brother in the side.

Opal rolled her eyes. "Tease him later, Elior. Nereza and Melanie are almost here, aren't they?"

The door opened again, and Melanie and Nereza walked in. Nereza bit her lip and watched something on the screen. "I did a search after I got off the phone with Elior a few moments ago," she said. "You guys won't like what I found."

"Can you put whatever you're looking at on the screen?" asked Leonis, turning on the TV.

Nereza tapped a few times on her phone's screen. A moment later, a video was playing.

They watched the video soar over the planes on the western side of Vidania and finally stop to hover over the city. It cut to a view inside the ivory tower where Taariq sat behind a desk in the highest office. His voice felt like molten silver as he spoke.

"This is a public service announcement for all citizens of the United Federation of Six States. Yes, we're all different, but we are linked by a common world, and now a common enemy."

Taariq stood and walked around the desk as the camera panned closer to him. "Over the greater part of this last year, a disturbing trend has become apparent. There are a radical group of terrorists working under the name of a criminal, Michael Rex, who we executed last year. Their true mission is yet unknown."

The camera cut away to show the bodies of fallen guards in the prison and several manufactured scenes of carnage, looted cities, and children starving in the streets as Taariq continued his voiceover. "However, we know they leave destruction in their wake. No one is safe."

Tense music played, pulling on the heart and increasing the sense of urgency. The camera cut back to a closeup of Taariq. "If you see something, say something. This radical group will destroy us all if we're not careful. Protect our country, protect our peace, protect your family, and protect yourself."

White text flashed across the screen. *This public service announcement has been produced and approved by the federal government of the UFSS. All rights reserved.*

Not one mouth remained open.

Elior was the first to speak. "It get's worse than that." He unfurled the poster on the table and those who had not seen it emitted sounds of shock.

"Elior, that's your face on that poster," Opal said.

Nereza laced her fingers in his. "You can't go out into town with these things hanging up everywhere!"

He turned to her. Her eyes were moistened with fear and worry.

"Obviously he's not going out again," said Nyx, "but what do we do about this? How are we going to make this problem go away?"

"How can we?" asked Melanie, slamming her hand on the table. "The citizens of the UFSS outnumber us by a hundred to one. We are in danger!"

Eliam cleared his throat. "If Elior can't go out anymore, I can always run my errands alone."

"No!" shouted Melanie, flicking his ear. "You share a face with Elior. You're not going to town either!"

Everyone started talking at once. Not one solid idea came through until Leonis held up his hand. "Enough!" The room fell silent. "I know we're all concerned, but there's someone who has been sitting quietly this whole time, and I want to know what Neander thinks."

Every eye turned to Neander. His lips were tight. The former servant of Taariq didn't move to speak for several seconds, but then he stood. "They're doing the same thing with Michael's movement that they did to him. They're villainizing us, and the only way to combat it is to show people who we really are."

"That's easy to say," said Melanie, "but how in the world do we do that?"

"We need an anti-propaganda campaign," said Opal. "We can put up counter posters and use the radio to get our message out there."

"It's worth a shot," said Nyx. "After all, if we're going to defeat Taariq eventually, we're going to need more support, regardless."

"The best question we can ask," said Elior, "is what would Michael do?" He stood up and pulled the poster to him. "Taariq said horrible things about Michael, and he got many people to believe him, and many people were and are on Michael's side. He went around healing and helping people, but Taariq only knows how to tear things down."

"Then," said Nereza, new hope in her voice, "let's show him how we build things up."

Nyx sat down in a huff. He'd spent the last four hours hanging counter-propaganda posters all around Wick's Flight, and he was exhausted. He slumped against the storefront he'd just posted his poster on, wishing he'd remembered to bring water. Sweat trickled down his temples even as it evaporated in the afternoon sun.

The shop owner, Ezra, came out and crouched next to Nyx, fluttering his wings to keep his balance. "You look like you could use a pick-me-up. Why don't you come inside and I'll fix you some lemonade?"

"That would be amazing!" said Nyx, pushing himself up. "I really appreciate that."

"It's no trouble." Ezra held the door open for Nyx. "After all, the refuge and all the business they've brought have reinvigorated our little town. I was going to close up shop before they started growing."

Ezra motioned to a stool at the counter, and Nyx sat down. "I know I speak for all of us when I say that we truly appreciate the support. I don't know what the government has planned for us, but a lot of us are scared."

"I don't blame you," said Ezra. He pulled a pitcher out from under the counter and grabbed several lemons and a handful of lavender buds and a little bundle of fresh mint from the shelves behind him. "Honestly, I've been scared since they united our countries. I didn't vote for Swiftwing in any of the last elections."

"I honestly forgot he even existed."

Ezra squeezed the lemons into the pitcher and muddled the lavender buds and mint leaves into the juice. "There's a rumor going around that he's dead. I'm friends with the mayor, and he's saying that Swiftwing's office has been unusually quiet for the past several weeks. I don't know what's going on, but I don't like it."

"I wouldn't put anything past Taariq or any of them, so maybe there's some truth to that rumor."

"Maybe," said Ezra, finishing the lemonade with sugar, ice, and sparkling water. "All I know is that there's a lot going on, and everyone is picking a side. This issue with the Refuge feels like it's right at the center of the whole situation."

Nyx accepted the glass of lemonade Ezra poured for him and sipped. The cool sweetness coated his tongue first, followed by icy refreshment from the mint and finishing with a light floral bitterness from the lavender. "Wow! That's the best lemonade I've ever had! Thank you, Ezra. How much do I owe you?"

Ezra put his hand up, stopping Nyx from getting out his wallet. "You've already paid me by putting up a poster I can support. I know what you're all about. You seek healing, justice, and freedom for all under the guidance of Aelon, just like your poster says."

Nyx smiled and held out a hand to shake Ezra's. "You're a good fairy, Ezra." Downing the rest of his drink, Nyx turned on his stool and stood up. "I should get back to the refuge before it gets dark. Those forest paths can get too dark to navigate once the sun dips below the peaks, especially if it's a new moon like tonight."

"I understand," said Ezra. "Stay safe, and I'll see you next time you're in town."

Nyx set his glass back on the counter and walked towards the door. A fairy dressed in all black walked past him and sat at the counter as he left, but he thought nothing of it.

Chapter 19
Wrath of the Inferno

"As much as you love the lemonade," said Ezra, "it's way past my closing time now. I'm going to have to ask you to leave."

"Oh, do you really have to ask?"

"I don't want to get the police involved, but I will if I have to, sir."

The fairy in black smiled and snapped his fingers. His body elongated, his skin darkened, and little fires licked along his skin as his wings disappeared. "I don't think you're in a position to ask anything of me."

Ezra backed away, bumping into the shelving behind his counters. "Who are you? What do you want?"

"What do I want?" Iblis stood, glowering at the fairy, who was miniscule in comparison. "I want to have never had my form taken from me, I want the spies I sent into the underground to still be working instead of dead, and I want to serve my master. I'll help him remake this world in his image, but people like you get in the way."

"I don't know what you mean," stammered Ezra. His heart raced, his palms sweat. He tottered back and forth between standing and hovering an inch above the ground, but neither his legs nor his wings could hold him for more than a second or two at a time. "How could a little drink shop owner like me get in your way?"

Iblis pointed to the poster hanging on Ezra's window, the one Nyx had put up earlier that day. Just as Ezra saw where he was pointing, the paper burst into flames so hot that it melted the glass where the poster had been hanging.

"Do you see what I mean now?" asked Iblis. "I can't let people who would allow such garbage up on their storefronts become a nuisance to us! I'm afraid you're going to have to pay."

Ezra bolted for the door, but Iblis was faster and more sure on his feet. He held the fairy up by the wings and smiled. His teeth were so white against his shiny black skin that he was almost more terrifying than he had been as a dragon.

Iblis threw Ezra through the glass door out onto the street. Raising his hands up to all the shelves and things hanging on the walls, the djinn sent everything flying around the store as Ezra watched on in silent horror.

Walking out, Iblis blasted the interior of Ezra's shop with black fire. The flames stayed the same for a moment, but as it caught onto the kindling of old receipts and dried herbs, it turned red and yellow and orange as it consumed the store.

Iblis stood menacingly over Ezra, glaring down at the bruised and bloodied face of the fairy.

"What are you going to do to me?" asked Ezra. "You've done

what you wanted. You can let me go!"

"I'm afraid that won't be possible," said Iblis, crouching down and pulling out a gun. "You're the key now to taking down this little underground that worships Michael. You are too useful dead to leave you alive."

Iblis pushed the gun against Ezra's forehead and pulled the trigger.

The morning was quiet. Elior and Eliam were buttering their pancakes, Nereza was pouring over technical books, Opal and Nyx huddled in a corner over hot cereal, and Leonis sipped on a black coffee. Neander grabbed a muffin and switched on the tv to watch the local news while they all ate their breakfast.

The news anchor kept tight eye contact with the camera as she spoke. "… found this morning, dead in the street. We have Ezra's neighbor, Sampson, here. Sampson, would you tell us what you know about the murder?"

"It can't be!" Nyx rushed over and stood in front of the screen. "That's the fairy that gave me the lemonade yesterday after I finished hanging posters!"

"That's not good," said Opal. "What are they saying about the murder?"

Neander moaned and turned up the volume. "If you'll all be quiet, maybe we can hear!"

They all turned to the TV to listen and find out what had happened.

"Like I said before," said Sampson, "I don't know much, but I know Ezra was supportive of that fringe group, Eternity's Refuge."

Nereza gasped as they continued to listen.

The reporter shoved the microphone closer to Sampson. "Do you think that Eternity's Refuge has anything to do with this murder?"

"Did you hear about the explosion at the maximum security prison a couple months back? Several guards had third-degree burns, and I heard one even lost part of their hand! That happened when they sent that bastard prince from Vidania to break out a couple of criminals. If they can do that, then they're capable of murder."

The reporter turned back to the camera. "There you have it. Terrorists who help criminals escape prison leave destruction in their wake, and now murder beloved local businessman. What's next for these people who call themselves 'Eternity's Refuge,' anyway? One thing's for sure. In this new era of unrest and distrust of our government, no one is safe, not even the small businessmen. Back to you in the studio."

Neander shut off the screen, fuming. "They're painting *us* as murderers? Just a few months ago, Taariq was having me systematically hunt the underground down and kill as many as I could find, but we're the murderers?"

"An execution feels markedly different from a gunshot to the head in the middle of the street," said Leonis.

Turning around to face Leonis, Neander said, "Are you defending what they've done or condemning me?"

Opal swept over to Neander and placed a hand on his. "No one condemns you, Neander. Your very name means 'new.' Besides, no one in the Refuge committed that murder. Taariq and his whole regime are responsible."

"You know," said Nyx, "I wouldn't be surprised if Taariq or even Iblis were directly responsible for the murder."

Eliam raised his hand like a schoolboy. "If that was the case, why use a gun? Couldn't they have just cast a spell to stop Ezra's heart or something?"

"I think that would be obvious," said Nyx. "The reason they didn't use magic is that they want to frame the Refuge. None of us wields any magic that can kill. *Aelon above,* my powers prevent death and ease suffering."

"Still," said Elior, "if it was a djinn, they couldn't resist burning something to a crisp. Ezra's shop looked like a lump of charcoal there in the background."

"What does this mean for us?" asked Nereza. "We came here because we thought it was safe, but we're obviously in danger now, right?"

No one could say anything else. A knock on their dining-room door interrupted any further discussion, and Moretta flitted inside.

"Leonis," she said, "the mayor of Wick's Flight is at the gate demanding to see you. I told him I was the local leader, but he knows you're here, and he's insisting."

"I'm coming with you," said Neander.

Leonis stood and strolled toward the door. "I was going to insist that you come with me, anyway."

When they had descended to the forest floor and reached the gate, Moretta, Leonis, and Neander stood outside the gate with a very flustered fairy. The anger on his face was so distinct that Neander thought if he turned any redder, blood would ooze from his pores.

"Do you know the trouble you're causing?" asked the mayor.

Moretta crossed her arms, "Like I told you before, Kessler—"

"I'M NOT SPEAKING WITH YOU!"

Leonis spoke softly, attempting to quiet the mayor. "Kessler, Moretta has already told you, but I'll tell you again, too. None of us had anything to do with Ezra's death. Many of us here loved him, and we're heartbroken by what's happened."

"Perhaps," said Neander, "you'd like to speak with our general, Nyx Cascata? He was with Ezra yesterday."

Kessler spit on the ground at Neander's feet. "I bet he was the one who murdered him then. No, I will speak with no one else. The Refuge is no longer welcome in Wick's Flight. We're done helping you."

With that, the mayor turned, jumped into the air, and flew away.

Taariq, Iblis, Minerva, Loki, and Steelwort, all wearing glamour spells, stood relatively close together in the crowd of fairies as the mayor of Wick's Flight, Kessler, spoke.

"They offer no apology! They offer no safety, and everything they say sounds like a lie to me now!"

"Watch this," whispered Taariq, as he maneuvered to the front of the crowd. He turned to address the townsfolk, "We should burn it all down! Every stick of their stronghold!"

"They're menaces! We won't be safe until they're gone!" Minerva yelled.

Loki joined in, "Being burned is what they deserve for burning down Ezra's store!"

"How long will we wait until one of them does the same to

another business?" asked Iblis

"Or to our homes?" added Steelwort.

The work was done. Every member of the Wick's Flight community was calling for flames, calling for the deaths of all those who lived in the refuge.

A cruel smile spread across Taariq's face as Kessler flew above the crowd. "Grab every bit of kindling and fuel to start a fire. We will meet at the edge of town at sunset, we'll march on the Refuge's encampment, and we'll raze it!"

What remained of the Dark Circle and Iblis reconvened in the square while the townspeople made their collections.

"Won't a fire in the refuge spread to Wick's Flight, Taariq?" asked Minerva.

Taariq, glaring through the eyes of his glamour, said, "Does it look like I care? This town aided our enemies. I don't care if a single stick of this place remains. They die with the traitors. Hopefully, Yrahkaz sees this as an opportunity to rejoin us."

Opal's eyes shot open, and she gasped for air. Allura knelt next to her.

"Your eminence, are you alright?"

Sweat drenched Opal's brow as she grabbed Allura's hand. "We have to gather everyone now. Sound an alarm, do something. Taariq has instigated the people of Wick's Flight to burn the refuge to the ground. We need to tell everyone or we're all going to die!"

Allura shot up and ran out of the sanctuary. Several minutes later, a bell rang. The deep, honey sweet sound beckoned everyone to the clearing at the center of the refuge.

Opal made her way there. Moretta, Leonis, and Neander already stood at the center. Moretta rushed to meet her. "Allura told us you needed everyone together, but she wouldn't give us any details. What's all this about?"

Placing her hands on Moretta's shoulders, Opal said, "It will be better if I only have to say it once. Trust me, I'm not trying to go over your head, I'm just trying to do my job."

Moretta opened her mouth to protest, but rethought her actions and stepped aside to let Opal through to the heart of the clearing. By then, everyone had gathered. Every fairy, all her friends, and everyone else from other refuges was there.

Opal stepped to the middle of the clearing and raised her voice so everyone could hear her. "Everyone listen! We're in danger. Taariq, a couple of Dark Circle members, and loyalist djinn were in the town when Mayor Kessler returned to Wick's Flight today."

"Taariq and those with him, disguised as fairies, convinced the crowd they should march on this settlement and burn it down. Even as I stand here speaking, they are gathering supplies to torch this forest and everyone inside it."

A voice from the eastern end of the clearing asked, "How long do we have?"

"Two hours, three if we're lucky," said Opal. "If we hurry, we can pack a great deal and get clear of the forest before they get here. The fire won't climb the sheer rock walls to the north and south, and it won't cross the river to our east."

Leonis stepped forward to stand beside Opal. "You heard her! Everyone, you have forty-five minutes to pack as much as you can from your apartments and living quarters. After that, you scatter.

Make your way to other refuges, make your way to where you can be safe."

The crowd dispersed, clamoring in their own spaces.

Leonis's face suddenly changed. He took on the appearance of one who had traveled with a heavy burden for many months. "I hope you're right about how much time we have, Opal. I don't want to see anyone die."

"Unfortunately," said Opal, "we won't have that luxury tonight."

Chapter 20
Salvage

ELIOR SLAMMED THE CLOSET DOORS open, scooped his clothes out, and shoved them into his bags. He took no care in going through drawers and just pulled them out of the dresser and dumped the contents into any open pocket.

"Eliam," he said, "are you almost ready?"

His brother raised his head as he swept his arm across his nightstand, knocking his things into his duffle bag. "Yeah, do you want to go check on Melanie and Nereza?"

"Yeah, they might need help." Elior swung his bag onto his shoulder and opened the door. "After you."

Eliam entered the hallway and led the way to Melanie's and Nereza's room. The clatter of falling pieces echoed into the passage from their open door. Melanie hurriedly emptied their dressers indiscriminately about whose blouse or skirt or shorts belonged to who. Nereza pulled, twisted, and cranked at the portal, desperate to take it down and compress it into boxes.

Elior stepped in and asked, "How can I help?"

"Just pack what I pull down," said Nereza, the threat of tears on the back of her voice. "There are so many pieces and not nearly enough time."

Melanie pushed her hair back and asked, "Eliam, can you help me empty our drawers while they work on that?"

The four of them worked, desperately trying to get every piece, every component, every article they needed ready to go.

Nereza screamed in rage and frustration as she pulled at the copper cables. "Melanie, you never told me you welded the bottom of the cables into the steel plate! How are we supposed to get these out?"

"What are you talking about?" Melanie asked. "I didn't weld anything. We agreed everything would be held in place by tension switches for simple movement, since we didn't want the portal to be anywhere permanently."

Nereza pulled, grimacing and straining so hard that redness shone through on her bronze forehead. Her sweaty palms caused her to lose her grip on the copper cables, and she fell backwards. "I don't get it then. I released the tension switch, and this side of the cables still won't come out."

"Ok, let me see," said Melanie as she zipped the last bag of clothes and kneeled down beside the portal. She ran her fingers over the place where the cables were attached to the inner workings of the steel base. She gasped, realization and panic painting themselves over her face. "We didn't factor in heat expansion in this hole for the cables! When we tested it, this side wasn't wide enough and the cables are stuck even with the tension switch off."

"What does that mean?" asked Elior. "Can we fix it?"

Opal and Nyx appeared in the doorway.

"Hey, guys, we have to go," said Nyx. "Are you ready?"

Nereza sighed and said, "We can't get the last cable to release from the portal's base."

"We have to be out of here in less than thirty minutes," said Opal. "How crucial is the portal right now?"

Nereza stared daggers at Opal.

Rolling her eyes, Melanie said, "We've spent the last month building and working on this."

"Sorry," Opal said. "All I meant was that I want you guys to live more than I want a way to Nox Terra."

"Of course," said Nereza, softening her expression. "If we really can't get it unstuck, we can replace these parts, but they were so complicated to make. I'd like to save them if it's possible."

Opal dropped her bag and put a hand on Nyx's back, signaling him to do the same. "What can we do to help?"

"What if the guy's pulled on the cable while we weighed the plate down?" asked Melanie. "That might be enough strength to loosen the cable."

"It's worth a try," said Elior, rubbing Nereza's shoulder.

"Let's give it a shot," she said, meeting his gaze.

Opal, Nereza, and Melanie stood on the steel plate, crouched and holding onto its edges, while Elior, Nyx, and Eliam lined up along the length of the copper cable.

"When I say pull," said Nyx, "we all pull back with everything we've got. Ok?"

"Ok," said Elior. "On three?"

Eliam secured his grip around the Cable and said, "Sounds good to me. Wanna count down, Nyx?"

"Yeah," said Nyx, digging his feet into the ground. "One."

They tightened their grips, Nereza muttered something like a prayer under her breath.

"Two."

The hardness of the cable dug into Elior's arms as he held tighter.

"Three!"

Nyx, Elior, and Eliam pulled, and the world went into slow motion. Every heartbeat was an eternity as they strained against the expanded metal. For several milliseconds, nothing happened. Then hope boiled over in their hearts as the scream of scraping metal rang forth from the cable's connection to the base. In another moment, the copper cable slipped out of the base, sending the boys tumbling backwards onto the floor.

Neander knocked on the doorframe. "It's time. Put those last things away, and let's get out of here."

They trudged along with a caravan of fairies. The side of the mountain was steep, but if they could make it to the crest, they'd be out of sight of whoever might come to burn what was their safety.

"Ironic, isn't it?" asked Nyx, extending a hand to Opal.

She took his hand, allowing him to help her climb a boulder that was more than half her height. "What is?"

"That we would have to flee a refuge because it isn't safe," he said, hoisting her up. "I just think it's funny."

Opal let a singular chuckle out. "If we weren't fleeing for our lives right now, I might agree with you."

They continued up the side of the mountain. Eliam and Nereza were ahead, hoisting bags and mountains over the crest with the help of the winged horses. Melanie and Eliam directed fairies towards the meeting area over the crest from the back.

As Opal and Nyx reached the top, she grabbed his hand. "I have to see what happens."

"Are you sure?" he asked. "I don't want you to get hurt."

She edged over to a flat rock that overlooked the wood below. "Don't worry. They won't even see me."

He followed her and laid down next to her. They peered over the edge. For several minutes after the rest of the caravan had passed them, there was no sound. Then, the trampling thunder of wings and feet approached the clearing where the refuge lay.

Leading the mob was Taariq. If she concentrated, Opal could see through his glamour. He yelled something she couldn't quite make out to the crowd. Everything he said made them angrier. Loki, Minerva, Steelwort, and Iblis all did their share of riling the fairies of Wick's Flight up in their own corners, too.

Then it started. The townsfolk lit torches and poured gallons of starter fluid all over the trees, the buildings, and everything in the refuge's gates. Opal held her breath. Many of the fairies from the town had been so vigorous they'd gotten the fluid on themselves.

Taariq stood in the center of the field. For a moment, his true form flashed through his glamour, his bloody smile sending a shiver down Opal's spine. He screamed so loudly and with such force that she could understand clearly.

"Burn it down!"

The fairies dropped and threw and launched their torches in every direction. In an instant, everything was blazing, even the fairies. Their screams echoed off the mountainsides. They couldn't fly away, with their wings so delicate that the flames melted and withered them instantly. The people of Wick's Flight were trapped in the clearing with no way out as Taariq laughed and frolicked, immune to the flames.

"Nyx," said Opal, "they're going to burn down the world if we don't stop them. They don't care who lives or dies! He worked them into such a frenzy that they are killing themselves."

Nyx reached for and took Opal's hand even as they continued to watch, weeping openly for the people of Wick's Flight. "By Aelon's grace, we will stop them. We will end Taariq's tyranny for good."

"I hope so," she said, moving closer to him and burying her face in his chest.

They stayed there, holding each other. Opal wept into and soaked Nyx's shirt until every tear in her body had been cried out.

Chapter 21
Hide Away

EVERY MUSCLE IN NEREZA'S LEGS cried out in agony. For eight days they'd hiked through the mountains of Faeland on foot, trying to make it through the mountains without being discovered. Initially, Elior had suggested that they go through Dragon's Breath Pass like he, Nyx, and Opal had on their first adventure. However, Opal reminded him that the only trails out of Dragon's Breath led into the heart of Nanony, to Atom. They couldn't afford to go there, not if Steelwort had gone home.

A cramp in her calf slammed Nereza to the floor, and she shrieked in pain.

"Nereza!" cried Elior, bounding back to her and cradling her head. "What's wrong?"

She pointed to the source of her pain. "It's a cramp, the worst one I've had."

"Here," said Opal, holding out a water bottle. "Drink. You might be dehydrated." She cupped her hand over her mouth and yelled, "Nyx! Come back here, we need your help."

Nyx picked his way over the rock and descended to where Nereza lay. "It's not the same leg I healed in the hole, is it?"

"No," said Nereza. "That one's been better than new ever since."

Nyx's smile warmed her almost as much as his healing. "Good. I'd hate to think I didn't do a good job."

"How much further do we have to go?" asked Neander.

"Same question," said Melanie. "I could really use a bath and a proper bed."

Opal took her bottle back from Nereza and slid it back into her bag. "It's not much further."

"Just tell me we can make it before the sunset," said Eliam, mopping his brow. "It's hot, and I'm sweaty."

"Which is why a bath would be nice," said Melanie.

Neander checked his watch. "Probably best to press on. It's noon now. We only have about five and a half more hours of good sunlight before the peaks obstruct it."

"Are you good to go?" Nyx asked Nereza.

She hadn't even noticed his healing light shimmering over her legs. She wiggled her toes and relief washed over her. "All the pain is gone. I don't even feel sore anymore!"

"Good," Nyx said. "Elior, help her up and let's keep going."

Nereza took Elior's hand, and they climbed, hand in hand, over the peak. Opal hadn't lied when she said it wasn't far. Granite Valley, the far north Nanonian refuge, lay sprawled out beneath them at the bottom of a sheer cliff.

"Uh, Opal," said Elior, "how do we get down there?"

She pulled herself up to where he and Nereza stood. "I sent a guard a message. He should be on his way over with repelling equipment now."

No sooner had she said it than a grappling hook embedded itself on the rocky cliff. A red-headed dwarf climbed with an agility that surprised Nereza carrying several harnesses.

"Afternoon," he said. "Hope you weren't waiting too long, your eminence." He bowed slightly to Opal.

"You're just in time. Thank you for meeting me here."

He pulled the harnesses off his shoulders and laid them out for everyone to grab. "It's my pleasure. Everyone put on a harness and attach it to the rope. Another of my men is at the bottom, and he'll help us repel down."

After a brief but thorough safety lecture, everyone was in their harnesses and they were repelling down into Granite Valley. When they had all reached the ground, the dwarf asked, "Shall I show you all where you'll be staying?"

"Yes, please," said Opal. "I know we'd all like to rest. It has been a long eight days."

"Just let me call down the horses," said Neander. He pulled a whistle out of his pocket and blew. No audible sound could be heard by most of them, but overhead, the two flying horses that had carried their things for them circled, getting ready to land.

As gently as twin feathers, they alighted on the ground and whinnied in unison.

"Now we're ready," said Neander.

Wet, shrunken coils dripped onto Nereza's shoulders as she reassembled the portal, but she didn't care. She wanted to get it put back together. She wanted to be sure she wouldn't forget the adjustments she made and put it back together wrong. As soon as she'd gotten to her room, she'd started, but Elior had insisted she take a bath and rest for a bit after what had happened. It was the one concession she'd allowed herself, and now her dripping hair was pulling focus from her delicate machine.

"Nereza?" Melanie kneeled beside her. "It's been hours. You missed dinner. Don't you think you can leave the portal alone now?"

For several moments, Nereza couldn't be sure she had heard anyone speak, but then Melanie's voice reached her inner mind. "I can't. I'm close."

She was. Only a few components needed to be reinstalled. Most of it was fully in place.

"At least let me help you," said Melanie.

Nereza tossed Melanie a tool belt and kept working. She and Melanie attached the remaining components, calibrated the computers, and input a new set of parameters they'd agreed on. Once again, the portal was together.

Sighing, Nereza leaned back. "Think we should test it?"

"It's a little late, don't you think? We've been working for hours."

"Has it really been hours?" Nereza grabbed her phone. Without realizing it, she'd worked for four hours straight. The window revealed the changing colors of sunlight on the grass outside.

"Let's just go to bed," said Melanie. "We can test it tomorrow."

Nereza sat for a moment. "You know what, we spent so much time calibrating this thing, we really should just test it now."

"You won't let this go until I give in, are you?" asked Melanie, slumping in defeat.

Nereza flashed her a toothy smile. "You know me so well!"

"Fine."

They flipped their switches and stepped back. The copper cable glowed pink as the light floated up in widening rays from the fibre optic cables. A sucking sound whispered and hissed from the air in the middle of the arch. Then the light solidified, changed color, and swirled.

"Toss something in," said Nereza.

Melanie picked up a pad of paper and chucked it into the slow turning vortex where it disappeared.

"You should put your head through it," said Melanie. "See if you can see anything."

Nereza walked up to the portal. Holding onto the arch of copper cables, she stuck her head through. White marble floors stretched out beneath her with green gardens. Beyond that, an endless sea of clouds backed up to an azure sky. Isengürd.

She backed out. "Melanie," Nereza said. "We did it. The portal works! I've gotta go tell everyone!"

"Wait!" Melanie yelled before Nereza could fully open the door. "Most of them have already fallen asleep. Wait for morning. Everyone will be happy to hear about it in the morning."

"I suppose you're right," said Nereza. Her eyes, suddenly heavy, she yawned. "I could use some sleep myself. Let's shut it off and show everyone tomorrow."

The smoldering remains of the Faeland refuge and Wick's flight lay blackened beneath Taariq as he stood on the edge of the cliff.

"He's not coming back," said Iblis. "Yrahkaz isn't playing a double agent, Taariq. He left with the others. He ran like a scared dog even though he could have reveled in the fires with us."

Taariq smoldered, the flames licking along his body growing brighter and hotter. "Don't you think I know that, Iblis?" He screamed and kicked a rock off the cliff knocking several branches off trees below him. "This is a grave loss to the Circle."

"He was only one human. Humans, as I remember, were the weakest of all the races the Sky Demon placed in this world."

Taariq summoned a chair and a glass of brown liquor. He sat down and sniffed the contents of the glass before chugging it and throwing it down, sending glittering shards everywhere. "Humans are the weakest, but Yrahkaz was special. He was the human version of what your dragon self used to be to me."

"And now he isn't using magic, he's helping the other side, and he's given up the power you helped him attain. Why does the loss of one human upset you?"

"In one month," said Taariq, "Yrahkaz killed over two thousand of Michael's supporters. In one month! He was good. Now that he's on the other side, I can't imagine the damage that he'll deal to us."

Iblis summoned a chair and sat across from his master. "Is there any way to stop him, though? After all, they have a seer. We can't count on spies working if Aelon protects them."

Taariq's mind drifted back several months. There was a glimmer of hope in a deal he'd made…

"I'll start worrying about him again if he becomes an obvious problem. At least for now, I'm going to see what happens."

"And if he becomes a problem? If he pushes a bit too far?"

Taariq summoned another glass filled to the brim. "Then I kill him and reclaim the power I helped him get."

Opal shivered as if suffering from extreme cold, but the room was comfortable, and the sun streaming in warmed her back even as Nyx rubbed it.

"Opal," he said, "you haven't stopped shaking for ten minutes. Are you sure you're ok? I can try to heal you."

Her teeth were still chattering, but she said, "No, I'm ok. It's just the effect of having a vision like that."

"Like what? What did you see?" he asked.

As soon as the question was asked, she stopped shaking. She turned towards Nyx and began describing what she'd seen. "I was at the top of a mountain so tall that it overlooked the entire world, both sides. Fires blazed everywhere, and I tried to call out, but everyone was so far away that they couldn't hear me."

"Then I saw three figures. One was Michael. As soon as I recognized him, I saw a flash of his death and felt the peace of seeing him alive again. The second was a being made entirely of light and water. When I saw that being, I remembered the light that flows through us when we use the gifts from the Well."

Nyx poured a cup of water and handed it to Opal. "And what about the third being?"

Opal sipped the water and continued. "That's where it gets strange. The third being was almost like a man, but so much taller that

I could barely see his face. Great big wings wrapped around his body with feathers that were iridescent and reflective and opaque white all at the same time. Whenever he took a step, pools of burning water sprung up in his footsteps, and the air sang around him."

"Sounds absolutely terrifying." Nyx leaned out and blew out, fluttering his lips. "What happened next?"

"The third being pointed to the world and the words *Terra Aeternitas Nova* wrote themselves in the air in blue flames. The fires that burned over the world grew and grew and grew until they covered the world. A huge fist formed out of the fire, and that fist reeled back to smash the world. Then, a man made of purple crystal shining with blue light stood up and raised his arms toward the beings."

"Thousands of little shadows fell off the world, and the crystal man reached out and wailed, mourning their loss. The world suddenly became engulfed in light, and when it dimmed, the entire world sparkled and the fist of fire was gone." Opal reached behind her. "And when I woke up, I had the urge to write this."

Nyx took the paper and read aloud, "Oh world, given over to fire. Woe to you, woe to all who are satisfied with consuming warmth and burning prosperity. Pull them in, pull them in from every corner to the valley of safety. Watch then for the strike. No one is safe from the fire bringer lest the anointed stand. Stand for right, stand for justice, stand for the promise of the lifesaver. Open the door for a gush of cleansing, and then shall eternity live again."

"What do you think, Nyx?" asked Opal. "I'm not sure I understand."

Nyx handed the paper back to Opal. "I don't either. All I know is that you're a seer. Soon this will all make sense because Aelon will help you interpret it."

"I just wish there were someone," said Opal, repositioning herself in her seat to be comfortable, "that was wise enough to know what this means."

There was a knock on the door. Neander opened the door and said, "We're all gathering in Nereza's and Melanie's quarters for some sort of big announcement. I told them I'd come get you two since you didn't answer your texts."

"Come on," said Nyx. "We'd better go. I'm sure Aelon has an answer."

Chapter 22
Where the Winds Blow

NEANDER SAT BETWEEN HIS SONS on a couch facing the portal. Nereza and Melanie whispered at the front while Nyx and Opal sat down.

Elior cleared his throat. "We're all here, Reza. What's going on?"

"Oh! Everyone's here," Nereza said. "I was so focused I didn't notice. Melanie and I have an announcement."

"Yeah," said Nyx. "Neander told us that. What's the announcement?"

Melanie giggled and stepped to one side of the portal. "Maybe we should just show them, Nereza."

Nereza smiled a big, toothy smile and kneeled down on her side of the portal. They both keyed something into the controls and then flipped the switches.

The air hummed as light gathered and changed color in the

portal's arch. Sparks glowed as they floated up from points of light on the base, and the smell of spring air perfumed the air. Then, in a lightning instant, the light swirled and shifted colors under the arch until a vortex of light spun in front of them.

"You got the portal to work!" exclaimed Elior, rushing up and spinning Nereza around in a hug. "You are absolutely incredible. I'm so proud of you."

"Thank you," she said, planting a kiss on his cheek.

"What does this mean?" asked Nyx. "What does having a working portal mean for us?"

"It means," said Neander, "that we have to go there."

"What?" Eliam's face contorted in concern and confusion. "Why would we go over there? I spent months over there just wishing to be home, and you think we should go there?"

Eliam's breath quickened, but Elior rushed back over and grabbed his shoulders. "Bro, calm down. There isn't a dragon over there anymore. There isn't a threat to you, and even if there was, you have all of us to protect you."

Allowing his shoulders to relax, Eliam breathed and dipped his head. "Ok."

"While I'm not as worried as Eliam," said Elior, "I would like to know why you think we need to go over there, Dad."

"I'm curious as well, to be honest," said Nyx.

Neander moved to stand in front of the portal. He gazed into the swirling colors and felt the subtle rush of wind around him. He turned around to address the rest and said, "I spent months looking for people in the underground and executing them for their trust in what Michael stood for. I am the reason so many are dead, but Michael redeemed me. Why would he do that?"

Blank stares passed between the others.

"Because," said Neander, "or at least this is why I think he redeemed me, he wants people on his side. Do you honestly think that Aelon is going to allow Taariq and his supporters to rule forever? And what happens to anyone that isn't on Aelon's side when he finally squashes the djinn like he did the dragons?"

"Of course!" blurted Opal. "Neander, you're a genius!"

Neander laughed and put his hand on his chest as his cheeks reddened. "Thank you, but what prompted the compliment?"

"I had a vision last night," she said. "I wrote it all down, but you're right. Eventually, Aelon has to stop Taariq or he'll destroy the world. One line of the prophecy was *'pull them in, pull them in from every corner to the valley of safety.'* We have to win people to Michael's side, or who knows what will happen to them?"

Neander stomped his foot emphatically. "That's exactly what I'm saying! We have the refuges on this side. The one in Faeland burned down, but people still know about us. We're growing *despite* what Taariq wants. But what if we went beyond his influence? There's a whole other half of the world that needs what we have."

"Then we're going? Today?" asked Elior.

"That's the most exciting thing I've heard in a long time," said Melanie. "After everything Nereza's told me about Nox Terra, I've just been dying to go."

"Good thing you helped put the portal together," said Eliam.

Neander raised his arms as if embracing them all. "Then it's decided? We're all going and we're going to win support for Eternity's Refuge?"

"Yeah, Dad," said Elior. "Let's get ready." He laced his fingers into Nereza's and added, "Let's meet back here in two hours, and we'll cross over."

The sensation of walking through the portal was much more pleasant to Elior than being sucked through the Mirror had been. That experience had ripped him off from the floor and sent him hurtling through a magical storm to the other side of the world. However, with all the calibration that Nereza and Melanie had spent painstaking hours on, the journey through the portal felt like a warm summer breeze and a jolt of excitement bursting through the gut.

Elior breathed in the clear air as they emerged. A sea of clouds stretched out from the edge of a green park as far as he could see. "Is this Isengürd?"

"I think it is," said Opal.

A gust of wind rippled around them and materialized. Aurus smiled brightly and said, "I didn't expect to see you back here. You three brought friends this time." He motioned to Neander, Eliam, and Melanie.

"We did," said Nyx. "We have a great deal to share with East. Is he busy?"

"East is always busy," said Aurus, "but he would never pass up the opportunity to see old friends. Why don't I show you all to his hall?"

"That would be great, Aurus," said Elior.

Aurus turned into a little cyclone, picking up stray grass clippings as he led them out of the park and through the city to East's hall in the citadel. When Aurus solidified again, he opened the door.

The same bright displays, swirling books and papers, and dark walls soared overhead to a dome where East hovered, every so often flapping his great green wings to keep himself aloft.

"Dad!" called Aurus, floating higher to get East's attention. "Dad, we have visitors."

East turned from what he was doing and a warm smile spread across his face, sending a warm, floral breeze towards them. Elior breathed deeply of the smells of peonies and fresh cut grass.

As the elder Ventus descended to the ground, he said, "Welcome! Welcome again to Isengürd, my friends." He held out a hand to Elior. "The last time I saw you, you were one. Now you are two!" he said, gesturing to Eliam.

"East," said Elior, "this is my brother, Eliam. He's the one we were trying to rescue when we were last here."

"For the part my kind and I played, I am honored. To be of service is the greatest of privileges." East released Elior's hand. Turning to address the group, he said, "You are double in number since you were last on this side of the world. What brings you back?"

Opal cleared her throat, drawing the eye of the ten-foot spirit. "We were hoping to gain some insight into that from you, actually."

"Oh? You don't know your own purpose?" East laughed and waved his hand, summoning a chair for everyone out of thin air.

"It's not like that," said Nyx. "We know why we're here."

"Yes," said Opal, pulling out the paper with the prophecy. "We know that we're here to call the peoples of Lox Terra to action, to stand against Taariq."

"That is going to be a hard sell, Seer," said East. "Remember, I told you we Nox Terrans were cowardly in the dragon war? I fear many hearts may still not have the courage to stand against Solarium, disempowered, as he may be in his new form." East's eyes twinkled, and he leaned forward, nearly whispering, "Unless you have something on that paper you'd wish to share with me?"

Opal read the prophecy to East and told him what they believed it to mean. When she was finished, she asked, "So, what do you think?"

East leaned back in his chair, his face tense and pulled in. Elior thought that if he suddenly went translucent, that he might have been able to see gears and cogs moving as East thought.

"You're right," said East, his voice heavy. "Obviously, Michael's movement must be supported, must be a torch we Nox Terrans take up with Lux Terrans. After all, while we exist on opposite sides of this giant coin in the ether, we share this world. If Taariq destroys one part, he destroys all parts."

Elior folded his hands in his lap and asked, "Then how do we gain support?"

Standing with a sigh, East plodded over to a display of light and put his hand on it. "The first step to gaining support will be to gain the support of the Venti. In order for that to happen, the council of four winds must be called." The brightness of the display split into four different colors: white, green, orange, and blue. In a glittering moment, each of the four squares turned into a sealed envelope and soared out of East's hall.

"What was that?" asked Nereza.

"That," said Aurus, "was how my father calls a council."

East stomped his foot and the dark walls faded to white and the displays turned into windows overlooking Isengürd's streets. "The four elder winds will be here tonight. Ready yourselves to fight for your cause. The anointed of Aelon must stand against the four greatest forces of nature themselves in order to gain support on this side of the world."

Opal sat at East's right, unable to remove her gaze from the door to the hall. "Are the other winds usually late?"

East sighs, the gust ruffling her hair. "Unfortunately, one downfall of my race is their loose approximation of time. I just hope they show up today rather than tomorrow or next week."

Then the door burst open and a female wind spirit with wings the color of sunshine and flaming orange hair sauntered in, her floral robes swirling around her legs as she glided to sit at East's left.

"South," he said, "I trust your journey was pleasant?"

South spread her mouth in a smile and said, "East, I had the most marvelous flight! The only thing that marred it was coming to an emergency meeting. Really, darling, must you take everything so seriously? What's this all about, anyway?"

"I'd really rather wait until everyone is here to discuss the details," he said, "but I promise I did not waste your time to get you here."

"I suppose I can live with that," South said, pulling out a nail file and delicately shaping her pinky nail. "The others should be along soon enough. I raced them here from the cliffs on the northern edge of the world. I always enjoy summering in North's palace."

Opal's attention was pulled back to the door when another imposing figure filled the doorway. A man who was remarkably similar to East, except his hair was black and moved like ocean waves and his wings were the blue of the sea, floated toward the table and sat beside South. He spoke slowly when he said, "I received your invitation, East. What was so urgent?"

"West," said East, "you'll know soon enough. Do you know when North will be along?"

He didn't have to wait for an answer, because at that moment, she walked in, ice forming wherever she stepped. Her skin, hair, and wings were all snow white. Everything was white, except for her eyes. North's eyes were icy blue, striking and formidable against everything else.

"Well, East," she said, her voice commanding and reverberating even though she might as well have whispered for the sound of her voice, "I'm here. What prompted this emergency meeting? We haven't all needed to be in the same room at a time in over a hundred years."

As North sat, East gestured to Opal. "This is Opal Stronghand. She's a seer, and has brought a message from Aelon that we all need to hear."

"And you're qualified to give this judgement?" asked North. "Have you already heard it, then and decided for us what we needed to hear?"

"North," said south, a soft giggle under her cheerful tone, "go easy on East. He's the eldest, after all. He wouldn't have called us together for no reason."

West ran a hand through his black hair and winked at Opal. "I think we should just hear the little dwarf seeress out, alright?"

North folded her arms and raised an eyebrow at Opal.

"You'd better tell them what you told me," said East.

Internally, Opal wished that Nyx could have been there, but protocols for the meeting of the Four Winds were very specific: no one but the winds and the most relevant party.

"Michael," she whispered, standing and circling the long table to face all the winds, *"help me."*

Strength filled Opal and her skin glowed slightly, throwing silver shadows as she said, "The Great Spirit Aelon sent a vision to me the night before last. As with the last great prophecy from Regalla, the Mare of Ten Thousand Tales, this prophecy concerns all of Terra Aeternitas." New insight flooded her as she spoke. "If left unchecked, Taariq will destroy the world and everyone in it, but for Aelon's faithful—those who stand with Michael and oppose Taariq's tyranny—there will be safety."

"What do you mean?" asked South.

"For those who align themselves with Michael, Aelon promises safety from the destruction Taariq is bringing. He will protect those who accept Michael's movement and join us."

"Who is this 'us' and who are you to instruct us ancient winds? Seems rather presumptuous, if you ask me," said West.

"On the other side of the world, in Lux Terra, I am the High Priestess of a group called Eternity's Refuge. Beyond worshipping Aelon, we also recognize that Michael redeemed the waters of Eternity's Well, thus triggering the events that wrapped up Regalla's last prophecy. My friends, Nyx Cascata and Elior BarVidania, all drank from the Well. Soon after, we came through Eternity's Mirror and restored the function of the Sky Wheel and defeated Umbra, removing him from his place of power here in Nox Terra."

"Opal," said East, "tell us—tell them—what you want us to do."

She swallowed, hoping that the urgency of the situation came across. "Eternity's Refuge needs more people. We need to be a force that can oppose Taariq and bring more people to Michael's cause. It's the only way to assure the survival of anyone. We need the Venti, the spirits of all the winds, to support us, join the cause, and help us bring others in, too."

The winds said nothing.

North's eyes bored into Opal, sending icicles up her back. "You expect us, the mighty Cardinal Winds, to believe and take instruction from you, a finite being? Of all the forms of audacity, the propensity of mortals to think they know what's really going on in the world is astonishing to me."

"Little lady," said West, "do you realize what happened the last time any of our kind got wrapped up in the dragon's drama?"

Opal cocked her head and frowned. "East said that no one had been involved with the war, and Virdor said that Nox Terrans refused to stand with Lux Terrans."

"That's not what I mean," he said. "I mean that many of us got involved with Umbra. There were spies among all Nox Terran races, there were horrible consequences to being involved with a dragon, and we're just now sorting all of that out and getting back to true peace."

"I'm not asking you to be involved with Taariq or any of his allies," Opal said. "I'm asking you to stand against him. Do what you should have done before."

North scowled and stood. "No. I refuse to give credence to this superstitious nonsense." She turned to go, but South disappeared and re-materialized in front of her with a blast of warm air.

"Are you so cold that you've also become heartless, sister?" South asked. "You were created last, yes, but you still saw the breath of our maker take shape as the lesser venti. How can you call this Seer superstitious?"

"Please," said East, "if we pledge our support, the worst thing that will happen is that Opal is wrong about what Taariq will do. However, if we don't pledge our support, the worst thing that could happen is that we'll sentence every wind spirit in the world to death."

"West, North," said South, "can you live with those consequences?"

"I'd like to say something," said Opal. "North, it's true. You were created on the day the venti were born. I'm a lot younger and I'll die sooner than you might imagine, but my message is not my own. If you have faith in Aelon, have faith in me because this gift is from him. I know what will come to pass because the Great Spirit gave me the gift of sight. I do not guess, I know."

At that moment, Opal's glow intensified enough for the others to see it from so high above her. North's hard face softened, and a tear trailed down her cheek. West put his hand over his heart.

"Wow," said South, "It's been eons since we've seen Aelon's light!"

Opal looked down at herself, unsure of what South meant. Thankfully, East sensed her confusion.

"Aelon's light is a divine blessing," he said. "It signals that the bearer is within his will."

West stood and bowed. "You have my support."

East and South pledged theirs as well. Only North remained.

"North," said South, "just agree. We're doing this with or without you."

She softened and sighed, "Fine. Just don't say I didn't warn you if something goes wrong."

The winds and Opal applauded.

East smiled broadly. "Opal, you have the venti's support. Get some sleep, and in the morning, I'll help you figure out how to get the other races' support, too."

Chapter 23

Path Through the Forest

SUNLIGHT FILTERED THROUGH THE GAPS between the buildings of Isengürd as Elior swung his backpack over his shoulder and faced East. "Thank you for all your help yesterday. I know we're all grateful that we have the venti among our supporters."

The wind at the edge of the clouds whipped through East's beard, spreading the smell of wild flowers everywhere. "I'm simply glad to be of service."

"Your modesty is admirable," said Neander, "but your help truly is invaluable."

Opal turned back to the group from where she had been observing the lightening sky around the sunrise. "Do you have any advice for us before we descend to the world below? Is there anything we should know?"

"Ask Aelon for opportunities to show his power," said East,

waving over six venti who had taken the forms of horses and gigantic birds.

"What do you mean?" asked Nereza. "What opportunities should we be asking for?"

"The world," said East, "isn't empty of problems since Umbra's defeat. The darkness the dragons brought into Terra Aeternitas makes itself known in lesser conflicts, disease, natural disasters, and other ways, too."

"Nothing's perfect," said Melanie, kicking a tuft of cloud swirling at her feet over the pavement. "Isn't that just life?"

The air seemed to grow heavier on their shoulders as East scowled. "Before the Dragon War, we didn't know disease. We didn't battle the elements. We lived in harmony with no written law and there was no conflict of any kind before the Dragon War."

Eliam put his arm around Melanie. "I think that what he's saying is that we need to ask for specific opportunities where our skills can help."

"Exactly," said East. "Especially you, Nyx, Opal, and Elior. You drank from Eternity's Well, and Aelon blessed you with rare gifts. Perhaps, if you ask, Michael and his father will grant you opportunities in which to use the gifts he gave you to bring others to the safety you speak of." He folded his hands and smiled again, and the air grew light again.

"Thank you for the advice," said Nyx. "Where will the venti you summoned be dropping us off?"

"I thought meeting with two races at once might be useful for you. I understand a centaur delegation is visiting with Virdor in the Living Forest, so they'll be taking you there."

"It will be nice to see Virdor again," said Nereza, pulling back her hair to prepare for the flight. I don't think we'll have any trouble convincing him to support us."

"Maybe not," said East, "but the dryads can be stubborn. How often have you seen a tree move or change position?"

"He has a point," said Elior, mounting his steed, "but hopefully there's a way to use our gifts to help them accept the safety the Refuge offers."

"Then let's get going," said Opal. She mounted a smaller ventus, and the others followed suit.

With nothing but air between them and the ground, the wind spirits dove through the clouds, rushing their charges to the Living Forest.

Every time Elior walked into the forest, it was different. Sure, yellow sunlight streamed through the branches overhead, sending scattered shadows dancing down to the ground, but the forest itself was still. Not one tree moved. A forest was supposed to be alive, but if he didn't know better, Elior might have mistaken the Living Forest for an elaborate replica of the dryads' home.

As they plodded into Virdor's clearing, they were the only source of sound. Wind didn't blow, it wouldn't dare, not now.

Soft gasps passed their lips as the reason for the forest's silence came into view. Virdor's tree, once the only sign that the forest was alive, had black streaks running up it, oozing whatever the tree equivalent of puss was. The scent was acrid and burning. The sound of Opal gagging pulled Elior's attention away. She covered her mouth, meeting his eyes with watery trails carving their way down her cheeks. He wasn't sure if she was crying or if the stench was that bad for her. It didn't really matter.

Three female dryads surrounded Virdor's tree, dabbing at the black streaks, spreading green salve over them while the Lord of the Centaurs mixed more at his gnarled roots.

Elior wrinkled his nose, but approached. "What's wrong with him?"

"Black blight," said the Lord. "We haven't seen it in centuries."

One dryad spreading salve said, "Until now, many of us thought that we'd gotten rid of it for good."

"Will the green salve cure him?" asked Nyx.

The Centaur Lord stood, dusting off his palms. "I don't know. It has been so long since we treated this disease or had need of the herbs that help that the exact recipe is lost to us."

"You called it a blight," said Opal. "When we had an apple blight in Nanony a few seasons back, we had to burn an entire section of the orchard to keep it from spreading. Will this spread to the other trees?"

The Lord hung his head. "I'm afraid so. The last time the Black Blight came to the forest, it wiped out half the dryads before the healthy ones and the ones who had recovered finally consented to burning the ones who would not recover. The Living Forest used to go all the way to the gates of Stonebridge."

"Nyx," said Opal, "you have to save Virdor."

"I've never tried to heal plants," said Nyx.

"It's worth a try, isn't it?" asked Neander. "I mean, they aren't even sure if what they're doing is working."

"Maybe," said Melanie, "but how long have they been trying?

Maybe they should keep trying the green goop to make sure they have a cure in case it comes back."

"If I'm being honest," said the Centaur Lord, "I'm about to give up and tell them they need to—" he stopped, leaning in to whisper, "burn him before he infects the others. Virdor's tree is so large and old that he'd infect every tree within fifty feet of his clearing. From there, it would destroy the rest of the forest."

"Try, Nyx," said Elior. "We can't afford to lose all the dryads. They're an important part of the world."

Nyx dropped his bags and picked over Virdor's roots to the base of his trunk. He knelt down and held up his hands, but no blue glow came.

"What's going on?" asked Melanie. "Those gifts you guys have don't have an expiration date, do they?" Her face was pinched in worry, but Nereza still elbowed her and whispered in her ear while Elior went to kneel beside Nyx.

"Hey, man," Elior said, "Melanie doesn't get it. She only gets magic she can explain."

Nyx dropped his arms. "I don't know where to start."

"If the gift comes from Aelon," said Elior, "let the Spirit guide you. He made Virdor, so he knows how to heal him, right?"

Nyx closed his eyes for a moment and then raised his hands again. This time, he touched Virdor's roots and hummed. As he hummed, the moss covering the roots around Virdor glowed blue. Light poured out of the moss like a fountain, bathing Virdor in light.

Slowly, the oozing black streaks shrank. New leaves grew from Virdor's branches, replacing the ones that were gray and browning with ones that were as green as a field of spring grass. With a pulse, the light cascaded out and Virdor emerged from his tree, stumbling and laughing, and looking younger than he'd been the last time they'd seen him.

Virdor laughed as he ran around his clearing, and the light followed him in waves, bathing the other trees and making them look just slightly fuller.

"You broke the curse!" cried Virdor. "You healed me so much that you gave the rest of the forest immunity! I can feel every tree getting stronger, Nyx. Thank you! Thank you for saving me and thank you for protecting the forest."

"I didn't," said Nyx. "I didn't know what to do, but the Great Spirit did. He helped me to heal you."

Stunned dryads emerged from all their trees. Blue silvery sparkles coated their forms, casting strange shadows.

Virdor faced his friends. "If the Spirit cured the entire forest, then he still used you, Nyx. Accept our thanks."

The old Dryad extended his hand, and Nyx took it. "Then I suppose I should say 'you're welcome.' "

Pivoting, Virdor addressed Opal. "What brings you all back to this side of the world, seer?"

"I had a vision," she said. "Taariq's power is growing. He has all of Lux Terra under his grasp with only a thin veil of separation of power between him and the other Circle members. He *will* attempt to take over the entire world, and in order for any of us to be safe, we must stand against him."

The dryads around the edges of the clearing murmured and whispered. Virdor spoke for them. "We remember our own reaction when Solarium went to war before. We will not be cowards again."

"You healed Virdor," said a red maple dryad, stepping forward. "Truly, if you can do this in the name of the Great Spirit, then he is great enough to protect us from the fire."

"You have our support," said Virdor. "We will stand with you against Taariq and all his plots."

After a full night's sleep and a lovely breakfast provided by the dryads, everyone stood just outside of Virdor's Clearing, talking with the Centaur Lord.

"I've sent one of my centaurs ahead to Stonebridge to get a carriage for you all. I'd have offered to take you there ourselves, but I only brought two others with me. I don't think you would be comfortable riding two to a steed with all your bags," he said.

Neander tutted, "Your Lordship, don't worry. We're not offended in the slightest."

"Good," the Lord replied. He knelt to speak with Opal. "After you shared your gift with us, we need no other convincing. You have the centaurs' support, your eminence."

Opal placed her hand on the Lord's forehead. "Don't kneel to me. Thank you, though, for believing in what we're doing. May Aelon bless you for your support."

"Of course," he said, standing up. "I will rally all the centaurs. If we can be of assistance, please, let us know. If the winds are on your side, they can carry messages quickly."

"We'll keep that in mind," said Opal.

The Centaur Lord trotted off, leaving them to wait for the carriage.

Chapter 24

Defense of Stonebridge

ELIOR JOLTED AS THE CARRIAGE went over a pothole. For a moment, everyone and everything in the large carriage floated in mid-air. Though when six unicorns are sent to pull a carriage, you can't expect anything but jarring, breakneck speed. Gratitude burst out of Elior with a huge smile when they finally slowed.

"You know," Elior said to his brother, "there's a reason going that fast in a car is illegal."

"Yeah," said Eliam, "that was pretty much horrible all the way around."

Melanie pushed them out of the way to get out of the carriage. The sound of puking behind them rattled Elior's stomach.

"You should go check on her," said Elior.

Eliam jumped out to follow Melanie while the rest of them unloaded their things and got a look at the city. The carriage had not stopped at the main entrance. Instead, they were standing over some kind of hole in the ground with a crude gate laid over the opening and locked in place.

"What's this?" asked Nyx. "I wonder why we aren't at the main gate."

The grate over the hole in the ground clicked open, and Davi poked his head out. "The venti told us you were on your way. Hurry, come inside!"

The six of them descended into the hole. When they had all passed the threshold, Davi locked it behind and led them deeper in as he explained, "The unders are at the gates holding us under siege. No one can go in or out by the main entrance. So far, they haven't discovered all of our tunnels, but some of them are barricaded."

"How did this happen?" asked Elior. "We met some of them when we were here before, and they made it seem like they couldn't walk around on the surface if the sun is shining on them."

"They can't," said Davi, "but they constructed these canopies that shade them from the sun so they don't have to worry about what time it is to terrorize people."

"You can't sustain holding out against a siege forever," said Nyx. "How long do you have until you have to give into their demands?"

Davi's shoulders slumped, and he turned back, his face pinched under the weight of the last weeks. "That's a question for the mayor. She isn't telling us much. The only reason I'm the one who came to retrieve you was because I know the tunnels better than anyone else."

They kept going until they emerged in the city square. Goblins and golems puttered about aimlessly. There was a scent of uneasiness and paranoia in the air. Even from the square, Elior could see the soot-blackened siege engines of the unders outside the gate.

A goblin woman in scarlet robes with gold trim approached them. "What took you so long, Davi? You were supposed to be back with them fifteen minutes ago."

"My apologies, Madame Mayor," said Davi. "They were slightly later than I expected."

"It doesn't matter." Addressing the travelers, the mayor said, "I'm sorry we couldn't greet you under better circumstances, but the little shadow imps are bent on taking over this city. There are so many of them, I'm not sure how we're going to stop them."

"Do you have any weapons?" asked Nyx.

The mayor motioned to the surrounding city. "We are known as a center of learning! There is not a single bow, arrow, sword, or anything else within my gates."

Elior thought quietly that the danger from outside was exactly why a place like that should have weapons, but he kept it to himself. Instead, he said, "I'm not sure how it would work, but I could try to protect the city when they attack."

"Are you a one-man army?" asked the mayor, raising one eyebrow and placing her hand on her hip. "No matter how talented you are with that sword on your hip, you won't best an entire army of unders."

"Maybe not," said Elior, "but I wasn't planning on fighting them. Unlike the legendary King Eliseo, I won't be fighting to rescue the city."

"A warrior is what we need," said the mayor.

Opal's eyes flashed with silver light and she said, "Actually, I foresee great suffering if you or any resident of the city tries to fight the unders."

"You're a seer, dwarfess?" she asked. "I saw the flash of light in your eyes."

"I am," said Opal. "I'm also the high priestess of Eternity's Refuge in service to the Great Spirit, but we can discuss that later. I suggest you let my friend Elior try to protect the city."

"While he does that," said Nereza, "Melanie and I can work on creating some weapons that will drive the unders away, hopefully with no bloodshed."

"Fine," said the mayor. "I have other duties to attend to. Davi, help them with whatever they need."

Eliam put his arm around Elior's shoulders and whispered, "I've seen you do some amazing things, man, but I've never seen you protect an entire city. Are you sure you can do that?"

"I have to try, right?" whispered Elior. He stepped forward, letting his brother's arm drop behind him. "Davi, are there any books on protector magic in the library?"

If it was possible, Elior could have sworn that the library had grown in the months since they visited to find out how to return the sky wheel. Davi led them through rows and rows of books after leaving Nereza and Melanie to work on their bomb and Neander, Nyx, and Opal to come up with diplomatic strategies to talk to the unders.

Finally, they reached the section Elior needed. On the second floor of the library, on the most forgotten shelf, was a book about Eternity's Well and the Protector Blessing it sometimes conferred.

"Do you want me to help you look?" asked Eliam.

Elior pulled the book from the shelf. "I don't know. Isn't this the only copy?"

"Actually," said Davi, "I keep a second copy of the rare books to make sure only one is on the floor at a time, but I suppose I can make an exception."

Elior winced. "Where do you keep the second copy, Davi?"

"Same place I kept the collection reserved for you guys last time."

"Gross. I'm gonna look away," said Elior, turning to face the bookcase.

"What? Why?" asked Eliam, but the sound of retching stopped anymore questions. Eliam gagged and said, "By the Spirit! How in the world did you get that in there?"

"Goblins have a second magical stomach that they can keep things in," said Elior. "I saw him do that last time, and I didn't want to see it again."

"Just make sure I get that copy back before you leave," said Davi. "If it's gone for too long, my filing system shifts in there, and I really don't want to swallow someone to reorganize in there when I can't find the next book I need."

When Davi left, Eliam asked, "Do you think it's safe to touch?"

"Yeah," said Elior. "It isn't even wet. Look at it!"

They leafed through the pages, desperately searching for answers. The blessing of the protector was more than Elior had thought it was before. Yes, it was defense, yes it functioned on faith like all blessings from the Well, but it was also directly tied to Aelon's will. The *will* of the Great Spirit could amplify the blessing.

"Wait!" said Elior, tugging on his brother's sleeve. "Look at what I just found. It says *If the protector obtains a blessing from a seer,*

Aelon's blessing will grow in strength for the protector, allowing the blessed to drive back any enemy. We know a seer, right?"

"We need to talk to Opal, then. She's talking with Dad and Nyx downstairs."

The twins rushed downstairs, deposited the extra book with Davi, and ran to Opal.

"Opal," panted Eliam, "we have something to ask you."

She squinted, pursing her lips. "What is it?"

"It's this," said Elior, still breathless. He passed her the book and pointed to the passage he'd found.

She read and said, "I'm sure that's true, but I can't just give you my blessing. Allura's been teaching me about my gift in our spare time, and if I give my blessing without communing with the Great Spirit, I could lose my gift, or worse."

Neander thumped his fist on the table. "We've got some good work done here, Opal. Nyx and I will finish the draft of what we talked about. You go see if you can get that permission before the gates give out or the unders launch an attack on the city."

"Ok," she said. "Let's go to the temple, then. If I give you that blessing, you'll need to be there to amplify your gift, anyway."

Opal ran her fingers over the quartz inlay in the wooden columns of the temple in the heart of Stonebridge. Elior and Eliam trailed behind her as she approached the altar. Fountains flanked it and subtle blue fire burned in braziers, casting a soft, unearthly glow on the steps.

"So, how do you get permission from Aelon to bless Elior?" asked Eliam, sitting down in a pew in the front row.

Opal sat on the dais, mist from the fountains coating her hair. "I'm going to ask Aelon. Hopefully, he or Michael will respond. Allura's been teaching me about how to surrender or commune. There are a lot of different words for it. Bottom line is that I'm going to sit here and talk and listen."

"We'll be quiet," said Elior. "I'll make sure we aren't disturbed."

"Thank you," said Opal. She closed her eyes and ran her hands over the cold stone beneath her. When she'd been in the temple in Granite Valley, Aelon had lit the candles in the shrine she'd prayed at. Was it a good sign that blue fire already burned here?

It was so silent that she could have heard a piece of paper hit the floor on the other side of the sanctuary. She listened, listened for what seemed like hours for Aelon or Michael to say something.

Please, she thought, *we need your help.*

Several more moments passed. She was about to give up, say that the lack of an answer was the answer, but then warmth washed over her body and light flooded her eyes, blocking her from seeing anything else. A breath passed. As she exhaled, Michael's face came into focus against all the whiteness.

"Opal," he said, "how can I help you?"

She stood, shaky from sitting for so long. "I need your help, Michael. The unders are trying to take Stonebridge, and Elior wants to help. He read Aelon can expand his blessing, allow him to protect the entire city, but he needs a seer's blessing."

"So you need permission, then?" He was beside her, offering his arm when she blinked.

She looped her arm into his and said, "I do."

"Then we should go ask my dad together."

Michael led her through the blinding white light until it turned into lush grass so green it hurt to look at dotted with purple buds. Then they were on a road so polished Opal wondered if anyone had ever walked on it before.

"Michael," she said, "what are these roads made of?"

He chuckled. "I'd think that a royal would know gold when she saw it."

"Golden streets?" she asked, not really needing an answer. The grandeur of the place came more into focus. They were walking towards a white city, every building pure white and capped with sapphire domes. The doors and window shutters shiny black and dusted with diamonds. The city was amazing, but even in the surrounding country, fruit trees stretched to the sky, nearly twenty feet tall and burdened almost to breaking with apples, oranges, grapes, and varieties of fruit she'd never even heard of or imagined.

"Michael," she said, "what is this place? Where are we?"

He gestured over her head and swept his arm across the landscape, saying, "This is the Unseen Realm where Aelon rules from. Do you see the river that runs out of the center of the city off that cliff in the distance?"

She followed his hand and said, "Yes. Why?"

"That is the spring that feeds Eternity's Well. It flows from beneath Aelon's throne."

He walked her through the city, so dazzlingly white that she thought that if she wasn't in a vision, it would have blinded her. Beings she had no name for, clothed in light, wandered with purpose through the streets as they passed. Then they reached the center of the city. A palace so big she didn't know how a physical structure could be that big towered over them, blocking out the sky. Without being touched, the doors swung in to reveal a central hall. At the other end, on a throne made of stardust and fractured light, was Aelon.

Aelon's face shifted constantly. He was a man, an elf, a dwarf, a merman, a lion, a dragon, a ventus, he was everything. He was everything at once and none of them at once, but in his eyes, piercing blue and deep like the waters of the Well, were kind and wise.

He raised his hand and suddenly Michael and Opal stood before his throne. He towered over them by at least three hundred feet, but she wasn't afraid. The sound of gushing water forming beneath his throne and flowing out drowned out everything until Aelon spoke.

"I know why you're here, Opal. You want to bless Elior with a seer's blessing."

She couldn't open her mouth. Shock and wonder pelted her mind with a barrage she couldn't bring herself to withstand. A single tear fell from her eye and splashed into the river rushing beneath her.

"My dear priestess, you have my permission," said Aelon. "You also take with you a request. Don't tell the unders what you were planning to tell them. Tell them what you saw here and try to win them to our side. They may be the smallest of my children, but they are mine. I don't want their bitterness to endanger them."

Opal curtsied, something she was rather clumsy at having never had to do it herself. A choking sound came from her throat, but she couldn't quite form words.

"Come on," said Michael. "Let's get you back."

In that moment, Opal found her strength. "I want to stay. Don't send me back!"

"Oh, Opal," said Michael, pushing a stray strand of hair behind

Opal's ear, "One day the Unseen Realm will be seen by all, but not yet. Your friends need you. Close your eyes, and everything will be ok."

Opal obeyed, and when she opened her eyes, the Unseen Realm was gone. The brightly lit interior of Stonebridge's temple might as well have been darkness to her, but she stood.

"Opal? What's wrong?" asked Elior. "Did Aelon refuse permission?"

"No," she said. "Elior, you have your blessing."

He crossed his arms. "Ok. Thanks, but are you ok? Something seems off."

She walked down the aisle towards the door. "I'll be fine. Stand on the dais where I was and you'll be able to protect the entire city from there. I have to go see if I can parlay with the unders."

"Are you sure you're ok, Opal?" asked Eliam.

"No," said Opal, "I'm not sure I'll ever be ok again."

"You can't be serious," said the guard. "We can't let a seer out into an active war zone!"

"I don't recall asking for your permission," said Opal. "Besides, do you see the blue force-field? It extends fifteen feet beyond the wall. If I stay within that boundary, I'll be safe."

"Just let her out," said the mayor, approaching from behind Opal. "We've tried to talk to them, but none of us has her gift. Let her try."

Grudgingly, the guardian golems opened the gates. Outside, the unders were a roiling cloud of shadow under huge awnings of leaves and pieces of discarded wood and metal.

Without hesitation, Opal strolled forward until she was at the edge of the force-field Elior was holding up from the temple. Standing at the very edge, the blue was as clear as water in a tropical sea. The unders hissed at her with whispers between them, their animal-like heads bobbing as they talked.

"I'm here to negotiate with your leaders," said Opal. "Who among all of you claims control?"

The sea of blackness parted and an under bigger than the rest, almost as tall as Opal herself, with the head of a snake wearing an iron crown, came forward. "What could you have to say to us that the goblins haven't already said?"

"I am a seer, I drank from the waters of Eternity's Well. I can tell you many things that the goblins could not tell you." Opal met the under king's eyes, red and beady under shadowy hoods.

Like any regular snake, the king's forked tongue jutted out. "What makes you think we care for Aelon?"

"You may not care for the Great Spirit, but do you wish the dragons were in control? Do you want the djinn to take over the world?"

"I care not," he said, stomping his foot. "All I care for is to have more for my people. We're always scraping, always just getting by! Stonebridge has what we need."

Opal put her hand on the force-field. It was cool and nearly wet under her hand. "You think the answer is in a city, but it isn't. I had a vision, and if the races of our world don't unite against the djinn, their actions will destroy the world, burn it down entirely. Is that what you want?"

A tremor of laughter rumbled from the unders, the king's laugh being louder than all the others. "We are born from the ash from the fires that created the dragons, dwarfess! If the world burns, we will not suffer."

"No," said Opal, "you'll burn, too! The only safety is on the Great Spirit's side. Please stop this siege and unite with us. If we stand together, and if we stand with Aelon, then the djinn can't possibly stand against us!"

"You have pretty words, seer, I'll give you that," said the king, "but they mean little to me." The under king turned to return to his hiding place.

"What if I told you I saw the Unseen Realm, Aelon's kingdom?"

Turning back to Opal, the king said, "Describe it to me. What was it like?"

"It was the brightest—"

"Stop!" he yelled, holding up his hand. "Already, I know it will never be what my people need. We are creatures of shadow. How could we expect to find favor with a deity who finds comfort in light?"

Opal's heart sank, but she had to try saving them. "The brightest lights cast the darkest shadows."

"We're done," said the king. He retreated into the crowd of unders huddled under the awnings and disappeared.

Defeated, distraught, and despondent, Opal turned and slumped back into the city.

"I've never worked so fast in my life," said Nereza.

"Let's stop," said Melanie, dropping her tools in front of her. "I think this is more than enough."

Nereza and Melanie leaned back, a collection of haphazard bombs sitting in front of them on the table. At least fifty of them were armed and ready to go off by remote detonation or by direct input.

Eliam slipped into the room, and Melanie smiled, her shiny white teeth glinting at him.

"Are you guys ready?" he asked.

Melanie twisted a lock of hair around her finger and said, "We just finished the last ones. Why?"

"Opal wasn't able to talk the unders down," said Eliam. "We need the bombs now. Elior can't hold the force-field up much longer."

"Then let's get these all to the walls," said Nereza. "Help us load them into the baskets the golems brought."

The three of them loaded all the bombs and left the library, heading straight for the walls overlooking the unders' camp.

Opal and Neander stood with the mayor, looking out over the unders.

"Madame Mayor," said Nereza, "we're ready to deploy these when you are."

The mayor turned to Opal and Neander. "Do you have any objections or any diplomatic approaches you'd still like to try?"

"No," said Neander. "If they're rejecting what Opal said, then the biggest thing we have to worry about is protecting Stonebridge and everyone inside."

"The bombs aren't lethal, are they?" asked Opal.

Nereza carefully placed the basket down. "I made sure that none of the bombs would actually kill them. It will disperse them, and hopefully it will be enough to keep them from coming back."

"Actually," said Eliam, "I found something Elior could do. If he uses his gift in a certain way outside the walls, he can protect the city from another siege for a hundred years."

"If that's the case," said the mayor, "then I don't care that you're not killing our attackers, but let's just get on with it."

As soon as they bent down to pick up bombs, the force-field fell. The unders were confused for a moment, but then they charged. From on top of the wall, they rained the bombs down. Some of them exploded on impact, others Nereza threw and waited until several unders were in range before detonating them remotely.

Every explosion sent unders flying hundreds of yards away. The ones they could see landed and ran as fast as they could in the other direction to avoid the sun. In three minutes, it was all over. Every single under had left, and they were standing on top of a wall looking at an empty field. Stonebridge was safe.

Elior wrote Aelon's name in the dirt outside the city, using ancient glyphs as the last piece of the ritual Eliam had found outlined. Kneeling to the ground, he breathed on the glyphs and prayed, "Michael, the unders are going to want to come back. I trust you to keep this city. These powers come from the Well that flows from Aelon's throne in the Unseen Realm, and I know that the creator of our world can protect this tiny piece of it from harm."

He stood back up, waiting. The air sizzled with blue electricity. The glyphs around the vast circle he'd drawn around the city glowed and filled up with water. Then it all faded. A faint glimmer shone from the glyphs and circle in the dirt, but it was quiet otherwise.

"Is that it?" asked the mayor. "Is Stonebridge safe now?"

"It is," said Elior. "For the next hundred years, no one will harm the city or come within ten miles with evil intentions."

"That's a tremendous relief!" she said. "How can we ever repay you?"

Opal cleared her throat. "There is one thing. Now that this threat is passed, we need your help."

"We came here," said Nyx, "to gain Stonebridge's support against Taariq."

Neander said, "We need all the support we can get."

"You see," said Opal, offering her hand to the mayor to lead her back inside the gates, "Taariq wants to take over the world, and he won't stop with Lux Terra once he figures out how to get to this side of the world. He will come here."

"You just said that Stonebridge would be safe for a hundred years, so why should we worry about that?" asked the mayor. As if punctuating her point, the gates shut with a thud, bearing the weight of finality.

Nereza crossed her arms. "That might mean that Stonebridge is one of the few safe places. Would you shut out the world? Would you keep out centaurs, venti, naiads?"

The mayor was silent for a while. "Stonebridge has stood as a beacon of knowledge for as long as any of us can remember."

"Then why life in darkness or ignorance?" asked Opal. "With the support of the goblins of Stonebridge, we can create a haven on this side of the world safe from Taariq's reach. I foresee great suffering and destruction from the hands of the djinn. We need to all stand against him, Madame Mayor. After all, what's a hundred years for a djinn?"

"She's right," said Neander. "Taariq has been around for millennia. He can wait a hundred years."

"I met his father, Methuselah," said Elior. "He's even older and is still alive and thriving."

The mayor turned and considered the streets of her city, crossing this way and that, bustling peacefully now that the danger, or one danger, had passed. "I wonder what goblin-kind can accomplish in a hundred years. Would we be able to withstand him?"

"No one can outside of Aelon's protection," said Opal. "That's the only reason your city is safe right now at all."

"What you say makes sense, seer," said the mayor. "Very well. I don't know what it means right now, but you have our support. Is there anything you need help with immediately?"

"Actually," said Nyx, "do you have a ship? We need to get to Misthaven."

Chapter 25

Voyage through the Storm

ELIOR PUSHED HIS CURLS BACK against the sea breeze on the ship
Stonebridge lent them for the voyage along with a crew. The sea was
so different from the last time they had been there. With a sun and
moon moving in the sky, the tides had returned. The sea rose and
fell beneath them, undulating in the sea and rocking them into gentle
contemplation.

"Nice night," said Eliam, coming up beside Elior and leaning on
the railing.

"It is," said Elior. "After so much time spent at Gabrielle's beach
house, the sea has a special place in my heart."

Eliam yawned. "I get that. Plus, it was always a fun time when
mom took us to the beach."

Elior dipped his head, not sure what else to say. They kept their
eyes on the sunset in the horizon. The pink and orange and gold

and red swirled and blended into a deep navy band that was slowly growing thicker. Soon, the twin moons would rise above them.

"Hey, Elior?"

He took his eyes off the sky and turned to Eliam. "What is it?"

"Did I ever thank you for rescuing me?"

A smile spread over Elior's face, and he pulled Eliam into a hug. "You didn't have to thank me."

"Maybe not," said Eliam, returning the embrace, "but I'm glad I wasn't eaten or taken back to work for Taariq, anyway. Thank you. Thank you for not giving up and for getting me back to safety."

"You're always welcome," said Elior. He held his brother in that embrace. He wasn't sure how long it was before Eliam withdrew.

"I think I'm gonna turn in. It's been a long day, and I think tomorrow is gonna absolutely kill me," said Eliam, stretching his arms and arching his back.

"Yeah," said Elior, "the naiads can be a lot to handle. I'll turn in, too."

Below deck, Elior climbed into his bunk beneath Eliam and closed his eyes. The gentle rock of the boat kept soothing him until he was asleep. For a while, Elior knew nothing but the peace of a dreamless sleep.

With a sickening crack, Elior woke up, his wrist bent at an odd angle on the floor of the cabin he shared with his brother, Nyx, and Neander.

"Agh!" Elior screamed when he tried to put weight on his wrist to help himself up.

"What happened?" called Nyx, rushing over.

Eliam was right behind him. "Your wrist! It's broken!"

"But how did that happen?" asked Neander. The answer came when the boat tilted so dramatically that they all tumbled to the left. Elior landed on his brother and screamed in pain again.

"Nyx!" screamed Eliam. "Heal him!"

Without missing a beat, Nyx grabbed Elior's hand and pulled it straight as light glowed around the bones, knitting back together.

"Thanks," said Elior. "That was the worst break I think I've ever had."

"Enough," said Neander. "Something is wrong. We need to go up on deck and see what's happening."

They struggled against the shifting gravity to climb the five flights of stairs from their cabin to the top deck. Rain pelted the deck so much that there was nearly an inch of water sloshing around on the deck. Every so often, a wave would crash into either side of the ship, and they would have to hold on for dear life to the nearest fixture to keep from falling off.

"What do we do?" screamed Elior over the noise of the storm.

Neander spit out a mouthful of water and called, "Nyx, how many of those charms do you have?"

"Only one! Elior, can you try to protect the ship from the storm?"

"I can try!"

Elior opened his hands and tried to send a burst of wind opposite a wave that was hurtling toward them, but it didn't help. Without the amplification of a temple, he didn't know if he could put a force-field around the ship, but he tried.

Shakily, the force-field enveloped the ship. There was a collective release as the rain stopped falling on the ship and fell harmlessly off the side of the surrounding bubble. Then, the largest wave that

Elior had ever seen swelled to life off the starboard side. He held his ground even as the wave rose a hundred and fifty feet over the top of his force-field. Then it crashed.

Elior fought, thrashing against every drop of that wave, but he couldn't keep their protective barrier up under the thousands of gallons of water. The bubble burst, flattening all of them to the deck in an instant.

Nereza, Opal, and Melanie ran out on deck when the water had cleared. Nereza pulled Elior up and asked, "Are you ok?"

"For the moment," he said, the wind nearly drowning him out, "but if we don't get some relief before the next wave hits, we're going to capsize."

The rain pelted the boat, the goblin crew ran up and down, bailing water out of stairwells and frantically purging anything that the boat could spare in vain hopes it would help them float.

Everything moved in a blur around Elior as he tried to summon another bubble around the ship, but it wouldn't work. Nothing would work, but then a window in the clouds opened.

"Michael," Elior cried out to the sky, "help us! I've tried everything, but I can't keep this boat afloat on my own! You saved us from the storm in the mountains all those months ago, so save us now!"

Lightning struck the boat inches in front of Elior. He stumbled back, and when the blinding light subsided, Michael hovered inches off the deck. He offered his hand to Elior.

"Elior," he said, "we can't save everyone if you're lying down on the deck!"

Taking Michael's hand, Elior stood. Michael didn't let go. Instead, he squeezed Elior's hand tighter and said, "Follow my lead. Do as I do."

Michael raised his other hand in an open palm toward the sky, and Elior mirrored his moments.

They clenched their fists, and the rain stopped. They lowered their hands to the horizon and opened them, and the winds died. Finally, Michael and Elior lowered their hands to just in front of their chests and snapped.

It was as if a large rock had been dropped into the sea beneath the boat. Ripples raced outward from where they stood, glowing against the dark waters, but when the ripples stopped, the sea was calm. All was quiet.

Elior laughed, smiling brighter than the moons now beaming overhead, but when he turned to thank Michael, his hand felt suddenly empty. Michael was gone.

The others ran up to him and pulled him into a group hug.

"How did you know what to do?" asked Eliam.

Nyx squeezed him tighter. "I thought we were goners, man!"

"You saved us," said Nereza. She planted a kiss on his cheek.

Elior backed away from them. "What do you guys mean? Michael did all the heavy lifting."

"You can take credit for doing a good job," said Melanie. "It's ok to acknowledge your own work."

"If it was me, I would," said Elior. "Didn't anyone else see Michael appear out of lightning?"

"No," said Neander, "but that's how he appeared to me when he blinded me, so I believe you."

"Michael was with you?" asked Opal.

Elior squeezed the hand Michael had held. The phantom warmth of the professor's hand was still there, a familiar weight. "Yeah, Michael was with me. I called out when there was a break in the clouds and asked him to help us like he did in the mountains when we got caught in the blizzard."

"Then it doesn't matter if the rest of us saw him or not," said Opal. "He answered you, and he gave you what you needed to protect us."

Warmth spread from Elior's hand up his arm and to his heart. "We're never really without him, are we?"

"The more I see and the more I time I spend as a seer, the more I know that he never left. Because of what he gave us, he's with us more than he was when we were searching for the Well."

A thud broke the conversation.

"Melanie!" screamed Eliam.

Melanie had fallen to the deck. Her neck was bent at a weird angle and she wasn't breathing evenly.

"Don't move here!" yelled Nyx, pushing the others aside to kneel next to her. He straightened Melanie's neck and hovered his hands over her body. A blue, watery glow descended over her, and her breathing went back to a steady rhythm, but she didn't wake up.

"Is there something else wrong?" asked Eliam. "She's not opening her eyes."

"I'm not sure why she isn't opening her eyes," said Nyx, "but she's fine now. She just may need the sleep. We all do, actually. Let's get back to bed."

"That's a good plan," said Neander. "We'll be in Misthaven in the morning, so we should rest while we can."

Eliam scooped Melanie up, and they all returned to their bunks to sleep for what remained of the night.

Chapter 26

Mercy Has no Hold Here

"How's Melanie?" asked Elior.

Eliam sighed and rubbed his hands on his face. "No change. Still asleep."

Elior rubbed the back of his neck and kicked the bunk beside him lightly. "Do you think you could carry her off the ship?"

"Normally I'd flex my arms and make some sort of joke, but I don't think I have it in me. I can carry her."

Elior wrapped one arm around his brother and gave him a side hug. "I'm sure she'll wake up. She's been busy with the portal, bombs, and then last night. She probably really needs to recharge."

Scooping up the slumbering body of his girlfriend, Eliam said, "Let's just get out of here."

As they descended from the ship, Neblina materialized out of the mist. She was dressed differently from the last time they'd seen her. Instead of icy tones, she wore a teal tunic with streaks of a warm cream running through it. Her hair was braided with pink seashells, and she wore a grin that made up for the limited sunlight on the island.

"Welcome! Welcome back to Misthaven," she said.

Elior smirked at Opal. She didn't respond. Instead, she stepped forward and shook Neblina's hand.

"Thank you," said Opal. "I'm so happy to see you so radiant! I told you that letting us go would pay off."

Neblina swallowed back a sob and choked, "I never got to apologize for that night. You did what we could never do, though. You brought back the sun, and you got rid of Umbra."

"Well, as much as we could," said Nereza. "He's causing trouble as a djinn now, but that's not nearly as bad as a giant black lizard that flies through the sky trying to find you and eat you."

"I suppose so," said Neblina. She ushered them off the docks to walk up the pathway. "You'll be happy to know that we rebuilt the guest house from scratch. No more fire damage from the dragon attack!"

"That is good news," said Elior.

Neander pulled up to walk beside Neblina. "We actually have something rather important to talk with you about. Do you have time this morning?"

"I cleared my morning as soon as a venti arrived to tell me you all were coming," she said. "I have brunch being prepared as we speak."

"Is it alright if I go right to where we're staying?" asked Eliam. "I don't feel right about propping Melanie up in a chair while I eat."

"I don't see why not," said Elior, "as long as our rooms are ready."

"They are," said Neblina, as they rounded a corner to approach her home. "Just go to the house with the blue roof behind mine. It's unlocked and everything is prepared."

"Thank you," said Eliam, trudging off.

Neblina led them inside. The dining hall was different, too. Rather than the coldness of a room of mirrors, they found it framed in driftwood and the walls painted a deep blue-green. The table was made of polished driftwood, too. The effect was cozy and warm.

They all sat down and servants emerged from the hidden panels. The servants placed steaming bowls of porridge in front of each of them, along with plates of fresh fruit, fish sausages, and freshly baked bread.

Once they had all eaten their fill and leaned back in their chairs, Neblina clapped and servants whisked the empty dishes away. She asked, "So, what did you all need to discuss with me?"

"There's a new prophecy," said Opal, propping herself up on her elbow on the table. "Taariq will not stop his conquest. He won't be satisfied with Lux Terra for long. He will come after Nox Terra, too."

"We've talked with every other race on this side of the world," said Neander. "This is our last stop, and we hope you'll support our cause."

Neblina put a hand over her heart. "After what Elior, Nyx, Nereza, and Opal did for us, I wouldn't dream of withholding our support. What is it you need?"

"Essentially," said Elior, "we need you and your people to pledge allegiance to Aelon and to join with Eternity's Refuge to stand against Taariq and his conquest."

Neblina was silent for a moment. She bore the face of a leader weighing the fate of her people, but when she spoke, certainty was her foundation. "I can't in good conscience do anything else. You have Misthaven's support. Any who will stand with you from the Naiads will join me in supporting you and your cause."

"Thank you," said Opal. "We're so glad to have garnered so much support."

Neblina stood. "Of course. Now, you've had a long journey and an eventful few days. Please, go rest, and we'll see each other later."

Eliam sat beside Melanie, holding her hand. Her breathing was easy, but she still lay motionless.

Eliam kissed her hand as his stomach growled. He thought about the meal the others were enjoying with the naiad leader, but he couldn't bring himself to leave Melanie. No girl had ever been so quickly and easily drawn to him like she had. She made it easy to like her, maybe even love her.

A bird chirped outside and flew past the window. As if in response, Melanie's eyes fluttered open. "Where am I?" she asked, trying to sit up.

"No, don't sit up just yet," said Eliam. "We made it to Misthaven. I'm so glad you're alright, Melanie. You've been asleep since last night on deck. I was worried you wouldn't wake up!" He kissed her hand again and held it with both of his.

Sleep fogged her voice. She rubbed her eyes with her free hand and said, "Djinn aren't supposed to get wet. My inner fire had to recover."

"What?" Eliam dropped her hand. "You're a human. Nereza's friend from college? My girlfriend?"

"Oops," said Melanie. "I wasn't supposed to say anything to you, but I'm never quite myself thirty seconds after waking up." She snapped her fingers and everything Eliam knew over the past several months melted away. The softness of Melanie gave way for the choppy, angular purple hair, the severe eyes, the black clothing, and the purple tongues of fire flickering over the skin of a djinn.

Eliam got up and backed away. "Melanie?"

"Stop calling me that," she said. "Now that you know the truth, I should introduce myself. My name is Viola, and I work for Taariq."

Eliam turned to run, but Viola turned to smoke and blocked the door. "Where do you think you're going?"

"To tell my dad and brother who you are," said Eliam. "You know too much."

"Well, let's even out the score," said Viola. "I'm on a mission to hurt Yrahkaz—sorry, *Neander*—worse than anything Iblis and his schemes can."

"What?" Eliam froze. He'd never been face to face with a djinn, but now he could feel the heat from the fire licking over her skin. If she came any closer, he was sure he'd start cooking.

She raised one eyebrow. "Oh, well, now *you* know too much. The only bummer is that my boss isn't anywhere near here, so tattling can't be my solution."

Eliam blinked, and Viola had him pinned to the wall by his neck. "*Please!*" he choked, but when he tried to speak, she squeezed harder.

"Please? Stop. I've had to listen to the idiotic conversations, be sweet and cute with you, and none of the little roadblocks I put up seemed to deter you people. I'm sick of it. If I'm going to make a dent in this, I need to cripple Neander. I wonder what would happen if I took away one of the sons he finally got to reconnect with?"

Eliam kicked, but the harder he resisted, the higher she lifted him. He scratched and pulled at her hand on his neck, but she was too strong. Eliam might as well have been fighting a brick wall with a toothpick.

"It's always fun when they struggle a little," said Viola, "but I'm getting bored now."

She squeezed. Her nails were sharp. There was the icy feeling of air touching the warmth inside, and then the heat from her hand intensified. Eliam tried to breathe, to scream, but everything went black. And then…

"Let's check in on Eliam and Melanie," said Elior.

Neander opened the door to the guest house. "Why do you think I brought an extra plate of food? I think it's sweet that he wanted to stay with Melanie, but he needs to eat."

Father and son walked down the hall past the open doors. The only closed door was at the end of the hall. When they reached the door, a loud thud came from inside.

The hairs on the back of Elior's neck stood straight up. He grabbed the doorknob and flung the door open.

If he could have stopped his heart by sheer force of grief, Elior would have died right there, but despite everything, his heart kept beating even though what he saw broke it into a million pieces.

Eliam lay on the floor in a pool of his own blood, his eyes vacant and staring up at a djinn cloaked in purple flames.

Neander fell to his knees. "Eliam… Viola, why? You could have killed me instead? Why him?"

"That's an easy one to answer, *Neander,*" her mocking tone washed over them like a sea of nails. "Killing you wouldn't teach you anything about loyalty. This way you know what happens when you walk out on a great djinn like Taariq."

Neander lunged at Viola, missing by a slim margin when she stepped out of the way.

"You know what?" she asked. "I should really get to my seamstress before Eliam's blood dries on my clothes. I want her to match the color so I can wear a dress the color of your son's blood."

She turned into smoke and was gone.

Elior laid down beside his brother, heedless of the blood seeping into his clothes and whispered, *"We belonged to each other."*

Chapter 27

Rites of the Entombed

WHEN THE EXPLOSION SWEPT ELIAM to Nox Terra, Elior had gone into shock. He'd been taken to the hospital and sent home where he had been alone. He wasn't alone, but the muffled sounds of his father, girlfriend, and friends three feet in front of him weren't helping push away the loneliness.

His skin itched and burned where Eliam's blood had dried on him and his clothes. Elior's eyes twitched as the memory of Neander running to get Nyx played in his mind. It was no use. There wasn't any use. The light in Eliam's eyes had gone dark, his joy was gone, he was gone.

Neander had pulled Elior off the floor, blood dripping down his pant leg so Nyx could try to heal Eliam, but no amount of healing could bring back the dead.

Eliam is dead, thought Elior. Everything he'd done up to this point had been with his brother in mind. He'd found the Well to save him. He went through the Mirror to find him. Even when they joined the Refuge, Elior had insisted on working with him. Maybe if Elior had insisted Eliam come on the trip to Registaan, he wouldn't have bonded with Viola in her disguise as Melanie. Maybe, but maybe didn't change that Elior's brother's body was being cleaned by the naiads.

The conversation around him came into focus when he heard Nyx say, "Maybe we should do a tasteful burial at sea."

A jolt ran up Elior's spine. "No."

Every eye turned to him. Nyx asked, "Why not?"

"No BarVidania has ever been buried at sea because there are ways that members of the royal family are supposed to be buried."

Nereza pulled in close to Elior and put a comforting hand on his thigh. "I didn't think that sort of thing was important to you."

"It's not," said Elior, scooping Nereza's hand into his and squeezing it. "But our mother felt strongly about those roots for us. I may not have grown up in the palace, but we did things the way royals did." He pulled out his locket, rubbing his finger over the BarVidania family crest.

Neander sighed. "He's right. Emily was very sweet, but she was proud of her family and what they stood for, at least before Eliezer took the throne. But do you know how to prepare a body for a royal burial, Elior?"

"Yeah," said Elior. He swallowed to keep himself from throwing up, "I've done one before. We need to get him back to Lux Terra."

Even after the long journey back to Granite Valley, Elior wouldn't rest before taking Eliam's body to prepare for his funeral the next day. Neander tried to offer help, but Elior insisted on handling it himself.

He worked all night. He painstakingly braided gold wire in a circle on Elior's hand to symbolize a crown, placed sage and violets in Eliam's mouth to honor the wisdom of a king, and dressed him in white linen with purple embroidery for purity and royalty. After that, he soaked him in a sweet smelling oil overnight while he dug a hole and poured water into it to symbolize Aelon's power. Over the hole, he built a pyre. At first light, he put Eliam on the pyre and went to gather the others.

When they were all gathered around the pyre, Elior said, "Opal, would you mind performing the rites? A high priest is supposed to perform the service."

"Oh," said Opal, "I've never done one before."

Allura tapped her on the shoulder. "It's alright, your eminence. I brought a script for you just in case."

Opal took the piece of paper, following the instructions as she read. "From the remnants of the other races, Aelon created man, a unifying force. The trees with their height, the water with its depth, the air with its freedom, the stones with their strength, and the fire with its passion all became part of the first man and woman. From that first man, an unbroken line of BarVidania kings led humanity and bolstered the other races. From this line, Eliam was born."

Elior's expression didn't change during the whole funeral. He kept his eyes on his brother's face. Despite the fear that he'd had painted on it when they found him, he'd made Eliam look at peace.

"Eliam," Opal continued, "was a beloved son and brother. He

fought valiantly for what he believed, even running into a building, heedless of danger, because he believed that 'every life is worth the risk.' I have only known Eliam for a couple of months now, but we've all been through a lot in that short time. His presence will be missed."

She grabbed a torch that Allura had lit for her while she spoke and held it over Eliam."Just as man was created from pieces of the other races, so too shall he return when life ends. Resting on a wooden pyre over a hole in the earth filled with water, we say goodbye with fire in the open air."

Tenderly, Opal placed the torch beside Eliam's body. His oil soaked clothes caught fire and kindled the flames to catch on the pyre. In only a matter of minutes, the entire pyre was ablaze and disintegrating into ash.

Out of the corner of his eye, Elior caught Neander walk away, wiping tears from his eyes and sobbing. Elior hadn't cried yet. He wondered why.

When the fire had consumed the pyre and Eliam's body, it went out and those that remained watched Elior sweep everything into the hole with water and cover the hole with dirt once more.

"Goodbye, Eliam," said Elior.

The last word was said, the hole was closed. The wind picked up, sweeping over the peaks of the mountains surrounding Granite Valley.

"We should get inside," said Nereza. "There's going to be a storm."

Elior let Nereza take his hand and lead him away from the gravesite. "Nereza?"

"Yeah? What is it?"

The first tear slid down his cheek and splashed to the ground, even as the first raindrop fell from the sky. "I died a little today, too."

Chapter 28
Wilderness

Stumbling through the door of his room, Neander collapsed on his bed. He counted the ridges above him on the ceiling while contemplating his life and how he'd lost a love and now a son.

After what Eliezer did to Emily, Neander would never have guessed things could get worse. Foolish. He'd been a fool to think that Taariq would let him go without repercussions, that he'd just let it all go. After what he'd found out about the Fire Oath Ceremony, Neander couldn't guess why Taariq hadn't just killed him.

But, as long as he still breathed, there was an opportunity to stop Taariq before he took anything else. Avenge Eliam, protect Elior. If there was a chance, he had to take it.

"Suitcase," said Neander. "No, backpack. Go lighter."

He ripped a backpack out of the closet and stuffed random items of clothing and necessity inside. Pants, shirts, granola bars, underwear, socks. Everything he might need in the few days it would take to get to Sumara. As far as Neander could tell, the only reason Taariq hadn't killed him yet was because he didn't know where he was. Taariq didn't know where he was because Neander hadn't used his powers.

"That must be why 'Melanie' tried to get me to use magic when we exposed the Faeland spy. She was trying to expose me to Taariq without openly communicating with him." Neander kicked the bedpost. "Idiot! If I'd recognized it, my son would be alive."

Tears blurred Neander's vision. This had to end. Taariq couldn't be allowed to do this anymore. He had to be stopped for good. Neander sat down at the desk in the corner of his room and left a note for Elior before shouldering his bag and sweeping out of the room.

Neander grabbed the set of car keys to the car they'd been given to use while in Granite Valley. Driving would be the fastest way out of the mountains if he wanted to remain invisible to Taariq for as long as possible.

He got in the car and turned the key. The engine purred to life, and as he pulled out, another wave of emotion crashed down on him. Eliam, Emily, his own parents. Taariq wouldn't take anyone else away. Elior and his friends had to be safe, and this was the only way.

He pulled up to the gate, and the guard flagged him down. "Going somewhere, Mr. Novak?"

"Yes," said Neander, "can you open the gate?"

"Normally I'd want to get some sort of confirmation that your trip was approved, but seeing as you're one of Leonis's advisors and you travel with Her Eminence, Queen Opal, I think I can make an exception."

Neander chuckled, releasing a breath he'd held. "Thank you, sir."

The guard walked back to the controls and opened the gates, unbarring the way for Neander to leave.

Elior knocked on his father's door. "Dad," he said, "I'm not upset that you left the funeral early. Everyone grieves in their own way, but please don't shut me out."

No answer.

"Dad, this isn't funny. Open up!"

Elior twisted the handle and found it wasn't locked. As the door swung open, Elior's blood turned to ice. The room appeared to have been ransacked. Clothing lay strewn across the floor, the bedcovers were crumpled and pitted as if someone had been thrown down on them, and every drawer and storage cabinet was open.

"Guys! Help!" screamed Elior into the hallway. "I think my dad's been kidnapped!"

The thunder of footsteps charging toward him echoed in the hallway. Nereza, Opal, and Nyx reached Elior at once, panting. Without waiting for them to catch their breath, Elior led them into Neander's room.

Elior waited in silence while his friends took in the scene. Then, Opal said, "How could anyone have even gotten in here, though? We have protections here that none of the other refuges even do."

"She makes a good point," said Nyx. "There has to be something more here. Let's have a look around."

Nereza put her arm around Elior and guided him to the bed. "Let us search. You've already dealt with more than enough today."

Elior's face contorted as half-formed protests teetered on the cusp of his speech, but he gave up and muttered, "Ok."

Nereza slipped her arm off him and searched with Nyx and Opal. They picked up every piece of clothing from the floor, searched drawers. Finally, Opal picked up a stray shirt from the desk and gasped.

"Elior," she said, "your dad wasn't kidnapped. He left!"

Elior's mouth tightened into a thin line, and he huffed out his nostrils. Could his father be abandoning him again? "What do you mean, he *left*, Opal?"

"It's all in this note he wrote you," she said, holding the piece of paper up.

In one stride, Elior was in front of Opal and ripping the note out of her hands. All the anger he had at the thought of his father deserting him again faded when he read his father's writing aloud.

Elior,

Watching Eliam's burial was too much, and I'm sorry I left. Unfortunately for my poor heart, you two are twins, and I couldn't help but think about you on another pyre, just like it if something were to happen. Taariq has taken too much from too many people, and I can't sit here behind a barrier of safety and wait for him to hurt us again.

I have to go confront him, Elior. I have to protect you, your friends, and everything the Refuge has built. I couldn't wait until you got back to tell you because I knew you'd want to come with me, and I can't let you do that. Stay here where it's safe. Once Taariq is no longer a threat, I'll be back. Once he's dead, we can really build a future.

I love you, Elior,

Dad

"I can't believe he's going to face Taariq on his own," said Nereza. "Do you think he's too far to stop him?"

"It didn't register with me until now," said Nyx, "but the car they gave us is gone. He could be over fifty miles away by now, and unless we get another faster car, we'd never catch him."

Opal sat down on the bed. "Besides that, there are over a dozen roads he could take that would eventually lead him to Registaan, and we don't have a clue which one he took."

"So," said Elior, "we're just going to let him face Taariq on his own?"

"Of course, we won't do that!" Nereza pulled her sleeves up and crossed her arms. "Though we are going to need a better solution than simply chasing after him. Opal's right. With too many routes out, we'll never catch him, so we need a smarter plan."

"Leonis is supposed to arrive tonight," said Opal. "I heard that before the funeral."

"That's good," said Nyx. "We can talk to him about it. Either way, Neander is one person. He won't be able to travel all that distance straight through on his own. He'll need to sleep."

"Once Leonis gets here, we'll figure something out immediately, right?" asked Elior.

"We won't waste a minute," said Opal. "None of us wants to see Neander hurt. He's overrun with grief, and he should have talked to us before hid did this, but I get what he's doing."

"We should call the leader of the Registaanian refuge up here," said Elior. "Methuselah might help with anything that might involve djinn magic, and I'd rather have a djinn on our side if we need it."

"I'll make the call myself," said Opal.

Nereza moved next to Elior and curled her fingers into his. "Don't worry. Until Leonis gets here, though, you need rest. You didn't sleep all night, and it's been a hard morning."

Elior's lids were suddenly heavy. He opened his mouth, yawning as widely enough to fit a small apple inside. "Fine. I'll go rest." Though with all this stuff going on around him, how much rest could he really get?

Sweat etched salty paths down Neander's forehead as he drove through the mountain passes, connecting Nanony to Registaan. Even at the high altitude above the desert, the air was heating beyond what the car could handle. It had been hours since the fan had stopped blowing cold air.

Neander wiped his brow and said, "I might as well sit in front of a panting dog for as much as this piece of junk is cooling me off."

He shut the fan off and rolled the windows down and let the rushing wind cool him down. It worked well enough until he came to curves where he had to slow down. The moment he dipped below sixty miles an hour, the air felt searing hot.

When Neander passed over the border into the northern range of Registaan's mountains. The road twisted sharply around a narrow peak. He had to slow way down, but the heat was too much. More sweat poured, making it hard to see.

"Maybe I can balance speed enough to keep from sweating into my eyes," he said to himself as he increased pressure on the accelerator. The round and round, spiraling pathway continued. Then, the sound of shifting gravel underneath the driver's side front wheel condemned Neander to fate.

The car slipped and went off the side of the road. He gripped the steering wheel so hard his knuckles popped from effort as he careened down the side of the mountain. He was driving down a nearly vertical plane with no purchase on the wheels.

Fifty feet from the bottom, he hit a boulder, smashing in the front fender and inflating the air bag just in time to keep him from hitting his head from the impact with the ground past the boulder.

Neander didn't move, didn't make a sound. If he moved, would he die? Was anything broken?

Adrenaline slowly dissipated, and he was fully in his mind again. The sandy wind howled through the open window of the car. He'd only been able to close half the distance between Granite Valley and Sumara in the car. He'd have to go the rest of the way on foot. But how?

He hadn't planned on being in the direct desert heat for more than a few minutes here and there at most. There was no way he'd survive, unless...

"I'm going to have to use magic." Hope sank into his stomach as Neander pulled himself and his backpack from the car, useless and steaming in the sand.

"Just two minor spells, and I won't touch the magic again."

With a wave of his hand, he was covered in heavy wraps to protect his skin from the sun. He snapped, enchanting the bottle of water in his bag to never run dry until he could find a sustainable source of water.

"No more," he said. "From here, I go without help. I go to avenge Eliam and protect Elior."

The sand stretched as far as he could see from where he stood at the base of the mountains. Desert forever inside the basin of Registaan. "One step, then another, and another. I'll be there, eventually."

Elior pulled a sweater over his head as Nereza knocked on the doorframe of his room.

"What is it?" he asked, adjusting the sweater's hem to be comfortable.

Nereza held out her hand for him to take and said, "Leonis and Methuselah just arrived. Do you want to go down to see them?"

"Of course I do," said Elior, taking Nereza's hand. "We have to catch my dad before he does something stupid."

"I hope we can," said Nereza.

The two of them went downstairs to where Nyx, Opal, Leonis, and Methuselah were waiting.

"Elior," said Leonis, "I was so sorry to hear about Eliam. I wish I could have made it here sooner."

"It's ok." Elior held up his hand, dismissing Leonis's regret. "It was just a small ceremony, and I know how important your job is."

"Which leads nicely into what we came here to talk about today," said Leonis, dryly.

Elior sat down with Nereza and asked, "Why do I feel that this isn't good news?"

Methuselah stroked his beard and coughed. "There really isn't any good news possible in this scenario."

"What do you mean?" asked Opal. "I'm not sure I follow how there couldn't be some plan we could make that would work."

"I agree," said Nyx. "It's such a long journey to Sumara from here that we should be able to overtake him if we use magic, right?"

Methuselah leaned back in his seat, heavy worry lines deepening on his brow as he spoke. "We could catch him, yes, but transporting Neander along with anyone who would accompany me would be enough of a magical ripple that Taariq would feel it, especially since Neander's magic is still bound in a Fire Oath." The old djinn cocked his head. "That is right, isn't it?"

"Yes," said Opal, "we haven't been able to figure out a way for him to cast off the magic yet."

"I don't know that there is a way of casting magic off after the way he gained it," said Methuselah, "but I doubt anyone who could take a djinn's powers would want to cast them off. He may be the first ever to pursue that goal."

"What are we really saying?" asked Elior. "Are we not going to get my dad?"

"No," said Leonis. "We can't risk it. By using magic on him to bring him back, we'd be opening ourselves up to an attack directly from Taariq, but we'd also alert him to Granite Valley's location. This place is our best kept secret. As far as we can tell, the spy sent here could never report back to Iblis from within the refuge because of the protections on it. No one can communicate magically to anyone outside of the Refuge's domain, and any outsider cannot remember its location without becoming a full member. We can't risk breaking those enchantments, even for Neander."

Elior's mouth felt like it was filled with paint. He wrinkled his nose and tried to expel the feeling, but he couldn't talk over the slimy bitterness.

Nereza grabbed his hand and rubbed the back of it softly. "So, what can we do?"

"For now," said Leonis, "we wait." He leaned forward on his knees. "Elior, with your gift, we can rescue him if he's captured, but we're going to need a while to put those plans in place. The best-case scenario is that Neander makes it to Sumara, kills Taariq, and returns. He'd end the conflict by ending the djinn's leader, and we'd avoid the worst part of Opal's prophecy."

"And what is the worst-case scenario?" asked Elior, bile fighting to come up the back of his throat.

Leonis stood and paced in front of the couch he'd been sitting on. "We might have to rescue him, and we can start planning for that now. At least with that, we aren't announcing the location of Granite Valley. We can be strategic about how we approach it."

"I don't like this," said Elior.

"I have to say, I'm not a fan either," said Nyx. "Shouldn't I get some say since I'm the general?"

"Ordinarily, Nyx," said Leonis, "I'd say yes, but not when it involves the safety of all of us, and you have an obvious bias to want to protect your friend. The bottom line is we've had heavy losses. The spies were an enormous setback, and now most of Faeland is against us. Did you know some towns close to Wick's Flight think *we* started the fire and then fled to escape it while it consumed the town and the townspeople?"

"More propaganda," said Opal. "They're relentless, insidious monsters, every one of them."

"With all of that," said Leonis, "I can't in good conscience encourage an expedition to catch and bring Neander back, even though I might want to."

Elior choked down a lump. He thought *I'd feel more secure standing on the edge of a cliff overlooking a lake of lava.*

"So," he said, "we wait?"

"We wait," said Methuselah

Chapter 29
Capture

A TINGLING SENSATION WASHED OVER Taariq's arms and legs. "Did you feel that, Iblis?"

Sitting on the couch across from Taariq's desk, Iblis opened his eyes and asked, "What do you mean?"

"There was something… moving… rippling somewhere. It felt familiar, but I can't put my finger on exactly what it was."

In a purple flash, Viola materialized. "I think I can help you figure it out. That little tingling is Yrahkaz, finally using his magic again."

Iblis stood, walked over to Viola, and circled her as if examining her for defects. "What would make you think that?"

"Not that it concerns you, Iblis, but I succeeded on a little wager of sorts I made with your *master*." Viola blew a smoke ring in Iblis's face, leaving him sputtering as she approached Taariq's desk.

"How did you succeed, then?" asked Taariq, pulling a glass of brown liquor out of thin air.

Viola raised one eyebrow. "I killed his son."

Taariq sprayed a sip of his drink over the desk in front of him. "Elior?"

"No," said Viola, "because I'm not an idiot. You tried to kill a Protector twice. It doesn't work because Aelon has basically erected an impenetrable shield of power around him. No, I killed his brother, the one that was lost I Nox Terra for all those months. I mean, it wasn't my original plan, but it still worked pretty well."

"What do you mean, it wasn't your original plan?" asked Taariq.

Viola smirked. "I was going to marry him and abduct him back here before holding a public execution, but when I got wet in the rain, it took all my energy and power to hold the glamour with the rain pelting my flames. That little brat was so tender and sweet, and it made me sick, so I ripped out his throat when I woke up."

"That's absolutely vile," said Iblis.

Viola turned her head, violet flames cascading from her locks. "I'll take that as a compliment, old serpent."

"I admire your cunning, Viola," said Taariq, pulling the conversation back on track, "but how do you know it's Yrahkaz using magic?"

"He's better by some standards than he was before," said Viola, "but he still has power, even if he refused to use it. He thinks he can take you out. I've been watching him. I waited until the perfect moment and then I sent his car off the side of the cliff. Without enough water or food to brave the desert, there's no way he isn't using magic now."

Iblis scoffed. "If she's right, and at this point it seems like a faint possibility, you'll be able to find Yrahkaz now, won't you?"

"Try it," said Viola, throwing herself into an armchair. "I delivered just like I said I would."

Taariq closed his eyes and concentrated on the memory of Yrahkaz's magic. Sure enough, as he waded through the magical energy flowing around him and the world, he found Yrahkaz stumbling through the northern dunes, the rusty residual of magic long abandoned, shaking off him with every step forward.

"You did it, Viola. He's coming."

Even as dark as he was, Ibis's cheeks flushed.

"Don't be upset, Iblis," said Viola. "Some of us just have more practice being djinn. If you're lucky, you won't be such a colossal screw up in a few hundred years." She tossed her hair and glared at him, daring the djinn to attack.

Iblis reeled back, clearly intending to pounce, but Taariq raised a hand, immobilizing him.

"Don't, Iblis. She delivered, you haven't kept your own assurances to me, so you have no room to be angry with Viola. One thing I know you can succeed at is relaying orders just as you did during the war."

"Your wish is my command," said Iblis. "I will be of service no matter what."

"Get the police force ready to capture Yrahkaz as soon as he enters the city. We have to be looking for him just in case his magical energy fades before he gets here."

"Yes, master," said Iblis. He turned and walked out the door, closing it behind him.

"So," said Viola, "I'm thinking amethysts and onyx for the stones in my crown. What do you think?"

Taariq swept over to her and scooped her up. "Above all my other servants, you have delivered something they couldn't. It isn't even the wager. Your fire is… is…"

"Hot?" asked Viola, hooking her arm around Taariq's shoulders and snarling seductively.

"Hot," he said. He crashed his lips into hers, both of their flames grew, wrapping them in a cocoon of fire. Arms writhed, grabbing for purchase, fighting for control as they kissed, sealing their deal.

When he pulled away, Taariq said, "Let's go get you fitted for that crown."

The last rays of the sun made the sandstone buildings of the city shimmer. The moons framed Sumara as they rose over the horizon. One full moon lighting its north side, and a crescent on its south as Neander watched from his hiding place behind a dune. Just a few more spells had got him here in half the time, but it stopped mattering after the first spell. Taariq knew he was out there, using magic. The only hope he had was that he might not know what he was doing.

As soon as the sky was truly dark except for the light of the moon and stars, Neander vaulted over the side of the dune and slid down. Magically enhanced speed carried him to the city wall in five minutes over several miles of space.

The walls of the city towered over him, but he jumped, floating higher and higher until he was on top of the wall. Neander climbed down and stuck to the shadows as he navigated the streets, moving closer to the palace.

As he rounded a corner down a side street that led to the back of the palace where servants entered, Neander felt the collar of his shirt pull back. An instant later and he was in the arms of a tall, burly djinn glowering down at him like Neander was a midnight snack.

Icy panic ran like a river through Neander's blood. He raised his arm to cast a spell to escape, but just as he was about to release the magic, a cold snap on his wrist cut off the flow of fire through his veins. A copper and leather bracelet gripped his wrist as tightly as a vise.

Neander pulled frantically at the bracelet, but it was so tight he was scraping his skin raw and thrashing in the djinn's arms.

"None of that," said Iblis, winking at Neander. "We don't want you to hurt herself or anyone else, Yrahkaz."

"They call me Neander now," he said, struggling to free himself from the behemoth of a djinn.

"They could call you Sad Sally for all I care," said Iblis. "My master, *your* master, asked me to collect you, so I shall." He snapped and said, "You can put him down now. Without magic, he isn't exactly a challenge to corral."

"Why can't I use my magic?" asked Neander. "What is this thing?" He held up his wrist and slapped it, furious at Iblis with every fibre of his being.

"That," said Iblis, "is a fire blocker. We put it on djinn before we execute them so they can't escape. At least, that's what I'm told. I've never seen one before today, but I think they're marvelous inventions."

"I'm not a djinn, though," said Neander.

Iblis laughed, "No, you certainly aren't, but you took the powers of one in order to gain your magic, so it still works. I'm tired of talking to you. Taariq wanted you as soon as we had you, so I'll be doing my job now."

Iblis blew a giant cloud of smoke into the alleyway that enveloped everyone. When it cleared, Neander sat in a chair in front of Taariq's desk.

Taariq tapped his fingers and scowled at Neander. "Why did you abandon us, Yrahkaz?"

"That's not my name," said Neander. "Michael made me new, and that's what my name, Neander, means."

Taariq's eye twitched, and he tutted at Neander. "Remember, Yrahkaz, our goal was always to take Michael and his father, the Sky Demon, out of the picture. What changed?"

"What changed is that Yrahkaz killed the brother of the woman he loved and thousands of innocent people who just believed in a man who you didn't like. Then I found out that you could recall my power by killing me. I didn't like my odds of living or finding happiness, and Michael appeared to me. He blinded me and sent me to find my son, the protector. His friends are both gifted, too. Opal is a seer, and Nyx is a healer."

Neander swallowed his tears, remembering the day. "Opal gave me hope and encouragement from Michael and Aelon, and Nyx healed me. Aelon gave me a new name, and a new purpose that went against everything you ever wanted for me."

Any pretense of warmth left Taariq. He cornered Neander inches away and breathed sulfurous breaths against the man's nose. "You knew I could kill you and take your power at any moment, yet you still rebelled against me? How foolish are you?"

"It's you who's in rebellion, Taariq! Aelon created us, Michael redeemed the waters and brought life back to a dying world! Magic was weakening, the life-force was draining, and he brought it back. Since he resurrected, can't you feel magic getting stronger and stronger?"

Taariq reeled back and slapped Neander so hard that Neander's lip split on his teeth. "Stop saying their names! I gave you power, magical and political! I gave you prestige! What have you had since then? A second-rate leadership position? Following around the ones who actually traveled with Michael? Your life is pathetic."

"If it were pathetic, Taariq," said Neander, "you wouldn't have had to exact revenge on me by killing my son through Viola."

"Viola fulfilled her promise to me to get you to come back. I hoped that by using the powers I helped you gain again that you would realize the truth, but I see now that I have to move up my plans. I can't keep you alive anymore, but I won't give you the dignity of a quiet death. You will be publicly executed for your crimes."

"Seems fitting," says Neander, "but I will not go down without a fight."

Taariq cackled and sat on the edge of his desk. "Don't kid yourself, *Neander!*" The djinn spat as if his former friend's name was a disgusting taste. "You're all out of moves. I have you pinned."

Neander stopped talking. He stared into Taariq's eyes, searching for any sign of life, real life, in them, but he couldn't find any. His eyes were dead and desperate.

"I'm going to broadcast your capture to the world. They'll know we are weakening the opposition. The perfect world I wanted will be mine, but you can no longer be a part of it, you will not see it, and you will miss out on everything I could give you."

Neander craned his neck towards the ceiling. He pictured Michael coming to him in lightning on a rainy day on a dirt road those many months ago, and he was not afraid. "If it's anything like what you gave me before, then I don't want it. I'd rather die than be part of any plan you came up with."

Taariq snarled and reeled his fist back. A moment later, everything went black while Elowynn's song played in the back of Yrahkaz's mind and then went silent.

Chapter 30

Lost Will be Found

THE SIGHT ON HIS PHONE'S screen made Elior glad he hadn't eaten any breakfast. Taariq sat talking beside Neander.

Elior's father's head bobbed, blood dripped from an obviously broken nose, and it was clear he was unconscious as Taariq spoke. The drivel was obviously something about the greatness of the UFSS, but Elior could tell a point about Neander was coming.

He rushed down the stairs into the kitchen, where Leonis was sipping on a cup of coffee and reading a stack of reports.

Elior shoved the phone on top of the stack of papers in front of Leonis and said, "Watch."

Leonis groaned but complied, setting down the paper in his hands and watching as Taariq spoke about Neander.

"Some of you may recognize the former Prime Minister of Vidania, Yrahkaz Almasi, except now he says his name is Neander

Novak. In this land, you can't change your name and escape your responsibilities. Yrahkaz, or Neander, as he prefers to be called, left his post, abandoned his people, and has been working closely with the terrors group that calls themselves 'Eternity's Refuge.' I, your senior sovereign, have captured and detained this man. His crimes against our great country are many, so I will not risk simply imprisoning him. No, for you, my people, I want the utmost protection. So, to protect the interests of the people, Yrahkaz Almasi will be executed for treason, terrorism, and public endangerment tomorrow afternoon."

The broadcast ended. Elior shook with anger as he said, "We had a window, and we lost it. My father is going to die. Haven't I lost enough already?"

"Elior," said Leonis, "I'm sorry about this. No one wanted this for Neander. I honestly hoped that Neander would have been able to defeat Taariq."

"He's just one man," said Elior, sinking into a chair beside Leonis. Elior's anger dissipated. "Please tell me we can try to rescue him."

Leonis pivoted his chair to face Elior head on. "We won't abandon him. We knew this was a possibility, which is why we planned for this. We will put our plan in place. Gather everyone, and we'll go over it."

Elior stood and went to everyone's rooms, pulling them down for the meeting.

"So," said Nereza, "what do we do?"

"Nyx, Elior, Methuselah, and I all worked together on this plan," said Leonis. "Would you care to explain, Nyx?"

"Of course. Essentially, we're going to need other magic users on our side since we're going in with no powers besides the three of ours," he said, motioning to himself, Elior, and Opal. "So, we'll stop first in the Registaanian refuge. Anyone who wants to volunteer will come with us, and we'll go to Sumara from there."

Methuselah yawned. "Don't forget about the tunnels."

"Right," said Nyx. "Methuselah told us there are tunnels under Taariq's palace. If we can infiltrate those, we can find Neander before they execute him and rescue him."

"Some of the djinn from the refuge will cause a distraction," said Elior, "but most will come with us. They'll be expecting us, so this won't be a stealth mission. We're going to have to fight."

"Good thing we kept the armor Michael gave us," said Nereza.

Opal leaned back, pushing her hair off her face. "How do we get out once we have Neander?"

"All the djinn will put together a charm," said Methuselah. "I'll give Elior the power to activate it so when everyone is safe, all he has to do is slap the script representing the charm on his hand, and we'll all be transported back to the Registaanian refuge's entrance."

"Does everyone understand?" asked Leonis. A chorus of yesses affirmed him. "Good. Then we leave in one hour."

Nereza bit her lip. The portal stood dormant in the corner. They'd been sending people back and forth to help the Nox Terrans learn about the Refuge. Viola, Eliam's murderer, had impersonated her old friend and helped to build it. "The djinn want this as badly as I did," she said.

Methuselah came up beside her. "You're probably right."

"I didn't hear you come in."

He chuckled. "I came in by smoke. Didn't make any noise as far as I know. I had to see for myself if it was true."

"Did you doubt me?" asked Nereza.

"I didn't know you before this week," he said, "but I didn't know if Aelon would allow this kind of magic to work. He didn't want the djinn to go back. That's why our mirror stopped working."

Nereza caressed the copper coils. It was almost like a child to her. "Do you think Aelon was wrong to keep the djinn from crossing over?"

"No." The response was fast enough that Nereza jolted and jumped back a bit.

"I'm sorry," he said. "No, Aelon did the right thing. So few of the dragons were actually good at the end, and those live on as djinn today, and they've had children and generations of grandchildren. Some have stuck with us and what we believe, but most have followed Taariq's misguided notion of freedom."

"Fire doesn't like to be constrained, I guess," said Nereza.

"Maybe not," Methuselah's eyes watered, "but a properly cultivated fire brings warmth, not destruction. My son leaves a trail of destruction wherever he goes."

"Then will you help me protect it?" asked Nereza. "Will you help me keep Viola from coming back to steal the portal?"

"I can make it so that no djinn can operate your portal."

Nereza cocked her head. "Won't that mean that no good djinn can go through there either?"

"Of course," said Methuselah, "but we don't mind not going to Nox Terra if it keeps them safe over there. Let me help."

"Ok," she said as she stepped away.

Methuselah stretched his hands over the portal and breathed. White, glittering smoke poured from his nose and formed a thin shell over the portal. Then the smoke glowed and disappeared.

"There," he said, "no djinn can touch or activate that portal. They're safe."

Nereza flung her arms around the wise old djinn and said, "Thank you. You're a good djinn."

"One of the few," said Methuselah, returning her hug. "Come now. We don't want everyone to be waiting for us for a long time."

Elior felt like traveling by smoke tingled. It was a strange sensation, but as the smoke cleared and they were in the hollow mountain of the Registaanian refuge, he involuntarily gasped.

"You mean to tell me," he said, "that djinn can go anywhere in the world and be there this quickly?"

"Of course," said Methuselah. "We were dragons before. We had wings!"

"Even wings are slower than that!" said Opal.

Nereza groaned. "I feel like I left my stomach back in Granite Valley."

"Humans often have that reaction," said Methuselah, "but it will pass in a few hours."

"Notify everyone to come together, Methuselah," said Leonis. "I want to get out there as soon as we can."

"Of course," said the old djinn, snapping his fingers. "Everyone will be notified. Let's go wait for them in the temple."

Even as they walked toward the djinn's temple, throngs of djinn merged with them in their journey forward.

Finally, they reached the temple. Every seat was full, and there were even some djinn standing in the back.

Leonis stepped to the front to speak. "Thank you, everyone, for coming. Doubtless, some of you have seen the broadcast that came out earlier today concerning Neander Novak. We believe we should rescue him, but we need more magic in order to do that. Would anyone like to volunteer for a mission to Sumara to rescue Neander?"

For a moment, nothing happened. Then, a few dozen hands shot up.

Elior breathed a sigh. There would be help. They could really rescue his dad.

"Thank you," said Leonis. "Those of you who volunteered stay by. We're going to go over the plan. The rest of you are dismissed."

Chapter 31
Storming the Castle

BEHIND A FORGOTTEN BUILDING ON the south side of Sumara, Elior, his friends, and thirty-six djinn materialized, ready to rescue Neander. Not one of them made a sound as they rounded the building.

Everyone was outfitted in armor, but after Methuselah muttered something under his breath next to Elior, everyone blended in with the bustling city and all the djinn going about their business.

"Good thinking," said Elior.

Methuselah harrumphed and said, "Better not to spook the deer before you're close enough to strike, young one."

Through the city, up the hill to the palace, they walked. When they reached a place along the outer wall where a few djinn walked, Leonis turned to address everyone.

"Thank you all, again, for agreeing to be here today. Without so many volunteers, this rescue wouldn't be possible. A third of you," he said, motioning to a group of djinn, "and our seer and magitechnician will perform the distraction. Create noise, protest, pretend to fight amongst yourselves, anything. Pull as many guards towards you as possible. The rest of us will be in the assault under the palace to find and retrieve Neander. Are there questions?"

No one raised a hand or interrupted the silence.

"I think everyone understands, Leonis," said Elior. "We're ready to go."

"Ok," said Leonis. "Everyone follow your assigned leader, and let's get going."

Leonis led the larger group, but Elior and Nyx stayed close to the front as they rounded the wall to the other side. Under the shade of a tree within the palace gardens was a bench. Methuselah motioned for a couple other djinn to join him and they breathed and mumbled over it. After several minutes, the bench's legs animated, and the bench got up and walked itself to the left several yards. It had been hiding a grate.

"Come help me pry the grate up, Elior," said Leonis.

"Yes, sir," he replied, grabbing the grate opposite from Leonis.

They pulled and pulled until it wiggled free. With a metallic clang, they revealed the opening and descended into the tunnels below Taariq's palace.

Opal and Nereza led the djinn assigned to them around the palace wall into the open courtyard. There was already a platform there ready for Neander's execution. Opal shuddered and wiped her palms on her skirts, trying to tamp down her nerves. She'd never been in a djinn city before and the fact that if they were discovered they could be killed made her nauseous.

Nereza reached out and took Opal's hand. "It's gonna be ok. Just keep it under control, and we'll all make it through this."

"I mean, I am nervous about creating a distraction, but I'm more nervous for Nyx and Elior."

"I've been there," said Nereza, "but Elior's blessing is pretty powerful. I doubt any of them will have a single scratch."

Opal breathed deeply, her armor tightening as she inhaled. "Let's do this so we can help protect them, too."

Opal, Nereza, and the djinn they led spread out into the crowd that was already growing, hoping to find some way to incite them into a riot or something.

Opal approached an old djinn woman with white hair and greeted her. "Hello," she said. "How are you?"

"As good as expected," said the old djinn. "I haven't seen a public execution in nearly a century. I'd hoped they'd extend one of the world leaders a bit more grace. Being a leader is hard."

"Are you crazy, old woman?" asked a muscular djinn who approached them. "He's getting what he deserves for committing treason! If being a leader is so hard, why has Taariq been able to do it so well for the last two hundred years? Before the dragons turned into djinn, Solarium led the war!"

"And how did that turn out? We have had to live on two legs because Solarium wasn't given any grace!" screamed the old woman. "Why would we act the way Aelon did and cause more pain like he did?"

Opal backed away as they continued to argue. All around her, groups of djinn argued, some were chanting 'Free Yrahkaz,' or 'Down with the traitor,' and still more were making a mishmash of noise that she couldn't quite place.

Nereza waved, catching Opal's eye. They came back together, and Nereza said, "That was even easier than I expected."

Opal squinted. "What do you mean?"

Nereza pointed up to a balcony with stairs coming down both sides. Already, the amount of guards had doubled. "If we keep this up, more and more of them will be diverted here, clearing more of the way for the assault."

"We better seem like we're arguing then!" screamed Opal, jamming a finger against Nereza's chest and barely containing a smile.

"Yeah!" screamed back Nereza, shoving Opal's shoulder and winking. "Let's really play it up!"

They continued to have a conversation while posturing it as an argument. With every passing moment, more guards lined the walls and balcony overlooking the courtyard.

"Shouldn't I be leading us in, Leonis?" whispered Elior from just behind him. "What if we need my blessing?"

"Not this time, Elior." Leonis rounded another dark corner and continued to step lightly. "The fact that we're here is my doing, so I'll lead. I won't rely on you to do my job or right my wrongs for me."

"Are you sure?" asked Nyx. "There are a lot of djinn up ahead, you know. No matter how big of a distraction Opal and Nereza can make, we're still infiltrating the palace. There *will* be guards with magic beyond your power to withstand."

"Enough," Leonis barked. "If you two want to have a conversation, then go back the way you came. We're running this mission my way."

Elior and Nyx backed off and let Leonis stay in front.

The tunnels wound this way and that like an undulating serpent finding its way through the sand of the desert. Then, the narrow passage suddenly widened into a cavern. On the other side of the cavern from them was a squad of djinn guards, all armed with whips and swords and axes and guns made of fire.

Elior grabbed the hilt of his sword and waited.

Not one living creature in that cavern moved a muscle.

"What's going on?" asked Elior.

"Hush, young one!" said Methuselah. "A battle between this many djinn doesn't start with the exchanging of blows. Until an attack makes it through, it's all spells and counterspells." Methuselah pointed to the ceiling.

Above their heads, a flurry of multi-colored sparks blazed over them like a miniature fireworks show. On the other side, the squad's foreheads were furrowed with concentration. They were so quiet that drops of sweat hitting the floor echoed in the dark space.

Then, a crack, a burst from overhead, thundered. Elior caught his breath and raised his arms just in time before molten rock piled itself on him and their company. When the spell ended, the squad let out a shaking battle-cry as they charged toward the front line.

"Attack!" cried Leonis, drawing a gun. He shot, barely heeding his aim into the crowd coming for them.

Elior raised his sword and summoned a shield as he charged with the front line into battle. Swing, duck, miss, connect, and the sickly soft movement of a blade through flesh. Every moment blurred. He protected as many people as he could, but he tried to focus on himself, Leonis, and Nyx as much as possible since the djinn could all use magic.

Fires blazed as if they were in a box of kindling. Everywhere, different colored fire balls zoomed overhead, crashed and exploded, seared the hairs off someone's head or face. Chaos reined. Still, Elior fought on.

Slowly, the numbers on the other side dwindled. They were winning! Elior was fighting one djinn. The sword of fire he wielded zipped around him, but Elior was fast. He could either dodge or raise his shield to meet every blow. At last, after several minutes of dueling, he caught the djinn's wrist, disarmed him, and ran him through.

Even as the djinn's body slumped to the floor, the awful sound of blood hitting the floor from behind him echoed on the hard surface. Elior turned around just in time to see a djinn rip a chunk of Leonis's gut out of him with his bare hands.

"No!" screamed Nyx, firing an arrow into the djinn's eye.

The djinn grasping Leonis's intestines dropped, but the damage had been done. Elior and Nyx rushed over.

"Can you heal him?" asked Elior. He searched frantically for the best place to put his hands to stop the bleeding, but with a wound like this, nearly all of Leonis's abdomen was bleeding.

Nyx searched with his hands, but so much was missing. "I can't heal this. I can't create new organs out of nothing, I—"

"Stop," said Leonis, still gasping for breath. "I was foolish. I know that now, but you can still win here."

Elior put his finger to Leonis's mouth. "Don't speak. We're trying to help you."

Leonis pushed Elior's hand away. "You heard Nyx. Nothing can be done. Lead now, Elior."

"No," said Elior, leaning away from Leonis. "Surely Nyx is more qualified."

"You're a protector, Elior," said Leonis. "The whole point of Eternity's Refuge is to create protection and to follow Michael and Aelon. My mind is made up. Don't argue with a dying man."

"Yes, sir."

Leonis smiled against the pain, satisfied with the response. A moment later, the life faded from his eyes. Nyx reached over and closed them.

"Are you ok?" he asked, offering Elior his hand.

Elior took Nyx's hand, and they stood together. "I kinda have to be, don't I?"

Nyx opened his mouth to argue, but thought better of it, letting the thought die. "Ok. You're ok."

"I am," said Elior, burying everything but determination deep down. Nothing could keep him from moving forward.

"What now?" asked one of the djinn volunteers.

"Now," said Elior, "we get to Neander before we lose him, too."

Chapter 32
Endurance

NEANDER WAS WAKING UP AGAIN. Every time he woke up, his jailers brought a new torment. He was burned up and down his body, and Taariq had him strapped to the table with rough, uncured leather. Taariq had Neander's naked body dipped in hot wax and then had the wax scraped off with salt rocks. At least he was alone. There was no one there to taunt him now. Perhaps he could get some rest before Taariq returned.

That hope shattered when the metal door opened and slammed shut. He strained his neck, trying to see if it was Taariq or a guard, but the two people coming in weren't who he was expecting.

"So," said Minerva, her hair billowing over her shoulders like ocean waves, "this is what it comes to, Yrhakaz? You're strapped to a table for treason against the wonderful country we all created. Why? Why betray your friends this way?"

Neander huffed and said, "My name is Neander."

"Ah, yes," said Steelwort, picking his teeth, "Taariq told us about that. It means 'new,' right?"

Minerva giggled. "I believe that's what he said it meant." She leaned over Neander. "Yrhakaz, if people could change because of Aelon's supposed goodness, don't you think I would have stayed serving him? I was a priestess, I bought into all that he said he was, but you know my story. You know how I suffered."

"I know it wasn't Aelon's fault, Minerva. Life sucks, sometimes."

She slapped him, and the sound echoed in his tiny cell. "Don't you dare blame me for what happened! Aelon could have stopped it with one little flick of his wrist! Now, because of Taariq, I can stop things like that from happening with one flick of my wrist."

"She's right," said Steelwort. "After all, you exacted your revenge on Eliezer, right? You killed him, burned him alive, right? Sounds like you got what you wanted."

Neander's stomach flipped, remembering how Eliezer's eyes had melted in his sockets as he killed him. "That was the old me. That moment was the beginning of the end. Emily wouldn't have wanted me to kill her brother, no matter what."

"Maybe not," said Minerva, "but because Aelon couldn't step in, Emily is dead. She can't tell you what she'd want."

Neander steeled his nerves. "Emily is dead because cancer is a disease that few people can stop. Even magic can only mask the symptoms. I've never heard of a djinn or djinn magic cure it."

"She suffered in pain, Yrahkaz," said Steelwort. "At the very least, her family should have helped her be comfortable."

"That's true," said Neander, balling his fist and shivering from the pain on his burned wrists. "Still, that's a problem with her family and not with Aelon. He set me free from a life where I had to kill and hurt people in order to survive. I was dying inside, and he rescued me."

"You're pathetic," said Minerva. "We might as well have some fun with him, then. Right Steelwort?"

Steelwort giggled and cracked his knuckles. "I'd love to."

Elior led the rescue team up a wide, spiraling staircase. Sunlight burned their eyes when they emerged from the tunnels as the sunbaked scent of flowers hit them. Rows and rows of topiaries, shrubs, flowers, and trees stood between them and the wing of the palace where Neander was being held.

Elior wiped the sweat from his brow as he searched for a clear path forward. "Do you know how to navigate through the garden, Methuselah?"

"The garden is organized in a series of smaller mazes that rearrange themselves to keep intruders from getting too close to the palace. Fortunately, I know how to counteract Taariq's magic, so I can disable the spell for a while."

Methuselah motioned for the others to step back from him. He breathed deeply. When he exhaled, glittering white smoke flowed from his nostrils so copiously that the ground below him appeared to be covered in a thin layer of snow. When the smoke reached the rows of plants around them, the flowerbeds themselves shuddered and rearranged themselves. The path was open.

"Let's go!" Elior called to everyone over his shoulder. They ran through the pathway, approaching the wing of the palace where

Neander was waiting.

As they passed the last topiary before reaching the tiled patio around the palace itself, a giant fireball formed over their heads.

"Everyone down!" screamed Elior. With barely a millisecond to spare, he summoned a giant shield over the team.

The force from the fireball crashing into his shield was so great that it forced Elior to the ground. He twisted his ankle so far to the right that he heard a snap. He cried out in pain, and the shield dissipated.

The attackers came into view, firing volleys of fireballs towards them, but this time Methuselah and the other djinn with them met the attack and rushed past Elior to join in the fight.

Elior stood and tried to take a step but fell back down immediately.

Nyx was beside him in a moment. "Let me help!"

"I can fight! I need to lead!" Elior tried to push Nyx off, but his friend pushed and pinned his shoulders to the ground.

"No, Elior, you can't fight. I love that you want to take responsibility for this, but you can't go on fighting if you're hurt. Let me heal you!"

It was futile to argue with Nyx. Elior couldn't even stand without pain, so he stopped fighting and surrendered to the merman's hands. The whole time Nyx worked, Elior could hear the clanging of weapons, the ripping sizzle of fire, and the blur of voices yelling and crying out.

When Nyx finished and Elior's ankle was better than new, he and Elior sprang up to join the fight,

A thousand tiny cuts speckled across Neander's body. He was raw, his breathing labored. How much more of this could he endure? While Minerva and Steelwort had their fun, he must have blacked out a couple more times. Nothing felt right. His whole body throbbed.

The door opened. Cal and Loki strolled in and closed the door behind them again. They wore smiles, only darkness and pain lived behind.

"Nice of you to join us," said Minerva.

Steelwort picked his teeth and huffed. "I didn't think you two were showing up at all."

"Loki couldn't miss the opportunity to visit Yrahkaz," said Cal, leaning against the wall.

Loki glided over to Neander, his robes barely moving with each step. He unclasped his hands and laid one on Neander's shoulder. "So, this is how the gem of Taariq's horde ends up. Strapped to a table, tortured and getting ready to be executed for treason. Tell me, Yrahkaz, how did you let this happen?"

Neander groaned, unsure of whether it was worth correcting these people again after so many times.

"Oh," said Cal, "but haven't you heard, Loki? His name's Neander now. He claims that he's a new person because of Aelon. Can you believe it?"

Loki laughed sharply. "I can't believe that Aelon could help someone change when he has never changed himself."

Neander glared up into Loki's face and said, "What exactly does the creator who sang your people out of the forest need to change? We don't even deny that he created the world, so why is Taariq trying to wrench it out of his hands?"

"You know as well as I do," said Loki, "that Taariq wants to give freedom back to the world, to escape from the constraints of Aelon's law, which I know all too well."

Neander laughed, but the sound turned into a cough. When the fit passed, his words were hoarse. "Aelon's law? Freedom? Loki, what constraints were ever placed on any of the races before Solarium's rebellion? We had freedom, but the dark disease that Solarium brought into the world with his conflict poisoned us. We wouldn't have needed the law if he hadn't broken it first."

Cal reeled back and spat on Neander's face, soliciting laughs from Loki, Minerva, and Steelwort. "You're a fool, Yrahkaz."

Neander refused to look at any of them anymore. He bored his gaze into the ceiling.

"You had all the power in the world," said Loki. "Why give it up?"

Neander swallowed, still not meeting their eyes. "Because all of that power was a lie. Remember the Fire Oath Ceremony? That made it possible for Taariq to kill us all and steal our powers without diminishing his in the slightest."

Cal was on top of Neander in a moment. "Don't say another—"

"No!" said Minerva. "Even if the torture has made him delirious, let him speak. I'm curious what makes him think that."

Cal got off of Neander. Neander strained against his bonds. "It was in a book in Taariq's library here. The Fire Oath Ceremony, in the way Taariq did it, binds our powers to him, not to each other. He did it so he could kill us. I noticed Swiftwing isn't here. What happened to him?"

Steelwort furrowed his brow and whimpered, "Taariq killed him."

"And do any of you feel any weaker because of it? Has his power left the Circle, or has it simply been claimed by Taariq?" Neander asked as Cal left, slamming the door behind him.

No one said a word.

Step by step, stroke after stroke, Elior and the others fought their way up the stairway. It was the last barrier between them and Neander.

We're so close! Elior thought. *Just the last thirty feet!*

The djinn guard was packed so tightly that every inch of progress cost the blood of an enemy to purchase. Spell sparked back and forth, djinn fell on both sides. Nyx cleaved to Elior's side, firing arrows into the onslaught of guards ahead while Elior protected him and sliced down anyone who dared come close.

Methuselah was a master of fire, breathing columns of flame into the ranks of Taariq's men. The sight scared some of them into fleeing, but there were still dozens blocking them.

Then, they reached the halfway point.

"We're halfway there!" cried Elior.

It was a rally cry. The djinn on their side surged forward, blasting a force of hot air up the stairs, sending many of Taariq's guards fumbling and falling down the steps into the weapons of the rescue team.

"We're almost there, dad," said Elior. "Hang on!"

The door didn't open this time. Taariq swirled in and solidified out of his smoke cloud. He grinned widely, his pointed canines gleaming in the dim light of Neander's cell.

"Sorry," said Taariq, "I would have used the door—knocked even—but your son is fighting my guards in order to get to you. Noble, really." Taariq sat down beside Neander's head. "Misguided, more so, but still noble."

Neander snarled, trying desperately to cast any spell, but his magic was still cut off. It was useless. "If you touch one hair on his head, Taariq, I'll—"

"You'll what, Neander?" Taariq's glare turned into a glare. "Yes, I used the name you keep insisting on if for only one reason." He leaned in and half hissed, half whispered, "It's more fun to kill something that's fresh than an old, loyal friend."

"Speaking of loyal," said Minerva, "Yrahkaz, Neander, whatever we're calling him, said that the Fire Oath Ceremony was just a way for you to gain our powers by killing us?"

Taariq, still maintaining eye contact with Neander, asked, "And do you believe him over me, Minerva? Do any of you believe him?"

"We don't know, Taariq," said Loki, bowing deeply.

Fire flashed in Taariq's eyes as he turned to face the rest of his Dark Circle. "Oh, my friends." He stood and strode over to them, slowly and deliberately, before saying, "That really was the wrong answer."

With a single snap, Taariq made duplicates of the bracelet blocking Neander's magic from working materialize on each of their wrists.

"Viola, my darling!" called Taariq. A moment later, violet smoke swirled into the room and revealed Viola dressed sleekly in a black dress that hugged her figure with a slit up to her hip and a black crown on her head adorned with huge amethysts and obsidian dust.

"What can I do for you, Riqy?" she asked.

"First," said Taariq, wiping obvious frustration off his face with his hand, "I told you not to call me that in front of anyone. Besides that, I need you to take Loki, Minerva, and Steelwort somewhere they can prepare to die. Their usefulness just ran out."

"What?" asked Steelwort, his jaw slack.

Loki gasped, "You can't be serious!"

"Neander was telling the truth," said Minerva. "We have to—"

But her thought was cut off forever as Viola disappeared with them.

Taariq turned around slowly, his face unreadable and manic. "You cost me some very dear friends, Neander. If I thought I was going to enjoy killing you before, well, now I know that I'll love it more than anything I've done in decades. I think I'll keep your eyes as a trophy. Maybe make some earrings out of them for my soon-to-be bride."

Neander wanted to spit in Taariq's face, but Elowynn's face popped into his head. She sang even as he prepared to give the order to hang her. She kept her eyes on Aelon.

"I don't fear death, Taariq. Opal foresaw that casting magic off would be difficult for me. Maybe dying is the way to do that, but I won't hold on to life if Aelon still has a plan. I will defy you until my last breath, but I don't fear death. After all, because of Michael, death has already died. Why should I be afraid?"

Taariq raised his hand to slap Neander across the face, but at that moment, Elior burst through the door.

"Dad!"

Taariq raised his hands, freezing Elior and Nyx in the doorway.

"Nice of you to join us. Unfortunately, I'm running late for a very important meeting, and your father has to come with me, so we'll be leaving. Please show yourselves out!"

With a flick of his wrists, Taariq swept himself and Neander away.

Chapter 33
It's More

"I can't keep this up anymore," said Nereza, her voice catching.

"Me neither," said Opal, her voice hoarse from yelling. "We gave them enough time. We should be good to go now, don't you think?"

Nereza pointed up to the balcony. "A lot of the guards have left. What do you think that means?"

Opal formed the first words of an answer on her lips, but a barrage of applause pulled their attention back to the platform set up for the execution. Taariq had arrived with a handcuffed Neander.

"By Aelon's grace," said Nereza. "What have they done to him?" Neander's face was puffy and swollen. His body oozed from thousands of tiny cuts, blood and pus making him look slick and gooey.

Smoke poured into the courtyard, djinn appearing everywhere. Elior and Nyx emerged from a smoke cloud. Elior's face was grimy with dried sweat and blood with streaks of tears.

"We didn't make it in time," he said, crashing into Nereza with open arms.

She held him and said, "We don't have to stay, you don't have to watch this."

"No," said Elior. "I can't leave my dad to die alone."

Taariq stood and clapped to gain everyone's attention.

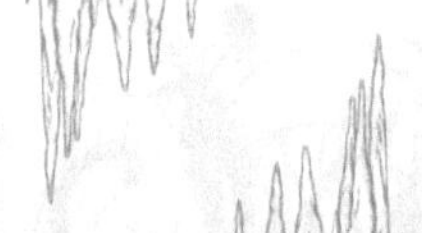

Neander watched the crowd for familiar faces. When he found Elior, Nereza, Opal, and Nyx, he kept his eyes on them while he listened to the first part of Taariq's speech.

"People of the United Federation of Six States, it brings me no pleasure to welcome you to the public execution of Yrahkaz Almasi, who insists on being addressed as Neander Novak."

Taariq stepped back as a hooded executioner stepped forward and placed a noose around Neander's neck.

"Yrhakaz committed heinous acts of—"

Neander would not be silent to listen to Taariq. For everyone he'd killed before Michael saved him, he had to make this moment count, so he sang the song that had haunted his heart since the day Elowynn died.

When waters flowed,
You flowed with them.
When the flowers sang,
You sang with them.
Oh, how could I fear
A flowing song

Sung by the maker of the mountains?

"No," said Taariq, "stop singing, you can't—"

But Neander didn't stop.

I was forged from the remnant,

I'm united in myself

That's what you intended.

Your heart carries me,

Oh, why would I fear

A flowing song

Sung by the forger of all peoples?

"Get out of my way!" screamed Taariq as he clawed his way toward the controls for Neander's rope.

Still, Neander sang on.

I watch the dawn;

It speaks of light.

I watch the dusk;

It speaks of night.

Oh, how could I fear

A flowing song

Sung by the lord—

The trap door opened, and the rope snapped taught, cutting off the rest of his father's song. Elior fell to his knees and let the tears flow. His father kept eye contact with him even as he died.

"I love you, Dad," Elior said, never taking his eyes off his father as he swung on the rope.

A glimmer of acknowledgment passed over Neander's face, and then he was gone.

The entire courtyard was silent.

"Why aren't you fools applauding?" screamed Taariq. "The traitor is dead! Our country is safe!"

Still, no one said anything. One by one, the djinn who watched the execution for entertainment turned around and left. Only the rescue team was left.

Methuselah came to Elior and said, "We'd better go now before Taariq realizes who we all are. He's deliriously angry now, and if he comes to any semblance of sense, we'll have a fight we're not ready for on our hands."

He was right. Taariq was tearing the wooden platform apart with his bare hands, yelling obscenities and raging about how someone would sing.

"Can you recover his body?" Elior asked. "I want to bury him. I can't leave him hanging like that if we don't have to."

Methuselah put an arm around Elior. "I'll do my best. I just need your order, and I'll initiate our retreat."

"Do it," said Elior.

Even as Taariq continued to rage, they all disappeared in white, billowing smoke.

Chapter 34

The Gathering

"Are you ready?"

Elior turned. Nereza was dressed in a tea-length black dress, her coils slicked back and straightened, hanging almost to her waist.

"Yeah," he said, straightening his tie one last time. "I didn't realize your hair was that long."

She looped her arm into his as they walked. "Are you ok, Elior?"

"Don't ask me that, yet," he said. "If I'm going to break down, I can't do it when I'm about to give a eulogy, to say goodbye to someone for the second time in a month."

"Ok," she said.

Nyx and Opal were waiting for them outside. Together, the four of them walked to the cliffs. At the end of the path was a beautiful waterfall. Wildflowers grew in vast patches, the sun shined with a magical happiness, and it exuded peace. Elior wanted his dad's funeral to be there because his dad's life had been anything but peaceful, and his death deserved to be peaceful.

A few dwarves shuffled about, but few people were there.

Elior's scowl deepened.

"Don't let the attendance bother you," said Nereza. "Your dad didn't exactly have a lot of time to build a new reputation."

Elior kicked a dirt clod. "All the same, I wish more people were here."

"We're here," said Opal, "and this funeral isn't for everyone. It's for you, it's for us, too. It's for the people that knew and loved him to say goodbye."

"She's right," said Nyx, affectionately clasping Elior's shoulder. "Just get as much love as you can out of this day. We'll keep loving you, but you're gonna need all you can get to get through this."

Elior bit his lip and bobbed his head once. His friends found their seats near the front, and he walked over to stand beside the casket. They'd had to put Neander in a high-collared shirt to hide the rope burn, but there wasn't much they could do about the bruises and cuts besides putting makeup on him, and that still cracked in places.

"Dad," said Elior, "it was nice to have you, even if it was just for a little while."

With one hand bracing against his father's casket, Elior turned to speak to the people who had come.

"My dad started out his life as Yrahkaz Almasi, the son of Irma and Hemosh Almasi. His family was wealthy and powerful, so at some point, they were invited to a palace dinner where he met my mother, Emily BarVidania."

A few more people rounded the corner and sat down as Elior

continued. "I didn't know my father until he showed up at my mother's deathbed in the hospital, but we still didn't know who he was until he came to mine and my brother's graduation. Turns out, he didn't know about us until my mother confessed that she'd gotten pregnant before he left on royal assignment."

Still more people came. A few dozen sat down, leaving only a few seats left. Elior went on talking. "So, I grew up without a dad, and it was hard for him to find a place in our lives. Eliam and I tried hanging out with him once or twice, but he was already working on his political career. What we didn't know was that he was working with Taariq. He was opposed to Michael and Aelon, and I was fortunate to be part of what Michael came to do here."

A steady stream of people of all kinds started coming in, filling in the last chairs and forcing people to stand behind the chairs they'd set up.

"My father was directly responsible for thousands and thousands of deaths of people from and related to Eternity's Refuge. Yet, Michael saw something in him. He blinded my father and sent him to my friend Nyx to be healed and to my friend Opal to receive a way forward. From that moment forward, he was a good man, a good father."

People shuffled, trying to make room for each other so that everyone had a good view. It confused Elior, but he kept talking anyway. "He took the name Neander Novak because it means 'new,' and he was new. He treated my brother and I like true sons, putting in the effort with us. He worked hard to bolster the Refuge to undo the damage he'd caused. He became so dedicated that he tried to avenge the death of my brother, his son, Eliam. And as Taariq killed him, he sang a song of praise to Aelon. He sang because he wasn't afraid."

Murmurs of appreciation and praise to Aelon escaped from the crowd. Elior couldn't even count how many there were now.

"I'm sorry," he said, "who are all of you? I didn't realize my dad knew so many people. Actually, how did you all get into Granite Valley?"

A young woman stood up and said, "I can only speak for myself, but I'd guess that we all came for the same reason."

"And what is that?" prodded Elior.

The young woman licked her lips and picked at her fingernails. "I saw your father's execution broadcasted as it was happening. I heard him sing, and I thought, 'anyone with that much peace, to sing while someone is killing them, must have something amazing.' So, I decided I had to come and be a part of whatever he'd been a part of."

"And do all of you feel the same way?"

Murmurs of assent moved through the crowd like wind through a field of wheat, shaking every stalk.

Electricity ran up and down Elior's spine, and he put his hand to his heart. Nereza stood beside him and put her arm around him and her head on his shoulder.

"What are you going to say to them?" she whispered.

Elior cleared his throat against the tears that were coming and said, "At the end, I know my dad wasn't trying to do anything but spread the message about the importance of standing with Aelon and against Taariq. If you're all here because of that, then I don't think my dad would be upset about his death at all. I think he'd have been happy to make the sacrifice."

"By Aelon's Grace!" someone yelled, and everyone echoed the

sentiment.

Elior turned back to his father's casket. Beyond the cuts and bruises, Neander was at peace. His lips upturned in a subtle smile, his brow relaxed. No, Neander had not been worried or upset when he died. He'd made peace, and in that moment, with so many there, ready to follow Michael because of Neander, Elior basked in the knowledge that it was all alright.

Elior closed the casket and waved Nyx up to help him lower the box into the ground beside the waterfall.

As the casket descended, Elior said, "Goodbye, Dad… and thank you."

Chapter 35
After

Elior sat alone on a couch in his room. Rain pelted the window, mimicking his mood. Nereza knocked on the open door frame and said, "May I come in?"

Without saying a word, Elior nodded.

She came in, sitting next to him in silence for a while.

"Do you need anything?" she asked

Every nerve in Elior's body came undone, and he sobbed. "I need the past two weeks to not have happened!"

He collapsed onto her shoulder, and she wrapped her arms around him. "Let it out, Elior. I don't know how you weren't sobbing at your dad's funeral. I mean, as great as it was that he inspired people, you still lost him."

"I did," he said, tears pooling into a wet spot on Nereza's shirt. "I lost my brother, who I haven't finished grieving, and then I lost my dad. I'm an orphan! I have no family left."

Nereza wrapped her arms around him and held him there, crying with him.

After a few minutes, she asked, "It pretty much sucks, doesn't it?"

"Yeah, and Leonis named me his replacement. There's so much work to be done, and I feel like I'm coming undone. I feel like there's nothing in me."

Nereza pushed him up and forced him to make eye contact with her. "Listen to me, Elior. You're not coming undone. This world, this movement, everything is so big, and you don't have to have everything on your shoulders. I am right here. I love you, and I'm walking through this with you."

"I don't know how I'm supposed to handle it all, Nereza," said Elior. "My family is gone, and I'm the last BarVidania left, as far as I know. I'm alone! I'm supposed to lead Eternity's Refuge! I've never led anything in my life."

Nereza simply guided him to lay his head in her lap while she stroked his hair. "Family can mean a lot of different things, El. You have Opal and Nyx. You've been through so much with them, and they love you. You have me, and I love you more than anything. Second, Leonis wouldn't have told you to lead if he didn't think you could. By Aelon's grace, you're a protector! I can't think of anyone better suited to lead Michael's people than you."

"I'm still scared," said Elior, hugging Nereza's knees.

"Why are you scared?"

He turned so he could look her in the eye. "I'm afraid of letting everyone down."

She laughed. "The world is already so far gone that there is nothing you could do to mess it up more, aside from surrendering to Taariq and his plans. Are you going to do that?"

"Of course not! I'll never let him win."

Nereza kissed his forehead. "There you go, you won't let anyone down, then. All that matters is that you keep fighting, and you have all of us behind you to help you do that. Is there anything else?"

"I'm afraid of being the last one in my family."

Nereza said, "Like I said before, family is a lot of different things, but if blood is what you're worried about, then you don't have to worry. You're going to be a wonderful father someday, and your family will grow again. Who knows? Maybe once Taariq is defeated, you'll be able to take Vidania back and be king."

"I've never aspired to be king," said Elior with a chuckle. "I would just want to see people out of Taariq's control. I don't need it."

"That's good. Is there anything else you're afraid of?" Nereza locked Elior in deep eye contact, begging with her soul for him to release his fear.

He thought, prodding his mind for anything that could hold fear inside him. "I'm afraid of losing you," said Elior, a strangled sob on the back of his voice.

Nereza leaned down and kissed Elior. "I promise you're not losing me. I'm here, and I'm not going anywhere."

"Really?" Tears welled up, tracing the routes on Elior's face they'd carved in the last several days.

"El, I promise you, for the rest of our lives, we will belong to each other."

END OF BOOK THREE

* * *

Preview of Eternity's Edge

IF IT HAD BEEN POSSIBLE to see inside Granite Valley from above, anyone might have assumed that it was any other quiet day there. Dwarves bustled about their shops, and their children ran around their feet in dizzying circles. But it wasn't a quiet day for Nereza Kahn.

Nereza stopped for a moment to catch her breath, leaning against a lamp post that was barely taller than her when Elior and Nyx walked by.

"Are you ok?" Elior asked, stepping over to her and putting a hand on her shoulder.

Nyx eyed her up and down from behind a huge bundle he'd been carrying. "You look like you've been running."

"I'm fine." Nereza stood back up and leaned in to kiss her boyfriend's cheek. "There's just a lot to get done today, you know? Did you get the list I sent you, El?"

Elior slipped the paper out of his pocket and shook the paper triumphantly. "I've been working on it. As a matter of fact, Nyx is helping me with double-checking the border right now. Right Nyx?"

Nyx shouldered the bundle he was carrying. "What good is a general if you can't get his help securing the border, right boss?"

"Knock it off." Elior rolled his eyes and shoved Nyx's shoulder.

Nereza sighed and smirked, barely keeping from chuckling. While she was slightly stressed, she didn't want to put that on Elior. His spirits were high, and he was joking with Nyx. Aelon knows that it took nearly three months before he even smiled after Neander's death. Her heart felt full knowing that six months had allowed Elior to get back to being himself in time for today.

Nereza shook herself. Today. She remembered her own list, crumpling it slightly in her hand. "I have to go. Are you sure you have everything under control, guys?"

"We've got it," said Elior. "Don't stress about it. Most of the things I'm doing are just precautions anyway. The border around Granite Valley is safe."

"I just want to be extra sure since you won't be standing guard or on call tonight." Nereza started walking away. "I'll see you guys later?"

Elior and Nyx left and she entered the florist's shop.

"Good afternoon, Ms. Kahn," said the shopkeeper, a portly old dwarf woman with a kind face and graying hair. "What can I do for you?"

Nereza's shoulders tensed. "I hope it's a small fix. The flowers were delivered earlier today, but there were supposed to be red velvet roses in all the boutonnieres, and the ones the shop sent were white roses."

The dwarf woman's eyes widened. "All of them? I'm so sorry, I don't know what happened. I'll have them redone right away, don't you worry."

"Thank you," said Nereza. "Will you have them done by this evening."

"Of course, and I'll deliver them myself, this time."

Nereza smiled. "That's a huge relief. Thank you, I'll see you there, then."

Walking out of the shop, Nereza crossed one more thing off her list.

"Almost finished with the preparations?" asked Opal, walking up to her from the direction of the town square.

"Yep!" Nereza stuffed the list into her pocket. "Everything else I need can be done at home."

Opal opened her arms to embrace Nereza, and Nereza stepped into the hug. "I'm so glad this is happening."

Nereza laughed and swayed back and forth. "You and me both!"

"Are you headed home, now?" asked Opal.

"I am. Where are you headed?"

Opal rubbed her head with the tips of her fingers. "To the temple. I feel like Aelon or Michael is trying to tell me something, but I'm too distracted at home to listen."

Nereza's jaw flexed and she balled one fist. "Nothing serious, I hope…"

"Hey," Opal took Nereza's hands and pulled her down to make full eye contact, "don't worry about that. I'm sure it's nothing that will throw off the plan. You just focus on your list, and everything will work out."

"Will it?" Nereza's eyes were as big as a puppy's.

"Of course it will. Relax, and everything will work out just fine."

#

"Are you sure they have to be here?" asked Viola. "They're so boring, now."

Taariq fastened the chains around Minerva's wrist and affixed them to the wall. "I want them to watch as we become the most powerful beings on the planet, don't you?"

Minerva, Loki, and Steelwort were all chained to the walls in the underground throne room of Taariq's palace. Across from them was Taariq's throne and the smaller duplicate he'd had made for Viola to occupy after their wedding.

Viola eyed them. "I suppose it's something. I do enjoy an audience."

"That's one of the many things I love about you, my dear." Taariq grazed Viola's shoulder with his finger, leaning in to smell the smoke on her skin and whisper, "Are you ready to do this?"

The purple flames dancing on her skin sparked as her eyes widened. "Finish them."

Taariq snapped his fingers. "Iblis!"

A column of black smoke emerged out of nowhere and coalesced into the form of an imposing djinn with shining black skin. "Yes, master?"

"Viola and I are ready for you, now. Where's Cal? He needs to collect the blood."

Muffled shrieks erupted from Minerva, Loki, and Steelwort.

Without missing a beat, Taariq summoned a whip of fire and

struck them all across the cheek. "That's enough out of you lot!" If you'd have left well-enough alone, you wouldn't have had to die. Well, at least not so soon. Don't complain or I'll make the death I've planned for you more painful."

Cal walked in with an empty cup in his hands. "Relax, I'm here. There's no need to torture the poor souls anymore than you already have."

"Easy for you to say," said Taariq. "You aren't the one they betrayed."

Viola pressed her body against Taariq's back. "Are we doing this, or not?"

Taariq turned around to face her and smiled, revealing his sharpened teeth. "Oh, we're doing it, alright. Let's begin."

Taariq snapped and he was instantly clothed in a crimson suite and Viola was garbed in a stunning violet gown with a black veil over her face.

"You look stunning," he said. "Shall we?"

About the Author

ZACHARY HAGEN is a Mississippii fantasy author, math teacher, and editor. He lives there with his wife, Claudia, and their dog, Flynn. When he isn't busy writing his next book, working with a client, or teaching, you can often find him walking around his neighborhood or up hiking.

From a young age he was enthralled with the world of story. From the stories his parents read to him from his blue bedtime story books (if you know, you know) to the first two series that he read, The Chronicles of Narnia and A Series of Unfortunate Events, Zachary's tastes continued to develop throughout his years of reading.

Connect with me on TikTok and Instagram @ZacharyHagen_Writes

Follow my Facebook page: Zachary Hagen Writes

Join my Newsletter!

Acknowledgements

First and foremost, I want to acknowledge my wife. Claudia is my biggest supporter, and she tells everyone that I'm her favorite author.

Second, I want to thank my readers and those who have reviewed my books. Reading and hearing positive things about my work is a huge deal, and I am encouraged to keep going because I know people enjoy my work.

I also want to acknowledge two people that aren't close to me, but they have still impacted this series. Cole and Evelyn, without your actions and choices, this series may not have made it this far. What you did gave me the time to write and inspired some of the chareacters and scenes in this series,

I also want to thank God. Every bit of this series is His before it is mine. He gave me the ability to write, and He is the master story-teller.

Other Books by Zachary Hagen

Eternal Chronicles

Lux Terra: an Origin Story (Available on Amazon)

Eternity's Well (Available on Amazon and B&N)

Eternity's Mirror (Available on Amazon)

Other

The Novel Planning Workbook (Available on Amazon)